Child's Play

Nancy Swing

For Kathy & Tom

Thank you for letting me be part of your family.

xo N

PARK PLACE PUBLICATIONS
PACIFIC GROVE, CALIFORNIA

First trade paperback edition March 2017
Designed by Patricia Hamilton
Manufactured in the United States of America

Published by
Park Place Publications
Pacific Grove, California
www.parkplacepublications.com

ISBN: 978-1-943887-44-6

Printed in U.S.A.

Cover photo: Shutterbox —Frank1Crayon

for

Harriet Shetler

*whose gift of an older woman's friendship
saved my young life*

and for

Russell Sunshine

who saved it again and again

ACKNOWLEDGEMENTS

WHEN YOU COME TO the end of writing a book, it's hard to remember all the folks who helped you make the journey. But I'll do my best, and if I've left you out, please put it down to an old lady whose memory ain't what it used to be, as we would've said in West-by-God-Virginia.

First and foremost, a major debt of thanks to Sally Spedding whose workshop exercise years ago at the Winchester Writers' Conference in U.K. spawned this book. "Draw characters out of the hats," she said, passing around one hat for victims, one for sleuths and one for murderers. I drew two young teenage girls and a mature woman. Wow, I thought, what can I ever do with that combo? Well, here it is, dear Sally, and I hope you like it.

Barbara O'Connor, Frank Olsen and Ben Steinberg read early drafts and responded with caring suggestions. Special thanks to Barb for her comments about toning down the squeamish bits.

Beloved West Virginians Bettina Bennewitz, Bob Swiger and Rick Wilson not only gave invauable feedback on the next-to-final draft, they were fonts of information about details of the life we lived in the Appalachian hills.

Terry Piotrkowski, book-lover and retired librarian, really knows how to read a manuscript and offer advice on everything from phrasing to plotting. Every writer should be so lucky as to have a Terry.

And of course, there's Russell, always Russell, husband, partner and friend, who read each draft with care, marking every page with thoughtful reactions, never pushing, always supporting. You truly are my Sunshine.

Finally, it's always a joy to work with Patricia Hamilton, who brings bountiful grace and expertise to the challenge of converting a manuscript to a book we both can be proud of.

As ever, any shortcomings or errors in *Child's Play* are mine alone.

1

WHEN THE NEWS COME over the TV about how Miz Gravesly's car went into the lake, I just couldn't believe it.

I could feel the wind beating up our trailer something fierce, one of them early summer storms trying to come over the ridge. Saw a program once on how West Virginia hills are real good at brewing up that kinda storm. But that ruckus outside didn't mean nothing to me, cause inside I was thinking, how can that be? Not the part about Mary Margaret Gravesly. Who cares what that stuck-up old biddy done? But they found Ray-Jean strapped as tight as she could be into that woman's swanky car.

Now, I knew Ray-Jean hated seat belts. Never wore 'em. Not even after her Daddy got a ticket cause she was riding in his front seat without one. That was afore he run off with that tramp over to Moorestown-way.

I remember it really well, cause he took a stick to her, but it didn't do no good. She still wouldn't wear a seat belt. "Eden," she said, "I can't abide 'em." That Ray-Jean Shackleford was one tough girl.

Well, I couldn't take it all in. My best friend dead? That scrawny tomboy with hair so short it didn't even ruffle in the breeze? So full of life I just had to follow her round. I was always trying to get outta gym class cause I was too fat to run. But she only had to say, "Come on, Eden!" and I was ready to dash off to the ends of the earth. If she'd just let me stop to catch my breath now and then. And she always did. That's exactly how good a friend she was to me.

I musta set there pert' near an hour, rocking myself back and forth on the sofa bed. Keeping time with the gusts wailing through the trailer park. We was in some kinda weird storm. No rain, just wind. Dust swirled up from the dirt road and coated all the windows, but it didn't matter none.

Nothing mattered. Not even my baby brother crying in the other room. Now that Lewiston Junior High was let out for the summer, I was supposed to be taking care of Cruz while Momma took her shift down at the mill. But I couldn't do a thing for him, and that's the truth.

Anyhow, I finally come out of it and started thinking about what that TV man said. And the more I thought, the more I knew I just had to do something.

〜

Bethanne stared into the open casket and tried to convince herself that all this was real. Mary Margaret lay there in her pale-blue linen like she was just asleep. The undertaker had painted her sister so she looked like a faded rose, all cream and mauve. Bethanne touched Mary Margaret's hair, as perfectly coiffed as it had been in life, a soft, buttery blond masking the gray. But it didn't feel like real hair anymore. Even so, Bethanne's heart said her sister was going to wake up from a nap and start scolding her for smoking in the house.

That made Bethanne crazy for a cigarette, so she went outside and lit up a Kool. Thank God the police were keeping the media half-a-block away. TV and press had latched onto the story like a puppy after a rawhide bone. Wife of prominent West Virginia lawyer found dead in her Mercedes with a poverty-stricken girl of thirteen—helluva a story, you had to admit. But Winston's friendship with the Police Chief was paying off, and the media couldn't get near enough to poke their cameras into anybody's face. Bethanne didn't like Mary Margaret's husband, but at least he had the connections to get things done.

The crush of mourners just kept coming. Doctors and lawyers, preachers from churches Mary Margaret hadn't even gone to. A full busload of senior citizens from the old folks home where Mary Margaret headed up the volunteer committee. Bethanne didn't know a one of them. Her sister's entire bridge club had shown up, cried over the casket and hugged Bethanne until she couldn't breathe. Out at the lake, someone had hung a wreath on the dock, and neighbors' kids had picked wildflowers and cast them into the water.

All this emotion made Bethanne want to puke. None of these people had really known Mary Margaret. Not like she had. They didn't know how Mary Margaret had grown up in a small clapboard house on the wrong street, how the two sisters had shared the second bedroom until they were full-grown, how they'd whispered hopes and dreams when they couldn't sleep in the hot Alabama night. These people just knew the woman Mary Margaret had turned herself into, not who she really was.

Bethanne put a hand to her queasy stomach. Jesus, she needed a drink. And there wasn't going to be one until after the funeral, after the graveside ceremony. Then they'd go back to the house where

Winston had brought Mary Margaret as a bride. All these people who didn't know Mary Margaret would crowd around, drink Winston's bourbon and tell everyone how sorry they were. After that, they'd go home and forget Mary Margaret in a week. Or maybe a month. For the rare few, maybe even a year.

Bethanne lowered her head and looked in the gutter. She tried to block the memory of the day she'd come to live with Mary Margaret last spring. But it kept grabbing her mind whether she wanted it to or not.

⌐⌐

Bethanne had driven up from Birmingham, coaxing her ancient Datsun all the way and breathing a sigh of relief when she saw West Virginia hills scarred by strip-mining. Just a few more hours to go. A closer look revealed most of the mines played out. Giant trucks rusted beside graveled roads climbing to where coal seams used to be. Down below, beard-stubbled men sat on unpainted porches, passing a jar of moonshine and watching the world drive by.

When she got to the outskirts of Lewiston, Bethanne was taken aback. What had been a high, green hill was lopped off like another strip mine. But this mutilation was different. Raw clay and shale backed a new shopping mall, its vast plain of asphalt corralled by places designed to separate folks from their hard-earned money. That's how Daddy would've put it. Fast food for fat people. "All you can eat for $14.95," bloated with carbs and lard. Tacky shops full of plastic and polyester calling out to families with lots of wants and little cash. The kind of places she was going to have to go back to shopping in, if this trip didn't pan out.

Just past the mall was a sign welcoming her to Lewiston. "Pop. 20,000. Home of the Mountain League Champs, 1997." Bethanne shook her head. Looked like nothing else had happened since. Next came a string of car dealerships—Chevy, Ford, Toyota. Even Volvo, so somebody besides Winston still had money around here. A giant home supply store was bracketed by a discount electronics warehouse and a full block of storage rentals. Suburban sprawl had come to Lewiston.

She skipped the bypass and drove into town, wanting to see what other changes had occurred since she'd last visited Mary Margaret. How long had it been? More than five years, less than ten. Anyway, it seemed like a long time. Except for the courthouse with its new jail wing, downtown was a ghost town, both hotels closed, the department store too, movie theaters converted into strange-sounding churches, stores with vacant windows, rubble-strewn lots where ornate Victorian buildings had endured for over a century. Even the drugstore looked down on its luck, lunch counter closed, floor space cut in half to make room for a pawn shop.

God, it was depressing enough to have to come back here without being witness to this endless degradation.

Things got better when she headed into her sister's neighborhood. Big houses still stood among big trees. Lawns melted into flower borders spilling over with spring's promise of summer to come. And in the middle of the most prestigious block, the biggest house of all, built by Winston's grandfather on three lots, just to make sure everyone knew he could afford the land. Mary Margaret's prize-winning roses drifted below the white-columned veranda rising two stories against red brick.

Bethanne pulled into the semi-circular drive in front and then along the house to the rear, parking in the concrete space between garage and kitchen porch. She got out and stretched the kinks from her spine. Two long days driving up from Alabama had about done her in.

She took a nip from the pint of Wild Turkey in her imitation-leather handbag and fired up a cigarette, squinting through the smoke at the old chauffeur's apartment above the four-car garage. Those Graveslys might have come down from the days when they had all kinds of hired help, but they still had the luck. She touched her jaw where Jack had hit her. Maybe some of it would rub off.

No sign of a car for Winston, so there was still time to talk with Mary Margaret before he got home. Bethanne took a last drag on the cigarette, crushed it underfoot and headed for the kitchen door. The colored maid wasn't there, probably finished for the day. Bethanne shrugged. That suited her just fine.

When she got upstairs, she found Mary Margaret standing in front of the mirrored doorway that led from her bedroom to her dressing room. Bethanne swallowed hard. Her sister looked years younger than she did. Last March, Mary Margaret had written a long letter about the dinner dance at the country club celebrating her sixtieth birthday. Bethanne had just spent the night of her fifty-seventh alone in a cheap motel.

Soft living, that's what did it. Mary Margaret never had to deal with not being able to hold onto three husbands. Never had one of them clean out the joint account the way Jack had done last week. Never had to worry about money at all.

Bethanne shook her head to send those thoughts flying. She stepped further into the room and made herself smile. "Hi there, sis!"

Mary Margaret's mouth got all tight. "Bethanne. I wasn't expecting you for another hour."

Bethanne tottered against the slipper chair and plopped down. "Thought I'd come a bit early so we could have us a little talk." She raised a hand to straighten rusty-gray hair blown by the car's open windows. It flopped back in her face, and she gave up the effort.

Mary Margaret went over to her vanity table and picked up the brush from her silver-backed set. "What's there to talk about? Jack's left you for good, and you need a place to stay."

"Well…I sure do hate having to impose on my only sister…"

Mary Margaret attacked her pale hair with a vengeance, smoothing down every tendril until her head was as sleek as an otter's.

"This isn't the first time," Bethanne continued, "but I'm hoping you'll help me make it the last." She rummaged inside the dark cavern of her purse and brought out a cigarette and a throwaway lighter.

"You know I can't tolerate smoking in the house," Mary Margaret said. "If you've got to have a cigarette, kindly go outside." She gestured toward the door to the second-floor veranda.

"Okay, okay." Bethanne stuffed the cigarette back in the pack and started looking for something else in her bag. "What I want to ask you is…" She smiled and pulled out the half-empty pint of Wild Turkey.

Her sister grimaced, turned back to her vanity table and took a gold bangle from her jewelry box.

Bethanne wasn't going to let herself be ignored. "What I want to ask you is…well, I don't want to stay here forever."

Mary Margaret sighed and faced her sister. "Now what? First and last month's rent?" She slipped the filigreed bracelet over her manicured hand.

Bethanne swigged from the bottle and screwed the lid back on. She tried to smile, but she knew it wasn't masking her wet eyes. "Nope. Better'n that. When I drove through Janesville, I passed some condos for sale."

Mary Margaret's voice came out shrill as a mill whistle. "Where do you think I'd get the money to buy you a condo?"

"Oh, come off it." Bethanne lolled back and crossed her arms. "Look at your clothes, your silver brush, all that jewelry. Winston gives you anything you want."

Her sister closed her eyes, leaned against the vanity table and slowly drew in a breath. Then she let it out just as slowly through lips tinted pastel pink. "He's very generous, but he keeps a tight hand on the cash. I get a monthly household allowance, and that's it. Nowhere near enough to buy you a condo."

"Then ask him for it." Bethanne took another nip from her pint. "There's nothing he won't do for you." She leered. "Must be all those little tricks you learned on your knees."

Mary Margaret looked like she was going to choke. "What do you mean?"

"You think I don't know? Where the hell you think I was when Momma was on the phone to Aunt Eunice? Asking how much you were showing and how much longer til it was all over?"

Mary Margaret sat down on the vanity bench and supported herself with a hand on the silk seat. "That's the only secret I ever kept from you"

Bethanne smirked. "Well, I found out anyway."

"I was in love."

"Course you were, college girl. And he must've taught you a lot." Bethanne smiled down at her pint. "So use those little tricks on

Winston tonight. And every night. He'll come around. You always get what you want."

Mary Margaret's backbone went rigid. She gripped the gold bangle with a white-knuckled hand. "But this is something you want. Not me. I'm not going to talk Winston into buying you a condo." She blinked and softened her tone. "You can stay here for a few weeks. Get back on your feet, find a job." She smiled. "Before long, you can buy your own condo."

Bethanne licked the pint's last drop and threw the bottle in the wastebasket. "What a shit you are, Mary Margaret. Everything's always gone your way—teacher's pet, scholarship to that fancy girls' school, beauty queen, rich husband. Meanwhile, I'm just dirt under everybody's feet."

Mary Margaret looked like she wasn't listening, like she'd gone back to the days of her lost love. But Bethanne knew how to get her attention.

She stood up and swayed back against the chair. Then she righted herself and lurched over until her face was only inches from Mary Margaret's. Her voice slurred, "You want me to go away, just like Momma made your nigger baby go away. Well, I'm not gonna, and you can't make me."

⌐~

Bethanne sucked on her cigarette and watched the people streaming into the funeral home. Who was she kidding? She was just the boozy sister, always getting in trouble, never holding down a job for long, marrying a string of losers. Or living with them if she couldn't get them to the altar.

Mary Margaret hadn't wanted her around for years, and Bethanne wouldn't have got that condo if she'd waited til Doomsday. The little bit of cash Mary Margaret had given her was almost gone. Pretty soon she'd be back on her own, too old to find a job. Or a man. Deep inside, Bethanne felt something quiver. She'd never felt so alone.

She tugged on her ill-fitting black dress, bought with Winston's money, so she'd have "appropriate attire" as he called it, ground out her cigarette and headed back inside. Time to get this over. Then she'd have to do something about her own life.

2

THEM TV AND NEWSPAPER reporters didn't even have the courtesy to wait til after the funeral. The very next morning after Ray-Jean was pulled outta the lake, they come right up to her momma's trailer door and started hammering til she dragged herself out and talked to 'em. They went on and on, wanting to know how she felt about losing her daughter. Any fool coulda told 'em that. What'd they think she was gonna say, she was glad Ray-Jean was gone?

And course they had to run all over the trailer park and try to get Ray-Jean's neighbors to say dumb things. I kept the door locked and wouldn't answer no matter how much they knocked and called. None of their business how I felt or what I thought.

But that Marlene was after the limelight, for sure. There she was, just the part-time help to the trailer-park owner, the trashiest girl who lived here. The only reason she lent a hand at the office was she finally graduated from high school and couldn't find a real job. Got her diploma a whole year late cause she had to repeat seventh grade. But that girl surely was ambitious for herself.

You'da thought she knew everything there was to know about Ray-Jean. Standing there on the office stoop, flipping her long black hair, sticking out her big boobs and going on and on about what a sweet child Ray-Jean was and who in the world would ever want her dead. She'd done a sight better to've taken care of them pots of scraggly daisies on either side of the door like she was supposed to. But them reporters couldn't get enough hints Ray-Jean been murdered.

Well, after Marlene blabbing about how somebody musta done her in, the reporters circled back to Ray-Jean's momma and asked her what she thought. I was standing back from the open window, watching everything and bouncing Cruz up and down so he wouldn't cry and give me away.

Miz Shackleford looked so care-worn, my heart like to melt. "I just can't imagine Ray-Jean had any enemies," she said. "My baby girl always was a little daredevil, but she never hurt nobody, ever."

"You think that's why she was in that car?" a man called out. "Because somebody dared her to?"

Miz Shackleford shook her head. "Ray-Jean liked to pick up odd jobs now and then so she'd have a little spending money of her own. You-all said on the TV that Miz Gravesly was going out to the lake to get her cottage ready for the summer. I 'spect Ray-Jean was tagging along just to help out."

"But she never told you that, did she?" said some bottle-blond with a tight suit and a fancy microphone.

I felt the sorriest for Miz Shackleford I ever felt for anybody in my life. They was trying to back her into a corner, and she didn't have nowhere else to go.

"Well, no," she said, "Ray-Jean didn't say nothing to me about going out there." They all started yammering, trying to get in the next question, but Miz Shackleford held up her hand for 'em to stop. "You-all know how girls of thirteen is. They like to have secrets from the grown-ups. You push 'em too hard, they ain't gonna tell you nothing.

I always thought, let her have her little secrets and maybe she'll talk to me about the big things."

That made me feel even worse. Ray-Jean musta had some secret that ended up killing her, and her momma didn't know nothing about it.

—

Bethanne peered through the living room's lace curtains along with Winston and the housekeeper—that's what the family called her, but it was just a ritzy name for maid as far as Bethanne was concerned. The woman was a good worker, though, even if she was round enough to roll like a ball. She kept Mary Margaret's antique furniture gleaming with polish and the brocade upholstery spotless.

The other two leaned forward, and Bethanne bent down to get a better look at how the Police Chief was handling the media outside. Mary Margaret's beautiful roses had been trampled into multi-colored mush, but Winston had held firm from the moment the news broke. He didn't have anything to say to the press, ever.

Chief Hastings had done a good job of keeping the media way from Mary Margaret's funeral, but it seemed like that'd just whetted the reporters' appetite. Here they were, only days later, baying for more. Hastings hitched up his belt over a stomach starting to hint at fat and smiled into the cameras. His bass voice held authority and likability at the same time. "I already told you all you're going to hear at the press conference. No evidence of foul play. Nothing wrong with the car. No alcohol or drugs in Miz Gravesly's system. This was just a tragic accident, and that's all you're going to get out of me or anybody."

Bethanne winced. It wasn't enough. How could Mary Margaret die for no good reason?

Hastings passed his smile around the cameras again. "Now why don't you folks go on about your business and leave this fine family to grieve in peace?" He made a show of waving, getting in his police cruiser and driving away. The reporters and cameramen ran after him a few yards, then milled in the street as if uncertain what to do.

Winston brushed past Bethanne and looked sideways at the housekeeper. "Mae, didn't you say you'd put the coffee on?"

"Yessir." She bobbed her head and smoothed her rick-racked apron. "I'll bring it right away."

He marched toward the breakfast room at the back of the house, Bethanne trailing along like she didn't know what else to do. She watched Winston sit at the head of the table and raise a well-kept hand to smooth well-groomed hair. Always was vain about his appearance. Mary Margaret had said he got contact lenses when he was fourteen. Must've been the first kid in town.

"Chief Hastings did a good job out there," Winston said. "Like I've been saying, if you don't feed the media, they'll get hungry and run after somebody else's troubles."

Bethanne moved to the chair farthest from his. Winston made her feel like she was just there to listen and applaud, but she had to put up with it. She had no place to go but Winston's house.

Mae brought in a tray, set it on the table and poured coffee into Mary Margaret's Crown Derby cups.

Winston went on like she hadn't even arrived. "Sure pays to have friends in high places. Billy Hastings and I go way back. Played football together at Lewiston High. I was quarterback." He smiled to himself. "Billy always was good at taking directions. Course, all those campaign contributions don't hurt either."

Bethanne sipped her coffee and tried not to let him see how he sickened her. Never a word about Mary Margaret or her mysterious death. About how that car he gave her only a few weeks ago rolled off the dock and killed her. That gift was as much about Winston as it was about Mary Margaret—a sporty Mercedes that shouted, "Look how much I can afford to indulge my wife." Custom paint job too, soft buttery yellow to match Mary Margaret's hair. Now all this selfish SOB cared about was protecting himself. How could her sister have made him the center of her life?

"Even before that, my daddy did his daddy a heap of favors," Winston continued. "Old man Hastings made the best white lightning in Lewis County, and Daddy got him off more than once." He winked. "Always got paid by the case."

Miz Shackleford sure was right about Ray-Jean being a daredevil. Soon as spring started warming up, my best friend commenced to sneaking into people's houses and taking away little things for souvenirs. Then she'd show 'em to me out at her hidey-place in the woods. Made me feel like a queen looking at them trophies.

But sometime later, she stopped showing me what she found, and I started thinking maybe she got another friend, better'n me. Ray-Jean swore that wasn't true, but it still made me feel bad.

After she died, I begun to wondering if maybe there was more to why she stopped showing me them trophies than I realized. Maybe there was a clue out there in them woods. Like in that book Miss Bailey assigned me to read. It told about this girl who had to find clues hidden all over the place. She was really shy, but afore that story was over, she found out she was pretty brave too. Miss Bailey said I had a lot going for me, but it was all hid inside, and she got me to reading all kinda things. Not Shakespeare, though. That man can't write English.

So when it come time to go to Ray-Jean's funeral, my body was twitching in this dress Momma made me wear, while my mind was restless with what might be in Ray-Jean's hidey-place. The service was at that small Baptist church over near the plant nursery, not the big old brick one downtown. Full of flowers and people crying their eyes out. Even her Daddy, who come back from Moorestown. Least he had the sense to leave his tramp at home. Anyhow, everybody crying 'cept me, cause I had me a plan.

Once the funeral was over, I put on my jeans and waited a couple hours so no one'd be paying attention. Momma was working the night shift, so she took care of Cruz during the day. I hightailed it way back into them woods behind the trailer park to where there's a couple big rocks leaning together. Them rocks got a little bitty cave underneath, hardly enough for a cat to get into. That's where Ray-Jean kept her treasures, in an old Maxwell House coffee can. Like our mommas save the bacon grease in so they won't have to buy so much Crisco. I pulled away the dry grass Ray-Jean used to plug the hole and got out that rusty old can.

I leaned back against the rock and felt that sun-warmed spot loosen up all the tension in my shoulders. Didn't even know it was there til it let go. Then I opened the can and dumped everything out on the ground. Touching them treasures got me to thinking about Ray-Jean. The time she beat up two girls twict her size cause they was mocking me for being so pudgy. And us making mud pies out in the rain when we was little kids. Her buying me ice cream and taking me to the movies.

Then I started to cry. For the first time. I never cried when I was watching the TV tell about how she died, and I never cried at the funeral. But I lay down on the ground, this fat girl with pigtails that nobody liked 'cept Ray-Jean, and I just bawled.

In the end, I got the hiccups, and I set up and laughed the way Ray-Jean woulda laughed at me being so silly over an old coffee can. Then I dried my face with the tail of my T-shirt and looked her things over real good.

I expected to see a lot of new stuff, cause I thought Ray-Jean been sneaking into houses without showing me what she found. But I recognized everything there 'cept a string of fake pearls. Where'd they come from?

Bethanne almost snorted when Winston assumed just the right posture for the role he wanted to play. Behind the imposing desk in his study, silver hair back-lit by the morning sun, looking over the half-moon reading glasses he affected since he'd had his cataracts fixed and couldn't wear contacts, an imitation of concern wrinkling his eyes.

"Bethanne, I wanted to spare you any embarrassment before the lawyer comes."

She managed to keep her nose from snarling as she looked at the old hypocrite. Less than a week after the funeral, and he had to get his jollies by gloating over her.

Winston went on as if he was totally oblivious. "I guess you know Mary Margaret didn't have much wealth of her own. Needless to say, the joint property stays with me until my demise."

She started to speak, but he held up a soft, pink palm and continued, "Of course Mary Margaret was free to bestow her jewelry as she saw fit. But I think that would naturally go to our daughter..."

Sure it will, you shit. Bethanne nearly gagged on the scent of his old leather-bound books.

"...clothes, shoes, handbags..."

Bethanne leaned back and lit a cigarette. Who the hell was going to tell her not to smoke now? She ogled the still-warm pipe on Winston's desk. Let the son of a bitch finish. Then she'd have plenty to say.

"...nothing much to bequeath. Still, everybody has to have a will." He leaned back, the very picture of probity. "I didn't want any hint of conflict of interest, so I suggested Mary Margaret go to Farnsworth's little firm down on Pike Street."

Bethanne felt restless, waiting for him to pause so she could get her two cents in.

"Farnsworth is also Mary Margaret's executor, and he'll be reading the will." Winston's smile at Bethanne barely turned up the corners of his mouth. "Don't feel hurt. Mary Margaret just didn't have much to give."

Bethanne leaned forward in her chair. "You made sure of that, didn't you? Figure you couldn't trust her? Or did you just want to tie her down tight?"

Winston blanched and drew breath to speak, but there was a discreet knock on the door. He swallowed his retort. "Come in."

Bethanne watched them cross the threshold. The fiftyish Sam Farnsworth she recognized from the funeral. The next generation of Graveslys, Lucinda and Clayton. And their spouses. All four in their thirties, all looking prosperous and appropriately subdued. Mae brought up the rear.

Bethanne's memory dredged up her sister acquiescing when Winston insisted that Clayton be given Winston's mother's maiden name. Even though Mary Margaret thought it was too big a moniker for a little boy. Now here he was, all grown up in a blazer and tie. It was Bethanne who started calling him Clay. Such a handsome boy, a towhead with blue eyes. They'd been pals.

Not Lucinda, though. Bethanne never could get next to the child who had the other half of Winston's mother's name. Lucinda looked just as unsociable today, her mouse-brown hair pulled back in a clasp, her suit so tailored she could have been a lawyer if only Winston had been willing to take a daughter, as well as a son, into the firm.

Bethanne gazed at Clay again, his little boy's long hair now turned dark blond and cut short. They probably weren't going to be pals now. Wills did that to families.

Winston made a show of graciously ceding his place at the ornate desk to Farnsworth. He moved the water carafe within the lawyer's reach and motioned the family to take their places in the semi-circle of chairs facing the lawyer. Clay held the center chair for his father, then slogged across the Persian carpet to sit at one end of the row.

Bethanne sat next to Mae at the opposite end, contemplating Winston's stagey gesture of cordiality to Farnsworth. It made her see the Graveslys in a new light. They were better dressed than she was. Better educated. Luckier too. But not smarter. She held onto that thought while Farnsworth droned on, reading the will.

It was just as Winston had said. Mary Margaret didn't have much, and it was all going to her children, except for a modest bequest to Mae. She had remembered Bethanne, though. Her sister was to choose any two pieces of jewelry she desired before Lucinda took the rest.

Well, at least it was a thought, Bethanne consoled herself. She wished she knew more about jewelry. How would she know which two pieces would bring the most at the pawnshop? She looked down at her left wrist. Maybe she could get her watch back. Daddy'd given it to her when she'd graduated from high school. About the only thing she'd ever done right.

She could see Farnsworth nearing the end. He paused for a sip of water, then read the last clause.

"To my only sister, Bethanne Whitehouse Swanson, I leave the contents of the savings account in my name at the National Bank of Moorestown in the hope that it will help her find a new direction in life."

Bethanne shook her head. A new direction? Who the hell did Mary Margaret think she was? Bethanne had spent her life starting over. Marrying that sailor she met in a bar because he got her pregnant. Losing the baby. Then losing him when he ran off with that redhead. Taking care of Momma after the car accident that killed Daddy and put Momma in bed for the rest of her life. Which wasn't that long. Having to sell the house Daddy'd left Bethanne to pay Momma's medical bills. Following Robbie Ray around the country music circuit until he beat her up one time too many. New directions in life, that was something she knew way too much about.

Behind those memories, she heard Winston say, "What?" His tongue hit the 't' so hard the sound crackled in the air. "How much money are we talking about?"

Farnsworth smiled, an expression so small it barely touched his face. "I checked the account. About twelve thousand dollars."

Winston leaned forward. "Why wasn't I made aware of this?"

Farnsworth touched his salt-and-pepper hair. "I represented your wife, Mr. Gravesly." He adjusted his wire-rimmed glasses. "That was confidential information."

Winston's face reddened. "Of course, of course." He eased back against the chair and crossed his legs.

Bethanne found herself split between guilt and gratitude. Her last days with her sister had been filled with the tension of her own demands on Mary Margaret. Yet her sister had remembered Bethanne in her will. When Bethanne thought it through, she felt pretty good about Mary Margaret giving her one more chance. Her sister still believed in her despite four decades of bailing Bethanne out of one crisis after another.

Twelve thousand dollars. It wasn't much, but it was enough. She could get the hell out of Dodge just as soon as she was ready. Fuck you, Winston.

3

I DON'T KNOW HOW long I set there in them woods with Ray-Jean's trophies, struggling to figure out what it all meant. Tried to empty my mind, so it could come to me. Leaned back against the rock again and listened to the birds' wings taking off and landing. If you listen real hard, you can hear their wind beat against the leaves as they pass through. All round me was the warm smells of early summer—new grasses, new wildflowers, everything new 'cept what Ray-Jean done to get herself killed.

But none of that helped. Eventually, I realized the shadows was getting longer and I had to hurry on home to watch Cruz while Momma went to work. Sometimes they got her working four to midnight and sometimes it's midnight to eight in the morning. Either way, I'm the one cleans him up in the evening, feeds him and puts him to bed, so Momma can take care of keeping us in house and home.

Me and Cruz got our names from a soap opera. Momma's a slave to the soaps, and I can understand how she needs a little romance, her life being tough right from the start. Well, she got herself infatuated with this girl on one of them shows, and nothing would do but she had to name her first child after that girl. That's me, and she named

Cruz after the guy who loved the girl in the soap opera. Ain't that something?

Course I have to put up with a lotta teasing about my name. And Cruz will too. But you know what? Even when the girls get nasty—"Why don'cha get naked, Eden?" they say and laugh at how I'd look with no clothes on. Even then, I don't pay 'em no mind cause my momma picked me a name that meant a lot to her. I'll bet them Judys, Janes and Marys can't say nearly the same.

Anyhow, the lowering sun got me to gathering up all the treasures and putting 'em back in the coffee can. That's when I saw the envelope wedged down in the bottom. Wrinkled and stained, like Ray-Jean musta took it outta somebody's garbage pail. Had one of them cellophane windows like bills come in. So I reached down, pulled it out and opened it up.

Then I shouted. "Wah!" Like that. The envelope was full of money. I lost all thought of Momma and Cruz. I just set there and counted them greenbacks. Tens and twenties and fifties. Nearly eight hunnerd dollars.

That made two clues, the pearls and the money. But I had no idea what to do with 'em, so I put everything back in the can. Stuffed the can in the hidey-place and covered it up with that wad of dry grass.

And hurried on home. Got there just in time, waved Momma 'bye, fell on the living room sofa bed and turned on the TV.

But I couldn't settle down to it. My poor old brain kept going over all the things Ray-Jean'd done just afore she died. Like buying me ice cream. And taking me to the movies. How come I didn't get suspicious? She never had that kinda money afore. She must took it outta that envelope. But how'd she get it in the first place?

I worried at those thoughts til I couldn't take it no more. Then I did the bravest thing. I went in Momma's bedroom and got her shears. I walked into the bathroom, turned on the light and cut off my hair.

I knew Momma was gonna be mad. But thirteen is too old for pigtails, and that's a fact. Momma was gonna have to get used to it.

I looked in the mirror, and my hair was just like Ray-Jean's. I figure some folks'll say I was in mourning, or I was trying to be her now she was gone. Well, they can think what they want. We didn't look alike—she was a little bitty thing, while I was big and fat—but we always was one mind in two bodies.

⁓

After Farnsworth read the will, Mae served tea in the dining room while Bethanne watched everyone's reactions. Once again, Clay held a chair for his father, then went off to sit as nearly alone as he could. He'd been Mary Margaret's golden boy. Now he seemed lost without her, like he was carrying a burden he didn't know how to lay down.

Lucinda grabbed the chair next to her father and tried to monopolize his attention. Always greedy for her father's notice, Bethanne recalled.

The housekeeper's dark face drooped with sorrow as she offered a cup to Farnsworth. Usually Mae wore cotton housedresses in bright colors, but today she had on a gray uniform with a white apron. The tight cuffs of the sleeves bit into her fleshy biceps. Probably Lucinda's idea. Made her feel grand to have a maid in uniform. Been like that ever since she was a little girl. Wasn't enough for Lucinda to be the oldest child, lording it over Clay every chance she got. She always needed to feel she was more important than anybody else in the world.

Thinking of Lucinda as a child made Bethanne remember the trashy girl she'd seen with Mary Margaret just days before her sister died. Bethanne had been on her way to the liquor store when she'd spied them in the G-Mart parking lot. Later on, she'd asked Mary Margaret about the kid in dirty jeans and T-shirt, but her sister had put her off with a tale about the girl asking for a dollar. Mary Margaret always was a fool for a sob story. Even when it was Lucinda trying to get the best of Clay.

Bethanne took a dainty teacake from Mae's silver tray, frowning at the memory of the girl in the parking lot. Was that the same one who'd drowned in the Mercedes with Mary Margaret? She reached for a cup of tea. A stiff bourbon would've been more welcome, but she knew the Graveslys would never offer alcohol before lunch, at the earliest. And then only wine. Or beer if they were having sandwiches.

She was bursting to talk with Farnsworth, but not in front of the Graveslys. The whole family soon wandered out to Mary Margaret's garden. It was like a shout that Bethanne and Farnsworth weren't part of their crowd.

Fuck them, she didn't want to be part of their family anyway. Bethanne started to speak, but Farnsworth reached into his briefcase and pulled out an envelope. Confidential, from Mary Margaret to her. The corners of his eyes crinkled with a gentle smile. "I suggest you read the letter in private." Then come by the office, and we'll talk it over."

After I cut my hair off, my soul was lightened. I could see things I hadn't seen afore. Put two and two together where there'd been only a bunch of zeroes.

Ray-Jean died in Miz Gravesly's car. That was a fact. There had to be some connection between Ray-Jean and Miz Gravesly for them two to die together. Them pearls was the only thing new to me when I opened that coffee can. So maybe Ray-Jean snuck into Miz Gravesly's house and took them pearls for a souvenir. Just like she always done from every house she snuck into.

But why would rich Miz Gravesly have tacky old drugstore pearls? Sentimental value, that's what. Maybe her family wasn't always rich. Maybe they been her granny's, and she give 'em to Miz Gravesly when she was baptized. Oh, I know them Graveslys probably go to the Episcopalian Church, just like all them rich folks. But maybe she was born a Baptist, like I was born a Pentecostal. I have to admit, though, I'm not so sure what I am no more, now that Daddy's gone.

Anyhow, there's lots of ways Miz Gravesly mighta got them pearls. Main thing is they meant something to her, and she was paying Ray-Jean to get 'em back. I asked myself if I was jumping to conclusions, but that explanation was the only way I could figure out a connection between them pearls and all that money in Ray-Jean's coffee can.

It shocked me some to think of my best friend being a blackmailer. But I could see how Ray-Jean woulda fell prey to the temptation. She always did want more than she could have.

But how come Miz Gravesly and Ray-Jean ended up drowned in the lake? Seems like family members is always the first suspects. Remember that little beauty queen got killed out west? The police was all over her family, trying to figure out which one done it. Maybe Miz Gravesly's husband found out she was cheating on him and messed up the brakes or something like that. Could be Ray-Jean's momma was right. My best friend just happened to be in that car at the wrong time.

All them ideas made me realize two things. I had to ask my cousin Buck—he fixes folks' cars in his backyard—ask him how you could do something to a car so it'd run for a while and then have an accident. And for sure I had to find out more about them Graveslys. Coulda been any of 'em.

Dear Bethanne,

So many years have passed since we used to whisper secrets late at night. Too many years when we haven't been that close, when I didn't have anyone to tell my secrets to.

Well, there's one secret left. All these years, I've been saving money from my household allowance. In addition to the amount in the Moorestown Bank, I keep petty cash—a few hundred dollars usually—in a lockbox. Most of the year, it's hidden at the back of my closet. But when we leave here for the summer, I put it in the niche behind the kitchen stove at the lake house.

Winston always bought me everything I wanted. That's why I feel I have to leave nearly all those beautiful things to Lucinda and let you have just a couple of keepsakes.

But he said the household allowance was mine. And that's the way I treated it, squirreling away what I could in case the day would come when I'd need to use it.

So take whatever you find in the lockbox. It was mine, and now it's yours. You'll find the key on a chain at the bottom of my jewel case.

Your loving sister,
Mary Margaret

Bethanne kept going over the letter, trying to see if she'd made a mistake. She stood in the middle of Mary Margaret's dressing room and looked around at the godawful mess she'd made—dresses crumpled and pulled to one side, shoe boxes all over the floor, drawers open with fancy lingerie spilling out.

As soon as Farnsworth had left, she'd gone to her room and ripped open the envelope he'd given her. Then she'd run to Mary Margaret's bedroom, locked the door and started searching. Locating the hidden key had been easy. There'd been two keys in the bottom of the jewelry case. One was tiny, a bit flimsy, a little bent from too much pressure. The other was bigger, stronger, on a chain like her sister had said. No problem telling them apart.

But finding the lockbox was something else. The closet was huge, fitted with drawers and shelves, bars at different levels for blouses, skirts, dresses and slacks. Even a special section for formal gowns and long dresses. Bethanne had combed every inch, but the lockbox was nowhere to be found.

She could hear Winston and the rest of the family banging on the door. Let them bang. Let them shout. And let them clean up the mess. Or let Mae do it, if that's what they wanted. All she was doing was looking for her money.

With an effort, she refocused her search. If the lockbox wasn't here, Mary Margaret must have already taken it out to the lake house. Maybe she'd hidden it before she went off the dock.

Heartache swept through Bethanne like it'd been doing off and on for days. She couldn't accept that Mary Margaret's death had been an accident. The Mercedes had been way out in the lake, like Mary Margaret had really put the pedal to the metal. The whole family seemed to want to keep the lid on any hint of scandal, and the Police Chief was doing his part to make sure they got their wish.

Bethanne inhaled Mary Margaret's Acqua di Gioia, its slight scent still lingering on the clothes she'd pushed aside. Her conscience stirred over what she'd done to her sister's beautiful things, but self-preservation soon got the upper hand. She'd better keep her mouth shut about her suspicions. And she'd better get out to the lake and protect her inheritance. She sighed. Might as well resign herself to the fact that the only way she was going to get inside that house was with Winston's cooperation.

Jesus, she should have thought about that before she'd locked the rest of the family out of the bedroom and messed it up so bad. She glanced out the window. Still lots of time to get out to the lake today. Best clean up the jumble, tell everyone she'd started to look at Mary Margaret's jewelry to select her two keepsakes and then just lost it, maddened by grief. After that, she'd see if someone would drive her out to the lake house and let her in.

No, that might make them wonder what she was up to. She'd just have to wait until they were going on their own and tag along. But when would that be? She couldn't bear to wait a minute.

A movement of bright color caught her attention, and she looked across the street. A girl was staring up at the house. She looked just like that other girl, the one Bethanne had seen with Mary Margaret at G-Mart. Except this one was fat.

4

IT SEEMED LIKE FOREVER, but it was only a couple of weeks before Bethanne was on her way to the lake house. Wedged in with two cardboard boxes on the backseat of Winston's black Range Rover, she hugged herself with relief. Winston and Clay were in the front, neither one doing much to keep a conversation going. Maybe Winston needed to concentrate on his driving while towing the boat. Maybe it was only natural Clay would feel awkward with his Dad now that Mary Margaret was no longer the bridge between them.

The family had debated long and hard about whether to go on with the usual summer move. Bethanne had felt like she couldn't bear all the chatter. Lucinda had argued that it would be gruesome to holiday where Mary Margaret had died. But Winston had countered that his wife would have wanted them to go on with their lives. It was Clay who suggested a compromise—move out to the lake a bit later, when the first sadness had softened.

Now Winston, Clay and Bethanne were going to finish readying the house. Lucinda and Clay's wife had stayed behind, because they didn't want the kids to confront the dock just yet. Lucinda's husband, John, had remained to fix a loose step. They were all spending a lot of time at Winston's house, so he wouldn't be alone in the first weeks after the funeral.

Winston turned off the highway onto a graveled road, and Bethanne leaned sideways to peer at the wrought iron arch over the entrance to Lake Charles. At last she could get what was coming to her. The thought made her feel guilty. Her better self, the girl she used to be, remembered why Mary Margaret hadn't finished her normal preparations for the move. The other self, the one who got drunk when things went bad, that one was itching to get into the kitchen and find the lockbox.

Winston pulled off the graveled road onto a steep drive that led past the house and down to the wooden dock. He stopped beside the two-story bungalow with its fieldstone porch. When Bethanne opened the car door, she found herself facing the lake. She got out and turned her back on the rippling water. If she started thinking about how Mary Margaret's car had soared off the dock, she'd never be able to go through with her plan. She reached in the backseat and snatched a carton of groceries. "I can set up the kitchen. That'll leave you men free to concentrate on the boat."

Winston seemed relieved to let her deal with the indoor chores while he handled the ones outside. Watching him march toward the SUV's boat hitch, Bethanne felt hope rise. She headed for the house.

"Bethanne!"

She turned toward Winston's call, fearful he'd follow her inside after all.

He came forward and put a hand in his pocket. "You'll need the keys."

Her arms went weak with relief, and she almost dropped the carton.

"Want a hand?" Winston asked.

"No, no, I can manage." Bethanne steadied the carton on her hip, grabbed the keys, opened the door and shut it firmly behind her. She paused, looking at the room which filled almost the whole first floor. In the weeks since Mary Margaret had died, dust had settled everywhere. Even the faded chintz on couches and chairs had a patina of fine golden particles, and the air smelled of ashes left in the fieldstone fireplace. Mary Margaret had once said she'd found it strange to have a hearth in a summer place, but then she'd come to appreciate it when cold thunderstorms crashed outside.

Bethanne crossed the wide planks of the wooden floor and entered the kitchen. She emptied the carton on a countertop and carried it to a white enamel stove that must have stood in its brick alcove since the fifties. Its flue climbed up a chimney left over from the days when the kitchen would've had a wood-burner. Bethanne put the side of her head flat against the brick wall and looked beyond the large gas canister that fueled the current stove. Sure enough, there was the lockbox in its niche.

The bump of metal on wood startled Bethanne, and she swirled around. It was Clay.

"Gosh. Didn't mean to scare you. Bringing in a new canister."

Bethanne sucked in a breath. "No, no. I mean, it's okay. I was just checking the old one." She worked to get her breathing under control. "There's still enough for several days. Why don't you put that one in the pantry, and we'll bring it out when we need it."

She hurried to the countertop and started putting the canned goods away while Clay wheeled the canister into the pantry. When he returned, he pulled out a pack of cigarettes and offered her one. Bethanne desperately wanted him back outside, but she didn't want to raise his suspicions. She took one, then nearly choked on a harsh lung-full. "Jesus," she said. "Whatever makes you smoke these things?"

Clay showed her the funny-looking blue label. "Started when I was backpacking around Europe. Order them through the internet now. That summer was the only time I ever felt completely free. Nobody knew I was a Gravesly or what that meant." He took a long drag and let the smoke trickle out his nostrils. "I could just be myself. You ever feel that way, Aunt Bee?"

She smiled at the use of his old pet name for her. "Maybe once. Long time ago, when I was married to Robbie Ray Vance. Remember him? The one wanted to be a country music star?"

Clay nodded, and she continued. "We were on the road a lot. I got tired of living in motel rooms, so I got a job in a little gift shop. Had my own money. Didn't have to worry about whether he was going to bring any home or not. That felt pretty free."

Maybe she was going to feel that way again, if only she could get her hands on the lockbox. She looked pointedly out the window to where Winston was fiddling with the boat.

Clay followed her gaze and sighed. "Guess I better get back to helping Dad."

She watched him saunter to the boat, then ran to the niche, took out the lockbox and hid it in the cardboard carton that had held the groceries. She carried the carton out to the Range Rover and put it on the backseat.

"Just getting the other box of groceries," she called out to the two men.

No way she was going to risk getting caught opening the lockbox here. She'd think of some excuse to take the cardboard carton up to her room once they got back to the Lewiston house. Then she'd have a little spending money.

⌐═

As soon as I thought of it, I called Buck and asked him about what you'd have to do to a car to make it go off the dock like Miz Gravesly's car done.

"Little buddy," he said, "I ain't gonna talk to you about something so morbid. I know losing your best friend like that was a shock, but you gotta put your mind on something positive." Then he hung up.

Well, that was a dead end, at least for now, but I'd find another way to bring it up. Meanwhile, I started watching the Graveslys' house whenever I could, studying their comings and goings, trying to figure out who was who. That was surely some house. Kinda like *Gone with the Wind*. I musta seen that movie a hunnerd times on one of them classics channels. But their house ain't really that old. My granny said Mr. Gravesly's grandpappy built it in the twenties just to show how much he could roar.

Anyhow, the more I watched that house, the more I realized I had to get inside. Even if it scared me just to think about going in there, I had to try and find me another clue. But there was always somebody to home.

I thought my chance'd come when their big old SUV pulled outta the driveway with a boat behind. There was several folks in the car, so I reckoned I'd mosey on out to the backyard and see if I could sneak in. Figured if Ray-Jean could do it, I could too.

But I was still nervous, prickly fingers running up my neck and across my scalp. Told myself to keep my mind on what I was doing and look for a safe way in. Didn't want no neighbors seeing me, if I could help it. Off to the side was this big rose garden, kinda beat down but starting to come back from whatever had messed it up afore. So I hunched down and scooted along a brick walk inside them roses, past this deep lily pond toward back where I wanted to be.

Thought I was doing pretty good, til I heard the hullabaloo coming from the backyard. I peeked round the roses, and my heart started beating like a woodpecker hungry for lunch. There was two women with their kids splashing in one of them blow-up plastic pools.

Biggest one I ever saw. Musta took all the wind them men had to get that sucker blown up. Then I asked myself what was I thinking? They probably had some sorta electric pump so they wouldn't get their lips dirty. That kinda calmed me down, thinking about them stuck-up guys trying to blow up a pool that big with just their lungs.

It was clear as day I couldn't get in at the back. But if they was all out there, maybe I could find another way in. I started scooting through the rose garden again, and then I heard a noise over by the house. Nearly peed my pants cause this man was coming outta the cellar carrying a toolbox. I barely managed to get down behind some bushes and pray.

He went on out to the backyard, and I saw he left the cellar door open. Maybe I could get in through there. So I crawled along, hoping the neighbors wasn't peeking outta their windows. Then I got ahold of my nerves and snuck into that cellar. Felt like Ray-Jean woulda been proud of me.

Sure was dark in there after being out in the sun. But in a little while my eyes got used to it, and I could see fine with the light spilling in from the one door and the little bitty windows just barely above ground.

It was some kinda big cellar, I can tell you that. Broke up into rooms all in a row, each one with a door that opened from a hallway at the foot of them outside stairs. I headed left, toward the front of the house. Figured the stairs up into the house oughta be near the front door. The first room I went into had a big old furnace and giant pipes going every which way. When I looked closer, I could see that it wasn't just a furnace. It was an air conditioner too. Nice to be rich and have the whole house heated and cooled without no noise like we have. When summer comes, all you can hear in the Happy Hours Trailer Park is the roar of air conditioners hanging on the side of everybody's trailer.

Work bench in there too. Them Gravesly men musta been handy, at least. Or maybe they just had some hobby they did down there. Next come a root cellar, dark as pitch, no windows, wood boxes and barrels all round. Smelled like potatoes'd rotted in there a long time ago and never been cleaned up.

I turned round and headed back the other way. When I got to the open door, I stood there, holding my breath and listening a spell. But all I could hear was some hammering and the kids screaming and splashing. So I went on and passed through a laundry room, big old wringer washer pushed over in the corner so there'd be room for the automatic. Double sink made of stone kinda soft to the touch, clotheslines all above but a big drier too, and an ironing board off to the side. Them Graveslys had the best idea for ironing I ever did see. The socket for the iron was up on that low ceiling, so when you plugged it in, the cord wouldn't get in the way. Ain't that something?

Well, on I went into another room with shelves all over, full of canned goods. Some of it was store-bought—Green Giant Niblets, Campbell's Pork 'n' Beans. But a lot of it was home-canned—tomatoes and green beans, pickles and relishes. Who'da thought Miz Gravesly been that kinda woman?

It took me a while to realize I'd come to the end of the line. I was looking at the other end of the house, and I hadn't found no stairway going up inside.

Just as I was standing there with my mouth open, I heard a floorboard creak up above, and my heart started jackhammering again. I lost any sense I had about being brave enough to sneak into folks' houses. All I could think of was getting the heck outta there.

I headed back for the cellar door. Nearly got there too, but just as I was getting ready to go up them concrete steps and head someplace safe, I heard a woman say, "Oh, Johnny. You left the cellar door open again."

I did wet my pants just a tiny bit then, cause the door slammed shut, and the bolt rammed home. There I was, nothing to do but sit in that shadowy cellar and wonder what I was going to say when they opened it up again.

5

As soon as WINSTON parked the Range Rover behind the Lewiston house, Bethanne jumped out with the cardboard carton and headed toward the back porch.

"Hey," Winston called, "what're you doing with that old box?"

"Oh…thought it'd come in handy for moving my stuff. Just as soon as I get the money Mary Margaret left me." She glanced at Clay as he closed the car door and started toward the two of them.

Winston shook out his pipe and came close enough she could smell the stale tobacco spilling from his lungs. "You're gonna have to wait a long time then."

"What're you talking about? You can't keep me from by money."

He smiled, but it looked like a smirk he was trying to control. "No, but the county can. Haven't you ever heard of probate? It'll take six months, maybe even a year, before you get that money." His face filled with gloating. "What're you going to do in the meantime, baby sister?"

Bethanne felt like he'd punched her in the stomach. She'd forgotten how long it'd taken for Daddy's will to be probated. It was all she could do to hold onto the carton, but the knowledge that she had to protect the lockbox inside gave her strength. "Well, I'll just have to stay here, won't I? If I don't have any money of my own." She smirked right back at him. "I don't suppose you'd want to buy me a condo?"

Clay came up to his father. "Aw Dad, Aunt Bee is Mom's only sister. You can't leave her dangling."

Winston made a low sound in his throat. "All right, I'll see what I can do about hurrying up probate." He started up the porch steps.

Clay called after him, "Where's she going to live?" His face lit up with an idea. "What about the old chauffeur's apartment over the garage? Aunt Bee could have some privacy, and so could you."

His father turned back to stare at him, and Bethanne gazed at Clay in wonder. Looked like they were still pals.

"Come on, Dad. Aunt Bee's family."

No, I'm not, Bethanne thought. I'm one of the Whitehouse sisters. Still, she hoped Clay would get his way.

Winston took out a monogrammed handkerchief and wiped his sweating face. "Okay. But only until the will is probated. I've stored some papers up there. Let me get my files out of your way first."

He pointed a forefinger at Bethanne. "In the meantime, don't bring that old box in the house. Leave it in the basement. I won't have Mary Margaret's beautiful home turned into a storeroom."

Clay grinned and gave her a thumbs-up. But when he turned to follow his father, his shoulders seemed to sag. He was putting up a brave front, Bethanne realized, but Mary Margaret's loss still hurt deep down.

Bethanne watched them enter the kitchen, then hurried around the house, savoring her small triumph. An apartment of her own, it seemed almost too good to be true. Okay, she'd still be tied down to Winston, but at least she wouldn't be living right in his house.

She tugged at the bolt on the cellar door, but it only budged an inch. A sound of scrabbling came from behind the door, and she wondered if there'd be rats. Never mind, she'd dealt with rats plenty of times.

⸻

Gol dang. That's all I could think when I heard someone starting to open the cellar door. Then I asked myself what Ray-Jean woulda done, and I got down behind a stack of boxes next to the stairs.

Just in time too. The door opened, and a pair of woman's legs come down, dressed in faded levis and torn sneakers. Couldn't have been one of them young Gravesly women. They only wore designer jeans and expensive shoes. I seen that for myself.

Then come her arms carrying a box and finally her head. I seen that face with them pouchy eyes and frizzy hair afore. Peeking outta the upstairs window.

I figured she was going to add her box to the pile I was hiding behind, but she fooled me. Walked into the laundry room—me peeking from my hidey-place—turned on the light, put the box on the ironing board and opened it up. She was smiling to herself, and that made me wonder what was going on.

So I snuck out from behind the boxes and into the dark corner where the old wringer washing machine was. She was so busy taking a metal box outta the cardboard one, she didn't even look up.

⸻

Bethanne set the lockbox on the ironing board and reached inside her polkadot shirt for the key on its chain. How much was inside? Probably only a couple hundred. But that'd buy booze and cigarettes.

Let Winston feed her. She'd use her money for the pleasures in life.

She giggled as she unlocked the box and raised the lid. The coin-tray was just a bunch of empty compartments. So what? Mary Margaret wasn't going to worry about petty change.

Bethanne's eyebrows raised of their own accord when she lifted the tray and found a diary underneath. Pretty, bound in dark green leather with a strap that buckled into a gold clasp and a small lock. Mary Margaret's money had to be underneath.

Bethanne pulled out the diary and choked. Nothing there. How could that be? Mary Margaret had said…Bethanne looked again. No money of any kind. She sat down on an old wooden chair and looked around. What'd happened to her money? How the hell was she going to have a drink and a smoke without asking Winston for a handout? She swallowed bitter bile.

⌒

I crouched down behind that old washer so long my legs went to sleep. And when I tried to ease the cramp, I toppled over. Too fat to be nimble like Ray-Jean, that's why.

The woman jumped up from the chair and come running at me. "Who are you? What're you doing here?"

"Hold on, Missus. Hold on. I was just looking for something to eat." That was pretty quick, if I do say so myself. Doubt Ray-Jean coulda done better.

But that woman grabbed my arm and bent down close. "Here, let me get a look at you."

I hung my head, cause I was afraid she'd recognize me, but she put a hand under my chin and made me look up at her.

"Wait a minute. I know you. You're the girl's been watching the house. The one who looks like that skinny girl with Mary Margaret. What's your name?"

That skinny girl? Did she mean Ray-Jean? With Mary Margaret, she said. I decided to own up. Just a bit

"Yes'm. I'm Ray-Jean's best friend."

"Ray-Jean?"

Yes'm. The one they found dead with Miz Gravesly."

All the air went outta that woman, and she set down hard. Right on the floor.

—

Bethanne flinched when Lucinda's voice echoed down the cellar stairs and into the laundry room. "Bethanne? Are you all right down there?"

Bethanne put a finger to her lips and looked at the girl. The kid's unnaturally pale skin blanched even whiter, and her hazel eyes glistened with fear. But she nodded her head in understanding. Bethanne levered herself up and headed for the bottom of the stairs.

Lucinda was already halfway down when she got there. "Who's there with you? I could hear voices."

Bethanne tried to smile. "Oh, just talking to myself. Trying to remember some things I need to do. I'll be up in a sec."

Lucinda turned to go. "Don't be long. The men are starting the barbecue. I'll wait here and bolt the door."

"I can do that."

"No, you can't." Lucinda's voice was firm. "You barely touched that mess you made in Mother's dressing room. Mae had to spend hours cleaning it up. I'll lock the door myself. Then I'll know it's done right."

Bethanne shrugged. Jesus, Lucinda was just as big a shit as Winston. "Okay, gimme a minute."

She hurried back to the girl, knelt down and whispered. "You and I need to talk, but we can't now." Her mind was racing, trying to figure out how to make all this happen. "I've got to go up and socialize. Lucinda's going to bolt the cellar door."

The girl's mouth quivered, and her jaw clenched.

"Don't worry," Bethanne said, "I'll come back while they're busy eating and unlatch the door so you can get out. But you have to promise to meet me tomorrow. We got a lot to talk about."

"You wondering too, Missus?" About how they come to die together in that lake?"

Bethanne nodded. "Could be we each know things that might fit together."

"Bethanne…" Lucinda called, sounding full of impatience.

"Coming now." Bethanne rose to leave.

The girl put out a hand to stop her. "Missus? You gotta let me out afore six o'clock. I gotta get on home and look after my baby brother. You promise that, and I'll promise to meet you tomorrow."

Luicinda's irritated voice punctuated the sound of her feet on the stairs. "Bethanne…"

"I promise," Bethanne said to the girl.

Her young face puckered with concern. "I don't see how I can trust no Gravesly."

"I'm not a Gravesly." Bethanne rushed to head off Lucinda.

Soon as I heard the bolt on the cellar door, I got up to look at that metal box the woman left on the ironing board. Boy, was that some disappointment. Just a empty old cashbox like they use at swap meets to keep their money in. Nice-looking diary setting beside it. I was thinking to check it out, but the diary was all locked-up with a fancy clasp. Maybe there was secrets inside, but I wasn't gonna get to read 'em. So I put it in the cashbox, closed that up and stashed everything in the cardboard box. Hid the whole thing in the darkest corner of the root cellar.

Then I got that old wooden chair, climbed up on it and tried to see through the little bitty high window at the rear of the house. That was pure frustration. Couldn't see nothing but the back of some bushes and a pile of nutshells where a mouse had left 'em.

So I settled down to see if that woman with the rusty hair— Lord, it was dry as straw. Didn't she ever hear about conditioner? My momma makes me use it every time I wash my hair, even now it's short. "Looks good." That's all Momma said the first time she saw me with my hair cut off. Guess she musta decided thirteen was too old for pigtails too.

Anyhow, I waited to see if that woman was gonna keep her promise. It was cool down in that cellar, but I could feel the sweat breaking out all over. I surely was having me some bad moments, I can tell you that.

꒰꒱

Bethanne followed Lucinda out to the backyard, relieved to see Winston seemingly mesmerized by the sight of his grandkids' wet bodies. He didn't even look her way when Clay brought her a beer.

Only the one, she told herself. She had to keep a clear head. She lit a Kool, settled back into the hard Adirondack chair and bided her time.

Finally Clay shouted, "Come and get it," and the kids jumped out of the pool. Their mothers were busy drying them off and getting T-shirts over their heads. Winston was pulling soft drinks out of the cooler. Bethanne knew it was now or never.

She stood up. "Gotta go to the little girls' room first."

No one even gave her a glance. She walked through the back door and ran to the front of the house, outside and around to the cellar door.

The bolt made such a screech she was afraid Lucinda would come running, but all she could hear was the kids shouting about mustard and ketchup.

She opened the door, and the girl's head poked out, eyes darting right and left.

Noon tomorrow," Bethanne said. "Outside lunch counter at G-Mart."

"I surely do thank you, Missus," the girl said and sprinted away.

6

SOMETIMES I'M ABOUT AS dumb as you can be. Miss Bailey said that happens to all of us, but I surely was dumb down in that cellar. It was only when I got home I realized maybe there was a connection between that metal box and the money in Ray-Jean's coffee can.

It was a cash box, right? Empty. So what if that's where Ray-Jean's money come from? Then how'd that rusty-haired woman get her hands on that box? I'd just have to find out. In the meantime, I hung onto the idea that maybe it was Miz Gravesly's box, and she took out all the money and give it to Ray-Jean.

I figured all this out while I was feeding Cruz. Helped me keep my mind off him spitting every other mouthful onto his bib. I surely can't make out why folks wanna have babies. If they're not puking out one end, they're pooping out the other. Who wants to spend half their life cleaning up all that? Not me, and that's for sure. Once I finish helping Momma raise this one, I'm done, period.

But I did have me something else to puzzle out. That woman said we should tell each other what we knew and see how it fit together. Maybe she wasn't no Gravesly, but how'd I know I could really trust her? Decided I'd get her to tell me what she knew but not tell her about Ray-Jean's money. Nor them pearls neither.

⟨⟩

"Mr. Gravesly's right." Farnsworth straightened the file folder on his desk. "You'll have to wait until the will is probated before you can access the money in the savings account."

Bethanne tried not to fidget in the hard oak chair facing his desk. She'd decided to talk with Farnsworth before meeting the girl at noon. She needed as much information as she could get. "Winston said he'd try to hurry that up."

Farnsworth smiled his faint twitch. "Mr. Gravesly would certainly have some influence if he cared to use it."

"You said there was about twelve thousand dollars in that account?"

Farnsworth opened the folder and took out a bank statement. "Yes, just a little short of that amount. There were a few withdrawals just before Mrs. Gravesly passed away."

Bethanne felt like something hard was lodged in her throat. "What do you mean, withdrawals? How much? When?"

"That's the strange part." Farnsworth studied the document. "The statements show small, intermittent deposits over many years, sometimes more, sometimes less. But never any withdrawals until some weeks before she died. Then she took out a hundred every Wednesday. Eight hundred dollars in all."

She looked at the window behind Farnsworth's desk. She could read the gold lettering even if it was in reverse. "Samuel Farnsworth, Attorney at Law." Winston's firm had twenty employees, but this office above the drugstore housed just one man and his secretary. "Mr. Farnsworth," she said, "are you really and truly my lawyer?"

His smile was warmer this time. "No, I'm Mrs. Gravesly's lawyer.

But I'd certainly keep confidential what we discuss here, if that's what you wish."

Bethanne gulped air and blew it out. "You know that letter you gave me from Mary Margaret? Do you know when it was written?"

"I can't be sure, but she gave it to me last year, after she reviewed the will I'd drafted."

"Last year," Bethanne said. "Such a lot can happen in a year."

⸺

I set there so long at the G-Mart's outside lunch counter, I about give up waiting on that wrinkled old woman. The smell of cooking burgers and fries was about to do me in, I was so hungry. It's not really a lunch counter, just a window they open in the summertime, so you can eat outside if you wanna.

Anyhow, I was thinking about scooting on back through the woods to the trailer park and opening me a can of pork 'n' beans. But just when I thought my bum couldn't take another minute on that concrete bench, this broke-down car pulled up, and out she stepped.

Said she was sorry she was late, but she wanted to talk with Miz Gravesly's lawyer afore we met. Wanted to make sure we had all the facts. I could tell she was nervous. She went on about her car and how she usually took the bus, but she couldn't have done that and got to both meetings. That woman was a powerful talker when she wanted to be.

Smoked like a chimney too. First thing she did when she got outta that car was light up. I like to bust my lungs trying to breathe, just standing near enough to hear her.

I kept my mouth shut and sized her up, trying to figure out who she was and what she knew. Was she the Gravesly's hired help?

Where'd she find that cash box? And what was she fixing to do with it?

Finally she stopped yapping and said we oughta have something to eat. Paid for it too. I got me a double cheeseburger and a chocolate shake. And double fries. But she just had a hot dog and ice tea. Made me think I oughta start slimming down, so I wouldn't get so winded like I was the day afore. Ray-Jean wouldn't had no trouble running away from that house.

The woman tried to find out more about me while we ate, but I didn't give her no more'n my name. "Eden Jones," I said. "What's yours?"

"Bethanne Swanson." She lit up another cig.

"And you ain't no Gravesly?"

"Nope. Mary Margaret Gravesly was my sister."

"You and Miz Gravesly was sisters?" I couldn't hardly believe it. They had a picture of Miz Gravesly on the TV when she died. So pretty and young-looking. For her age, I mean. This woman musta been years older, or else life had treated her some kinda hard. Had some heft on her. Not fat like me, but sloppy-bodied like she never took care of herself.

Miz Swanson nodded and said she needed to know how come her sister's car went off the dock. The whole thing didn't add up.

I could agree with that, so I told her about Ray-Jean being belted in so tight and her hating seatbelts and all.

That woman kept dragging on her cigarette like it was oxygen. Told me how her sister had left her some money in that cashbox, but when she opened it up, she didn't find none.

Her saying that set off alarm bells in my head. I tried to calm down by thinking about how Ray-Jean woulda handled all this. I set there a spell, then I said, "I hid that box away for you. Stuck it back in the cardboard one and put the whole thing in the root cellar." Didn't say a word about that diary. Didn't want her to suspect I mighta been snooping.

She smiled over at me. "That was quick thinking, Eden."

Her being so kind made me lose my head. "I found some pearls in among Ray-Jean's stuff. I knew they wasn't hers."

"Pearls," she said. "Not money."

"They was like drugstore pearls with the shiny stuff about wore off." I surely was skirting close to telling her a lie, and I didn't wanna do that. In case I'd have to tell her the truth later.

"Maybe they were Ray-Jean's, and you just didn't know."

"No'm. Ray-Jean wouldn't been able not to tell me if somebody give her them pearls." I thought for a while. Made out like I was busy with my cheeseburger, chewing and swallowing. "I been wondering if they been Miz Gravesly's."

"What made you think that?"

I drew in a mouthful of air and blew it all out. "I think maybe Ray-Jean snuck into Miz Gravesly's house and took 'em."

⁓

Clouds of dust threatened to choke Bethanne. She sneezed and sneezed again, then wiped her nose against her shoulder and looked around the large room with its alcoves for sleeping and cooking. The chauffeur's apartment hadn't been cleaned in years. Just walking through it stirred up dust on the floor so deep she left tracks beside those that must have been Winston's. Dust covered every other surface except the top of the dresser. His file boxes must have been there, and the dust'd never had a chance to settle.

She looked down at the cardboard carton in her hands. Inside was Mary Margaret's lockbox and the diary. She'd just retrieved them from the root cellar, gagging at the stink of decay.

Now she needed to stow them away before someone found her with them. Anybody might have a lockbox, so that was easy. She put it on the top shelf of the bedroom alcove's open closet.

But the diary was trickier. Obviously not hers. Probably Mary Margaret's. And how did she come to have it? The only space with a door was the bathroom. She hurried inside and hid the diary in the cabinet under the sink. Later, she'd get it out, get it open and see if Mary Margaret had anything to say about Ray-Jean and the string of pearls.

She pushed all that to the back of her mind and concentrated on getting her new place ready to move in. She took down the curtains, so gray with grime she couldn't make out what color they'd been, and put them on top of the bedspread. It might have matched the curtains long ago, but it was impossible to tell now. She'd wash all that later.

Footsteps sounded on the stairs leading up to her narrow porch. She looked out the window and saw Clay carrying a large wooden square marred by deep scratches. He entered through sunbeams strewn with floating dust. "Found this old card table up in the attic. Thought it might do for you to eat on." He opened the legs and set it down near the kitchen alcove. "Anything else you want me to cart away?"

"Not yet, but you might take a look at the bathroom." Too late, she remembered what she'd stashed under the sink. "Any old shaving cream in that medicine cabinet?" she said and hurried after him.

He opened the bathroom door. "Damn. Looks like kids broke

in again. Easy with that tree like an invitation outside the window."

She peeked over his shoulder and saw him fiddling with a loose latch. She'd been in such a hurry to hide the diary, she'd missed that.

"We'll need to replace this," he said. "And I'll scrub the footprints out of the tub."

She'd missed that too. Jesus, she was going to have to be more observant if she was going to get through this.

He looked down at the prints. "Pretty small. Definitely some kid."

Bethanne made an effort not to look down at the sink. "Thanks for helping out."

"Figured it was the least I could do once I got you into this mess." His shoulders sagged like they had so many times since his mother'd passed away, and Bethanne reached out to touch his arm.

"Are you okay?" she asked. "It's been hard on you, losing Mary Margaret like that. Would it help to talk about it?"

He tried, but he couldn't stop his face from crumpling "Chief Hastings asked to meet with me and Dad at the law firm. Said he'd been holding back all the facts until we got past the funeral and all."

"What facts?"

Clay swallowed and squared his shoulders. "Chief Hastings said Mom's car didn't roll off the dock. It must have roared off, full throttle, to end up like it did, so far out in the deepest part of the lake."

Bethanne frowned. Did Mary Margaret hit the gas pedal instead of the brake when she started to go down that steep hill toward the dock? Or did the gas pedal get stuck? That'd happened to her once on a hill, and she'd never forget the terror of that day. Had that same terror clutched Mary Margaret so hard she didn't do the right thing?

Clay wiped his eyes. "Oh, Aunt Bee, I miss her so much."

It almost broke Bethanne's heart to hear his voice quaver at the end. The little towheaded boy who'd loved her, now in despair. A man who still cared enough to help her.

Without thinking, she opened the cabinet, got out the diary and handed it to Clay. "I'm pretty sure this was Mary Margaret's. No one should have it more than you."

He held it with both hands close to his heart, eyes closed. Then he shook his head and brushed past her into the main room. "Lord, it's hot in here."

Clay tried to turn on the window air-conditioner. When nothing happened, he banged it with the heel of his hand. "I'll get a repairman to come take a look at this."

Bethanne wiped the sweat from her upper lip, thinking she'd been too hasty in handing over the diary. Why hadn't she read it first? It would've been easy to cut the strap and open it. But she knew the answer. She hadn't been eager to face up to what might be inside. She shrugged. Well, it was too late now.

She made herself focus on the air conditioner. "I don't hold out much hope for that old thing."

"Aunt Bee, if he can't fix it, I'll buy you a new one. And a TV too. What's your favorite program?"

"None of them. Got too much reality in my own life to be gawking at somebody else's problems." She smiled. "Appreciate the offer, though. Very kind of you, Clay."

He winked. "Okay, just an air conditioner. So we won't melt. In the meantime, I'll go get us a couple beers."

Bethanne watched him bound across the porch and zip down the stairs two at a time, the diary in his hand. Clay had always enjoyed a graceful athleticism. Even as a small boy, his body would do almost anything he asked of it—swim, play tennis, jump high, jump far.

She had a bunch of questions about Mary Margaret's car going off the dock, but if he wasn't ready to talk about what Chief Hastings had said, he wasn't ready. She turned to sweep the brown linoleum floor, but the dust just danced in the sunlight. Time to give it up and borrow the vacuum cleaner from the main house. She glanced at the minimal kitchenette. Probably hadn't been used for decades and wouldn't work any better than the air conditioner.

A spot of color under the bedroom dresser caught her eye, and she knelt to pull it out. "Christ."

Bethanne felt sick to her stomach. She collapsed onto the couch, despite its grime and looked again at the photo. A young boy lay on a bed, his naked body only partially covered by the rumpled sheets, face to the wall, head under a pillow, bare back to the camera.

She almost heaved. Who'd left this filth behind? The chauffeur? The Graveslys hadn't had a driver since before Mary Margaret got married. No one could afford such help after World War II. Couldn't have been the kids who'd smashed the window latch. They'd break in to smoke a joint or gape at girly mags. But kiddy porn?

She looked at the photo again. Slightly yellowed. Colors a bit faded. Edges starting to curl. How old was it? She turned it over. On the back was some kind of code: CG81.

CG? Those were Clay's initials. Surely the photo couldn't be his. He hadn't lived at home for years.

Clay appeared in the doorway, a frosty beer in each hand. She'd been so engrossed by the photo, she hadn't heard his feet on the stairs.

"What've you got there, Aunt Bee?" He handed her a beer and took the photo before she figured out what to say.

His tanned face lost all color, and he swallowed like something awful was stuck in his throat. "Jesus. That's totally disgusting." He set his beer on the dresser, pulled a lighter from his pocket and set the photo on fire. "I don't want anyone else to see this crap." He carried the burning photo by the tip of one corner and flushed it down the toilet once it had turned to ashes.

Bethanne felt her gorge rising again and just wanted to get away. She gulped her beer. "Thank God there was only one."

She bundled up the bedspread and curtains. "Better get these into the washer. Why don't you take that box of children's books? You and Lucinda can divvy them up for your kids."

Bethanne hurried down the stairs and along the driveway, striving to put distance between herself and her suspicions over the photo. Her hands were shaking so hard she had trouble opening the cellar door. Once inside, she loaded the washer and tried not to think about Clay and the photo.

But she kept seeing the nude boy and Clay's initials. Why had he rushed to burn the picture? Was it his? Or did "81" mean 1981? Was the photo of him as a boy? She felt faint and leaned against the washer as her own memories came flooding back.

HOT SUMMER NIGHTS ALONE in the bedroom because she was too young to go with Mary Margaret to Bible Camp. Her uncle, drunk and stinking of sweat, coming again and again into the room, telling her how pretty she was, touching her where she didn't want to be touched.

Later, when Mary Margaret returned home, Bethanne tried to tell her what he'd done. But her sister wouldn't believe her. "You're making it up to get even cause I got to go to camp and you didn't."

Then Bethanne told Momma, and she got so mad she was shouting. "How could you even think my brother would do such a thing? You're just jealous of Mary Margaret cause she gets all the attention."

But once Mary Margaret was home, their uncle never came back in the night, and Bethanne finally realized where she stood in the family. Bethanne was the ugly one. She was the stupid one. She was the one who didn't matter.

The cellar seemed to close in on those memories and push them back where they belonged. Bethanne stood straight and wiped her tears. She shook her head. No point in thinking about that now.

Mustn't think about Clay. Mustn't jump to conclusions. Just because she'd been molested didn't mean he had. Look how well-adjusted he was. Not like her. Besides, he'd acted like he'd never seen that photo before. Think about something, anything else

She forced her attention to what Eden had said. Ray-Jean'd had a habit of sneaking into people's houses. So maybe she'd sneaked into Mary Margaret's and taken that necklace. But why would her sister have a string of drugstore pearls?

A gasp parted Bethanne's lips. Eden had said they were old and worn. What if Mary Margaret's black lover had given them to her? That would be a secret worth paying to cover up. That would explain why there was no money in the lockbox, why there'd been withdrawals from the savings account. But where was the money now?

The next morning, Bethanne was making a cup of instant coffee when Mae came clunking up the stairs carrying a giant Hoover.

"Excuse me for bothering you, Miz Bethanne." Mae wiped the shine from her chubby face. "I wanted to help you clean up the apartment yesterday, but Miss Lucinda said I didn't need to take anything on except looking after Mr. Winston."

Bethanne opened the screen door and motioned Mae inside. "I know. She told me I didn't have enough to do anyway."

Mae tugged her orange-and-purple flowered dress back down from where it had ridden up over hips like basketballs. "Well, she isn't here now, and Mr. Winston's at the office. I can do what I want." She grinned. "And what I want is to help you."

"That's more than kind of you." Bethanne considered how getting to know Mae might prove useful. The housekeeper ought to be a good source of what was going on in Mary Margaret's life before she died. Besides, Mae had a way about her that hinted of more than what was on the surface. Better take it slow, though. Mae was no fool. Just be friendly today.

Bethanne smiled and led the way over to the kitchenette. "Let's have a cup of coffee first."

⸺

I surely felt funny being strapped into that rattle-trap old car. Faded to a no-color. Maybe it'd been light blue once. Or light green. But just no-color now, all washed out by the sun.

Anyhow, I was strapped inside and thinking about Ray-Jean being tied down by a seatbelt she'd never've worn unless she was forced to. But I told myself this was differnt. I wasn't in Miz Gravesly's car. I was in her sister's.

Bethanne, she said to call her. Not "Miz Swanson" like my momma would've said I should. I never called no grownup by their first name afore. 'Cept for Buck, but he's family. So I decided I'd just say "Miz Swanson" for the time being, til we come to know each other better.

Miz Swanson said we needed to get out to the lake and search for clues afore the family moved in for the summer. That was after I told her about them pearls. We agreed there had to be some connection between the necklace and the two of 'em drowning in that car. So once she cleaned up the apartment Mr. Gravesly give her and moved in—she didn't wanna make him suspicious by taking off afore that— Miz Swanson picked me up at the G-Mart, and we was off to the lake.

Well, as best we could be. I thought that old car was going to up and die afore we got there, but Miz Swanson managed to keep her going slow and steady. No air conditioning, so we kept all the windows open, but I was used to that. And wouldn't you know her car had to get overheated, so she had to stop at a gas station and get some more radiator fluid. But we finally made it, and I surely was glad.

I never been out to Lake Charles afore, so I just had to stand there awhile and take it all in. Sunlight bouncing off the waves like a thousand golden saucers floating up and down. Pond-waders skating over the water and dragonflies darting above. I don't think I ever saw a prettier sight. All them houses with all that space in-between, part-way in the woods and part-way lawn and flowers stretching all the way down the hill to their boat docks. Rich folks surely is lucky.

"You want to go for a swim?" Miz Swanson said. "I'll bet you could find a suit up at the house. Nobody'd know you borrowed it except me." She fired up a cigarette. "And I don't count."

"How come?" I said. "How come you don't count?"

She looked at me like there was something she recognized. "Cause I'm your friend."

Well, she wasn't no friend like Ray-Jean, but maybe she was another kind of friend, the kind you go on an expedition with. I saw that on the University Channel, folks coming together to go look for something. And that's what we was doing.

"No'm," I said. "I surely do thank you, but I can't go for no swim."

I was hoping she'd let it go at that, but of course she said why not, and then I had to tell her I didn't know how. "I'll teach you someday," she said, and I wondered if maybe our friendship was going to have a lot of parts to it, maybe go on and on. Me and that woman as broke down as her car. Now that was really strange.

Well, I didn't know what to say, so I just looked round. Saw these petunias all wilting in the sun and a watering can nearby. Decided the best way to get outta talking was to water them flowers. So I got the can, went down to the lake, filled it up and give 'em a good soak. The whole time, that woman was smiling at me like I was a prize heifer.

That got me through the embarrassment of the whole thing, so I was ready when she said we oughta search the house first. She stole the key from Mr. Gravesly when he wasn't looking. Well, not stole, exactly. The key was hanging on a hook near the back door of his house. She just picked it up and kept on going.

Anyhow, she ground out her cigarette in the gravel, unlocked the door and let me inside. I don't know what we thought we was looking for, but I guess we figured we'd know it when we found it.

The inside of that house was surely a surprise, like somebody hadn't finished working on it. Wood not painted, walls all rough, furniture worn and faded. So I asked Bethanne how come rich folks don't spend their money.

Momma has to spend every dollar she makes just to keep us three fed and clothed. That's cause Daddy run away after Cruz was born. Guess he couldn't handle two kids in a one-bedroom trailer. Said he needed some space. I don't know if he's coming back or not. He used to send us money now and then, but we ain't heard from him in a while.

Miz Swanson said Mr. Gravesly's father built the lake house

when rich folks had an affectation—that's what she called it, "affectation"—for the simple life. Said a lot of Miz Gravesley's friends was modernizing their lake houses, putting in fancy kitchens and such, but the Graveslys all liked their house just the way it was. Besides, they was always using the big stone barbecue outside to cook everything from steaks to corn-on-the-cob, so what'd they need a fancy kitchen for?

I kept on thinking about all that while me and Miz Swanson looked high and low, upstairs and down. But we didn't find a thing that looked like a clue 'cept some ashes in the fireplace. Looked like somebody'd burned a stack of old photographs. Everything was all black and crumbly, but you could see the shadows of pictures on a couple big pieces.

Them picture-shadows was surely peculiar. A couple boys wrassling, but they didn't have no clothes on. And another naked boy on a bike. What was they? Some kinda athletic club? I saw once on the TV that the ancient Greeks liked to exercise naked. Maybe these guys was copying 'em.

None of this seemed like clues to me. And I guess not to Miz Swanson neither, cause she broke all them ashes up real quick with the poker and put 'em in a plastic sack she got outta the kitchen.

After that, she looked like she could use a little air. Kinda damp and red in the face—you know how old ladies get on a hot day. I figured it'd be cooler down by the lake, so I said we oughta go check out where Miz Gravesly's car went off the dock.

Miz Swanson seemed of two minds about that. Like she didn't wanna think about her sister's car flying into the lake but also like she wanted to get away from that fireplace. In the end, off we went, me in the lead. That felt pretty good, like I was in charge.

We started at the land end and worked our way to the water end, inch by inch and foot by foot, along them wooden planks. It was just the same like in the house. We wasn't looking for nothing in particular, just something that struck us when we saw it.

But we never found a thing. No skid marks like when somebody throws on the brakes. And it was so steep from the main road down to the dock, there shoulda been some, if Miz Gravesly was trying to stop the car.

But when I come to think of it, I realized maybe that was some kinda clue. Maybe Miz Gravesly was asleep at the wheel, cause she been drugged. But who drugged her? And how?

I leaned way down over the far edge, trying to see if Ray-Jean mighta thrown something in the water for me to find. It woulda been just like her to do something like that—throw out her shoe, or any old thing to show she hadn't gone into that water of her own free will. Course I knew that anyway, but it woulda been nice to find the proof.

Well, the next thing I knew, I was under that dark green water, looking up at the light far above. I wanted to cough in the very worst way. Even more'n that time I had bronchitis so bad my momma give up and took me to the store-front clinic. But I knew I mustn't take a breath, and I started kicking as hard as I could toward that light.

Bethanne heard the splash and turned to look. The dock was empty. She ran to the end and saw frothy white in the center of expanding rings of dark water.

Just then, Eden's head broke the surface a few feet away. "Missus, Missus, help me!" Her blubbery, white arms thrashed without much effect, and Bethanne looked for a rope or a pole to pull her in. But there was nothing on the dock, and Eden sank again.

Bethanne didn't think. She jumped in. Down below, she saw a jerky puppet suspended in yellow-green light. Bubbles rose from Eden's head toward the surface. Her body was turned away from the shore. Her arms and legs lashed out, but her movements were uncoordinated and useless.

The one thing Bethanne prided herself on was swimming. She hadn't been underwater in a long time, but she felt like a frog come home. She jackknifed down to Eden, grabbed her by the collar and turned toward the surface. How far away it seemed, like they'd never, ever get there. Her lungs needed air, and her legs felt like someone had tied weights on them. She was too old and out of shape for this. The water's buoyancy should have helped, but Eden's body dragged like Bethanne was pulling her through jello.

Panic filled Bethanne's stomach. It was all she could do to hold onto Eden and keep kicking their bodies upward to where the air shone like the Promised Land.

⸺

I thought I was a goner for sure. Momma and Cruz and Ray-Jean was all jumbled up inside my head. They was the three people I loved, and my mind was full of 'em as the water took me away.

Then I felt something grab me, and I thought it mighta been the Devil. But it was Miz Swanson. She jumped down in that water, and she saved me like a guardian angel.

She pulled us out on land, and we lay there awhile, sputtering and heaving and coughing. I like to barf my guts out, and that's a fact. Decided right there and then I was never gonna eat no more of them cold pork 'n' beans. Least not two cans at a time.

Finally I could breathe, and I said, "Oh Missus, you saved me."

"I'm not Missus," she said, "I'm Bethanne."

"Yes'm, you surely are. But you're something else. You're my savior and my friend."

Then I told her everything I knew. The coffee can and the money and all my suspicions. I didn't hold nothing back, cause you can't do that and be friends.

⌐⌐

Bethanne lay on the bank next to Eden and let the sun's heat dry her clothes. For the first time in a long time, she could let herself relax. It was like a heavy rock had been lifted off her chest. She could stop worrying about her dwindling cash. At least for a while.

Mary Margaret's money was in Ray-Jean's coffee can, and as soon as the two of them dried off, Eden was going to take Bethanne to get it. Bethanne grinned. That dough was hers. She didn't have to say a word about it to Winston. Or Farnsworth either.

She looked over at Eden, eyes closed against the sun, stretched out, her whole body a smile. Bethanne thought about all those lovely banknotes, how she could do what she liked with them. Well, what she liked was to give Eden some. That child needed cash just as much as she did, maybe more.

8

BETHANNE POPPED THE TOPS on the drinks they'd bought at the gas station and handed Eden a grape soda. Then she took a long swallow of her beer and glanced around Ray-Jean's hiding place. Deep in the woods, just like where she used to play, building forts and hollering through the trees. Her gaze came to rest on Ray-Jean's treasures spread out on the sun-dappled rock.

Eden plunged her hand into the bottom of the coffee can. "Here it is, Mis…" The girl bobbed her head. "Bethanne. Just like I told you. I never touched a cent of that money. Eight hunnerd dollars. It's all yours." She passed it over.

Bethanne looked down at the cash in her hand. "I think I know what happened, some of it, anyway." She forced herself to raise her head and look Eden in the face. "It's not pretty."

"Have we got all the clues now?"

Bethanne smiled at the girl. So like herself at that age. Awkward, half-ignorant. Standing on the threshold of the grownup world, eager to be part of it. Eden was mature from all the responsibilities she'd had to take on, but sometimes the impulsive child inside took over. Easy to go wrong when you're so thirsty for life. Like she had.

"Not all the clues," Bethanne said, "but we've got enough to make a good guess. And you found most of them."

Eden squirmed like a happy puppy. "So tell me."

"Ray-Jean liked to sneak into people's houses and bring back souvenirs. You told me that."

Eden nodded. "And she took them pearls from Miz Gravesly, cause they was the only thing I never seen in Ray-Jean's can."

Bethanne shifted her weight, but she couldn't get comfortable. The wind pushed at her, bringing the smell of carrion from far away. "I think Ray-Jean was in the house and heard me say something to Mary Margaret. A terrible secret."

Eden leaned forward, her mouth open, tongue circling her lips, her grape soda forgotten on the rock.

"I came to see Mary Margaret last spring because I was way down on my luck." Bethanne couldn't look at Eden and swung her focus out into the woods. "I wanted her to talk Winston into buying me a condo."

"That's Mr. Gravesly?"

Bethanne nodded. "I must've been really desperate to think of something so stupid. Mary Margaret told me it wouldn't work. I got mad and said things I shouldn't have." She gulped her beer and turned her head even further away.

Eden reached out a plump paw and touched Bethanne's arm. "What'd you say? I'm your friend now. You can tell me. I won't tell a soul." She patted the arm. "Won't judge you, neither."

Bethanne stared at a distant tree, its leaves dark against the sunlight. "I shouted at Mary Margaret about having a black baby."

"You had a black baby?"

"No, Mary Margaret did. A long time ago. When she was in

college. Momma sent her to live with Aunt Eunice until the baby was born. Then Momma put the baby up for adoption."

Eden rocked back and forth. "You think Ray-Jean heard that and decided to blackmail Miz Gravesly?" She stopped rocking and grinned. "I already thought about blackmail myself. Even though Ray-Jean was my friend, I have to say she wouldn't been above doing that."

Bethanne swigged the last of her beer and hung her head. "In a way, that's what I was doing. I hadn't planned it that way, but when the words came out of my mouth, I saw I might use that secret to make Mary Margaret get me what I wanted."

"How do them pearls come into it?"

"I think they were the proof Ray-Jean needed. The father of that baby must've given them to Mary Margaret." She paused. "I think they really loved each other."

"So why didn't they get married, if they was in the family way?"

Betthanne shook her head. "You just couldn't do that in those days. Blacks and whites didn't mix, and they sure didn't get married. Not in Alabama."

"Then how'd them two meet in the first place?"

"I heard Momma say he was the leader of a screaming nigger band." Bethanne felt embarrassed even before she heard Eden gasp at the ugly words. "I know it sounds awful now, but that's what they called them then. Mary Margaret was social chairman at this girls' college, and all the students wanted that kind of band for the spring dance."

Eden leaned forward. "Was he handsome?"

"I don't know. But I heard Mary Margaret tell Momma he wasn't like the black boys Momma knew. He was studying to be a teacher at some Negro college. He just sang with the band to make ends meet."

Eden nodded. "I'll bet he marched with Dr. King. I saw that on the TV. All them black students marching for their rights. I'll bet that boy made something of hisself."

"Momma didn't care if he was Booker T. Washington. She had big plans for Mary Margaret. She was going to marry her off to a rich boy."

Eden smiled. "And she did too. Your momma musta been one smart woman."

Bethanne felt cold inside. "She was ambitious for both her daughters. I can see that now." She looked at the dark tree again. "I must've been a big disappointment to her."

⸻

I have to tell you I never had no conversation like that in my whole life. Here was this grown woman telling me all kinda secrets and me trying to understand everything and comfort her at the same time.

I set there and looked at her with her faded old clothes, her dried-up face and dried-up hair, and I felt sorry for her, I surely did. So I said, "Maybe things got kinda messed up in your life, but you got the money to fix 'em now."

Bethanne—after she saved me, I started thinking of her as "Bethanne," but I still couldn't bring myself to call her that outloud, 'cept that one time I passed over the money from Ray-Jean's coffee can. Anyhow, Bethanne kept going back over stuff we already knew. Said Miz Gravesly wanted her to have the money in that cashbox. But her sister had to give it to Ray-Jean to keep her secret safe, even had to dip into her savings account. No way Miz Gravesly could have her husband find out she had a black baby all those years ago. Let alone have the story get passed all round Lewiston.

I knew what she was getting at, so I said, "You think your sister killed herself and Ray-Jean too."

Tears made wet racks down her wrinkled face, and she said it was all her fault. If she hadn't screamed at her sister, they'd both be alive.

That seemed pretty far-fetched to me. I still thought one of them Graveslys murdered Bethanne's sister, and Ray-Jean was just along for the ride. I wasn't sure who done it or how, but I just couldn't accept Bethanne's version of how her sister and my best friend come to die.

"Seems like there's more to it," I said.

Bethanne shook her head. Said I didn't have all the facts. Her sister'd been trapped by Bethanne and Ray-Jean coming at her from both sides. No way out but something desperate. Besides, Bethanne's sister had tried to kill herself afore, when she was pregnant and her momma wouldn't let her see that black boy even to say goodbye.

I come back at Bethanne hard. Said her sister wasn't some silly college girl lovesick and in the family way. Miz Gravesly musta been one strong woman to rise above so many hardships. A woman like that wasn't gonna kill herself over a little blackmail, specially when she had more money in the bank.

"There's more clues out there," I said, "and we gotta find 'em."

Bethanne started to shake her head, and I figured I had to get her onto something else. So I said, "You're dwelling too much on the past, and that's a fact. You got all this money now, you oughta do something with it. Buy yourself some new clothes. Get that old car fixed." I give her a wink. "Then we can go looking for more clues."

That seemed to do the trick, cause she said I was right about the money and the first thing she wanted to do was give me some. Well, I couldn't take her money. What'd I done to deserve it? Kept it secret way too long instead of doing the right thing. But sometimes it's hard to know what the right thing is—give up an old friend's secret or help a new one? Anyhow, I said no and felt the better for it.

But she kept after me. Said there was something called a finder's fee, and I had surely earned it. Well, that was news to me, but it did make sense. She wanted to give me half, but I said that was way too much.

"How much is a finder's fee, usually?" I said, and she said ten percent. So we settled on that, and I walked home with eighty dollars in my pocket, trying to figure out what I was gonna tell Momma.

That evening, Bethanne sat on her narrow porch with a can of beer. She'd never liked air conditioning and always delayed going inside until she had to. The day's heat and humidity lingered into evening, but a soft breeze brought the scent of Mary Margaret's roses to caress her.

She reached down and touched the gold bangle on her arm. In the end, sentiment had won over avarice, and she'd let go of the idea of pawning Mary Margaret's jewelry. All she'd asked for were her sister's favorite bracelet and their mother's locket.

She could still hear Lucinda's shrill voice, "How do we know you didn't help yourself to more when you locked us out of Mother's bedroom?" But a survey of Mary Margaret's jewelry box had turned up nothing missing, and Lucinda had yielded the two pieces with ill grace.

Bethanne sipped her beer and looked at the main house. Winston was having another of his poker games. She'd already watched his buddies file in, the Police Chief, a doctor, some businessmen. She'd met them all at the funeral. Even with Mary Margaret so recently gone, Winston still had to have his weekly poker night.

Maybe he needed cards and his buddies to get through his grief. He didn't seem to be mourning, but Bethanne couldn't tell what he was really feeling. Mary Margaret had turned herself into the model wife for Winston, and there had to be a big hole in his life where she used to be. Who was going to run his house now? Hostess his parties? Make sure everything was the way he liked it?

She looked down the driveway to the window of Winston's study. Flickering light danced on the beige drapes. Why anybody would leave a TV on while they played poker was beyond Bethanne, but maybe it was just another of Winston's distractions.

The family was going to move out to the lake this Saturday. The lake house was so big that Lucinda and Clay's wife would live there with the children. The men would stay in town during the week and come out for the weekend. Bethanne needed to decide if she was going to the lake house or staying in her new apartment.

She lit a cigarette and pictured how pretty the lake was and how cool. It'd feel nice being out there for the summer. Be that long, at least, until the will was probated. Then she could withdraw the money in her sister's savings account and start a new life. God knows, she needed one, what with all the pain she was carrying. Guilt at the thought she'd contributed to Mary Margaret committing suicide. And taking Eden's friend with her. Grief that Mary Margaret would kill a child, even if she was a little blackmailer.

Bethanne rubbed the cold beer can across her forehead. No

wonder Winston wanted the Police Chief to cover the whole thing up. Let sleeping dogs lie, that's what Daddy always said when things got messy. But still, all this was hard to accept, let alone live with. Even now, when she thought maybe she'd figured the whole thing out, it kept coming back to worry her.

So maybe it was best just to stay in the apartment for now and not get near Mary Margaret's family any more than she had to. Avoid the temptation to blab her suspicions if she had too much to drink. Give herself time to think about where she was going in the fall. She could always move out to the lake later, if her cash ran out.

I let worries about that money Bethanne give me rest overnight. And the next morning, I knew the best thing was to tell Momma the truth. Or most of it, anyhow. Said I'd found some money and give it back to the lady it belonged to. She give me a finder's fee, I said. Momma was sidetracked right then, keeping Cruz from peeing in her face while she changed his diaper. Said honesty was always the best policy and concentrated on wiping his smelly butt with a wet washcloth.

I handed her the baby powder and said I wanted her to have the money. She dusted him down good and said it would surely come in handy cause we needed a few things and her check wasn't due til next week.

I laid them bills down next to Cruz, while she took ahold of his legs and slid a Pampers under him. "Here," she said, "you take twenty dollars and go buy a box of these here diapers. And some Spaghetti O's for your dinner." She looked up and smiled. "And if there's anything left over, you get yourself a Whitman's Sampler."

Well, I just about fell over. We usually only had a box of that candy for Christmas, and here she was saying I should get one all for myself. She surely musta been glad for me bringing in that money.

But then she said something that brought me up short. "Eden," she said, "in this whole wide world, ain't no daughter better'n you." I started to get a little teary, and she said, "Now skedaddle, dearheart, and get them diapers."

I took off as fast as I could, cause I didn't want her starting to think about how I found that cash in the first place. Walked down to the Busy Bee Market, that nearby, old one with the stale smells. Got Cruz the Pampers and me the Spaghetti O's. I was going to heat 'em up this time. No more eating stuff outta the can while watching the TV.

I pushed the cart over to the candy aisle and looked long and hard at the Whitman's Samplers. But I couldn't bring myself to get one, not even that small box with four pieces. I turned right round and went over two aisles to where they keep the shampoo and stuff. I musta looked at every bottle, trying to make up my mind. The fluorescent tube up on the ceiling kept sputtering, made everything look like an old-time movie. Why don't Busy Bee fix that kinda thing as soon as it happens? They surely had a new tube out back.

Anyhow, I opened all the bottles that looked good and smelled each one. Finally I found one that smelled just right. And that's how I come to buy a bottle of hair conditioner for my friend Bethanne.

9

The morning after Winston's poker game, Bethanne lay in bed, gnawing at all the details of how and why Mary Margaret had died. Chief Hastings had told Clay that the Mercedes must have roared off the dock full-throttle.

Murder-suicide? How could her sister have killed a child? Herself, maybe, but a thirteen year-old girl? Mary Margaret was soft on the outside but tough on the inside. She'd have found another way to deal with blackmail.

Hastings called it an accident. If so, how? The gas pedal got stuck? Brakes fail? Mary Margaret hit the gas instead of the brake?

Or did somebody make sure Mary Margaret would die in Winston's gift? Then who?

Bethanne's eyes lit on the lockbox, high on the open closet's shelf. Maybe Mary Margaret's diary had some answers. She sighed. Too late now. She'd given the diary to Clay. No way she could ask for it back.

Bethanne drew in a breath and bit her lip. What if he opened it? What would he find? Then she remembered he didn't have the key, and her pent-up breath puffed out. And sucked back in with the next thought. He could always just cut the strap to the lock. That's what she would have done, once she got the courage to read the diary. Well, there was nothing she could do about that now.

She was thinking too much, going round and round. "This is ridiculous," she told herself and got up to focus on something else.

She turned off the air conditioner and opened the windows and door to let in the cool morning air. Down below, Mae was washing the back porch and whistling under her breath. *Mae*, Bethanne thought. Maybe it was time to put their budding friendship to use. The trick would be to steer Mae toward the subject of Mary Margaret without alerting the housekeeper to her own suspicions.

Bethanne threw on some clothes and ran down the steps. "Mae," she called, "sorry to bother you. I've been trying to fix cornmeal pancakes, but I can't seem to make them as good as you do."

Mae put down her mop and smiled. "The secret is using bacon grease. Come on in, and I'll show you."

Bethanne smiled back and followed Mae into the large kitchen, its old-fashioned wooden cupboards shiny with coats of white enamel. In the center of the black-and-white tiled floor sat a pine table surrounded by eight chairs. Left over, Bethanne gathered, from when the hired help used to eat there.

She perched on a stool by the pantry door and watched Mae get out the ingredients. "You must be missing Mary Margaret even more than I do. You were with her everyday."

Mae broke an egg into a bowl and started beating it with a fork until it was solid yellow. "Yes'm, I sure do. No doubt about it, Miz Mary Margaret was a special lady. I came to help her when she was a bride, and I've been here ever since."

Bethanne realized for the first time how well Mae spoke. No

southern Negro dialect like she was used to. Mae had too much education to be working as a housekeeper. What was her story? But this wasn't the time to find out. Bethanne tried to stay patient and look attentive while Mae added the rest of the ingredients and recounted tales of Mary Margaret winning a prize every year for her roses, chairing various committees that benefitted the community, giving generously to those in need.

After a while, Bethanne judged the time had come and tried turning the topic. "I got the impression that she was giving money to that girl who was in the car with her."

"Don't know anything about that," Mae said, turning on the gas under a cast iron griddle. "Now you got to use bacon grease in the batter and on the pan. That's what makes the cakes crispy on the outside and fluffy on the inside."

"And an iron griddle," Bethanne said to prove she was following Mae's instructions. "Did Mary Margaret seem different to you in the days before she died? More worried, maybe?"

Mae gave Bethanne a sharp look. "Why're you going on like this about your sister? She's dead and buried. Isn't a thing you can do about it but keep on keeping on." She paused and gave Bethanne a weak smile. "Like we're all having to do."

Oh, hell, Bethanne thought and gave up trying to be subtle. "I can't let go of it, Mae. I think I know what happened, but I just can't accept it." To her surprise, she felt tears well up.

Mae pulled a couple of tissues out of a box on the black marble counter and handed them to Bethanne. "All right now, that's not going to help."

Bethanne blew her nose, trying to think what else she could say to get Mae to talk about Mary Margaret's last days.

Mae turned to the griddle and ladled in batter. "These'll make you feel better." She pivoted back to Bethanne. "I'll tell you one thing. When she came back from that first trip to fix up the lake house, her eyes were all red and puffy."

⸺

Nothing much happened in the week after Bethanne told me her suspicions about her sister committing suicide and taking Ray-Jean with her. Then one morning, she invited me to go with her to the G-Mart. Seemed like now she had a little spending money from Ray-Jean's can, it was burning a hole in her pocket. So I ended up standing in the ladies' department, marveling at Bethanne while she turned this way and that in front of the mirror. She looked like some teenager picking out a prom dress.

"You surely look nice in that blue blouse," I said. "Brings out the color in your eyes."

"Makes me look five years younger," Bethanne said. "I'm going to buy the skirt too. And that flip-phone we looked at. Don't think I'm ready for a smart phone. Way too intimidating." Then she give me this big smile. "Let me get you something. What about that T-shirt I saw you fingering?

My heart soared at the thought of something new to wear, but I knew it wouldn't work. "That's really kind of you, Missus," I said, "but I don't see how I could explain it to Momma. She'd wanna know where I got it, and I wouldn't know how much to tell her."

"Thought you were going to call me Bethanne."

That just added to my discomfort. I was thinking of her as Bethanne, but I wasn't ready to call her that. I commenced to shifting from one foot to the other. "I been trying, but it don't feel right somehow. What if I just call you 'Missus' til it does feel right?"

"Okay by me," she said and wheeled round toward the dressing room. I walked alongside to show we was still friends even if I was feeling strange about having to say no to her offer of a T-shirt.

But Bethanne just wouldn't let go of it. "You gave me a present," she said. "Now I want to give you one. That's only fair."

Lord, I thought, what do I do now? I wrinkled up my forehead and give it some thought. "What if you get me one of them pretty notebooks and a pen? I could…" I started to say, "write down all them clues," but then I recollected Bethanne didn't wanna hear no more talk about murder. So I finished up with "use it to take notes in school."

Bethanne smiled from the dressing-room door. "Good idea."

After they had lunch at the G-Mart, Bethanne paid for a taxi to take them to Eden's cousin's house. Nearly having a breakdown on the way to the lake had been the last straw. When Eden'd talked about what a good mechanic Buck was, Bethanne had decided to give him a try.

The taxi pulled up in front of a tiny wooden house—surely no more than one bedroom inside—with a low chain link fence all around. Eden pushed the gate open and led the way along a dirt path through scraggly grass to the backyard. A pair of work boots poked out from under Bethanne's Datsun, which was up on a makeshift platform of cinderblocks.

"Hey, Buck," Eden called.

The work boots scrabbled, and Buck's compact, muscular frame rolled out from under the car. He stood up and untied the bandanna protecting his long, dishwater-blond hair.

He sure looked like someone who knew what he was doing, Bethanne decided. She got out her wallet, but Buck refused to be paid for anything but parts.

"No labor?" she asked.

"No labor." Buck winked at Eden. "This here's a favor to my little buddy."

Bethanne glanced at Eden. She was beaming up at Bethanne like she'd pulled another fast one. Bethanne shook her head and smiled back. How was she going to keep this friendship in balance?

"Come on home with me," she said to Eden. "Let's get cold drinks and put our feet up. The family moved out to the lake last week, and we'll have the whole place to ourselves."

⌒⌒

Course I been out to the Gravesly's neighborhood afore, when I was watching their house. But I was impressed all over again when I went with Bethanne. Big old houses with big old trees and fancy gardens.

"Ain't nothing further from Happy Hours Trailer Park," I said, "and that's a fact." Bethanne give me the nicest smile.

She pulled round in back of the house, and we ended up beside this four-car garage with wood steps up the outside.

We grabbed our stuff and headed up the stairs. Bethanne was in the lead, me in the rear, carrying the bag with my notebook and pen. Maybe it was a rich neighborhood, but how'd I'd be sure no one'd steal 'em outta the car?

She stopped halfway and kinda moaned. I peeked round her and saw the screen door bust off its hinges and the main door standing open. Maybe the screen door was already broke, but it didn't seem like Bethanne, walking away and leaving her house unlocked.

Well, she took off up them steps two at a time, and I was right behind. We got to the top, and there was the door all stove-in like somebody took a crowbar to it. Bethanne put a hand back to keep me behind her, but I could see inside. There wasn't nothing but one room and the door standing open to the bathroom. Whoever done it was long gone.

Bethanne pulled in a lungful of air and huffed it all out. Then she led the way inside. You never saw such a mess, all the cupboards and drawers open, her stuff all over the floor. Mattress overturned, cupboards smashed. They even tore the bathroom medicine chest off the wall. Left a big hole behind it.

She was walking round, touching everything and saying, "Oh my God, oh my God." Kinda whimpery, like a wet kitten. I didn't know what to say, so I just kept patting her on the arm.

She checked for the cashbox, but it was gone. Good thing there wasn't no money in it after all.

Once we seen everything, Bethanne started to look a little funny, like she was gonna faint. So I turned up a kitchen chair and had her set down. Then I plunked myself on the sofa, cause I wasn't feeling any too good either. Couldn't figure out who'd wanna go after Bethanne. Or why.

This moldy old smell coming outta the sofa didn't help any with how I was feeling, neither. Bethanne had put one of them denim covers like you can buy down at the G-Mart over the sofa. Made it look better, but it sure didn't smell better.

After a while, she got up and opened this little bitty refrigerator under the kitchen counter. Come back with a Coke for me and a beer for her. We just set there, drinking our drinks and trying to take it all in. Finally I seen the light, and I got out my notebook and pen.

"Missus," I said, "we got us another clue."

Bethanne watched Eden writing in her notebook and wondered what to do next. Even before that time she'd got picked up for shoplifting, she'd never had a satisfactory contact with the police. Like those nights the neighbors called the cops when Robbie Ray was beating her up. The police never really helped and always wanted to know more than she wanted to say. She wasn't sure she needed the cops involved now. But she'd have to tell Winston.

The sound of a siren took the decision out of her hands. Somebody next door had seen two guys heaving things around inside and dialed 911. Winston wasn't far behind.

Everyone started gabbling at Bethanne at once, asking questions, wanting her to repeat herself over and over. Winston's face looked like all the color had been washed away. He could barely say a thing to anybody. Fortunately, Clay showed up and got his father a stiff drink. He offered one to Bethanne, and she downed half of it in one gulp.

"Who's this girl?" First the cop asked that, then Winston. Eden shrank back into the couch as far as she could go, clutching her notebook to her chest like a shield.

Bethanne contemplated the sweat dripping off the hectoring men and decided sweltering served them right. Besides, there was no point in turning on the a.c. with the door stove in. Then she looked at their hard faces and realized she'd better go slow on the booze and keep her wits about her. She moved to sit beside Eden and said the same thing to everyone. "We met at G-Mart awhile back. Found we had a lot in common."

Winston harrumphed and sneered. The cop looked skeptical and wrote down Eden's full name, address and phone number. He leaned over the girl and narrowed his eyes. "I'll be by to see you later." Bethanne felt Eden burrow behind her shoulder.

Finally it was all over. Winston told the police it was probably druggies looking for something to steal. The house was alarmed, he said, but not the apartment. By then, the whiskey had helped him regain his composure, and the cops seemed to give his hypothesis some credence.

"Yeah," Clay said, "or those kids who broke in before."

Winston started, and his voice rose to a screech. "Who broke in?"

"When?" the cop said.

Clay explained about the broken window and the footprints when Bethanne moved in. "The kids do it all the time, daring each other to break into an empty house just for fun."

The cop gestured at the disarray all around them. "This was more than a couple kids out for fun. And the apartment wasn't empty."

"Druggies then," Winston said. His voice sounded normal again, but it seemed to cost him some effort.

"What d'you think, Missus?" Eden whispered.

"I'm not so sure."

"Me, neither. I think this is connected to your sister's car going off the dock."

Clay came over. "What're you two whispering about?"

Bethanne's brain went into overdrive. "Trying to figure out how to get a new door at this late hour."

"My old college roommate runs a construction business now. Let me see if he can send someone right away." Clay grinned. "Bet we can get a screen door too. And new cabinets."

Bethanne watched him stride out of the room with his cell phone and recalled the photo with his initials on the back. Was that what the bad guys had been looking for?

—≈—

I'm sorry to say that there break-in caused me and Bethanne to have our first fight. Not that friends don't fight. I know that. Me and Ray-Jean used to have fights aplenty. But somehow the first fight with a new friend feels a hunnerd times worse than the last fight with an old one.

Anyhow, as soon as everybody cleared out, I said, "There's something else going on. Them two was murdered, and we gotta find out who did it."

Bethanne snapped at me. I can see now it musta been cause she was nervy and all. But it surely did hurt at the time.

"Eden," she said, "you got to get that out of your head. We don't really know what happened. Maybe we never will. We're going to have to learn to live with that."

I was trying really hard not to get mad back at her. "No'm," I said, "That car went off the dock for a reason we don't know yet. And when we find out, we're gonna learn there's a lot more to it than a little blackmail over a string of drugstore pearls."

Bethanne frowned and started to say more, but just then the truck pulled up with the new doors and stuff, and she had to go make sure the job was done right.

It was time for me to get home anyway, so I just slipped by and waved. Bethanne looked at me kinda strange, but I couldn't figure out what that look meant, so I kept on going. As it was, I had to run to catch the bus.

Heard they was gonna stop running the buses next year, what with so few folks riding 'em nowadays. But at least there was a bus now, when I needed it. I was practically the only white face on it. Most of the seats that was taken was filled by hired help going home. The Graveslys' maid was talking on and on. Everybody listening, eyes and ears open. I could see that break-in story was going to be all over town afore morning.

Meanwhile, I was jiggling with worry. That old bus pulled over to every stop, letting folks off or picking them up. I just barely got home in time to look after Cruz. Lord, I love that child, but I wish he'd get old enough to take care of his own self.

10

AFTER THE MEN INSTALLED the new doors, Bethanne found herself checking the solid one again and again to make sure it was locked properly. It was dark now, and the whole place felt spooky. She tried to clean up the mess, but it was hard to find the energy.

Trust Winston not to offer to help, even if he was in the main house. He was paying for all the repairs, though, she had to give him that. Clay had apologized. He had to get out to the lake where one of his boys was in a tennis tournament. Said being a good father was his most important job.

Bethanne sighed and hugged herself. Maybe she could get Mae to lend a hand in the morning. Then she recalled Lucinda forbidding the housekeeper to help her clean up before she moved in the apartment. Sure, Mae had sneaked up the stairs with the Hoover, but they probably shouldn't push their luck anymore.

She pulled the mattress back onto the bed and searched for clean linens in the pile on the floor. Winston had let her have some of the old ones from Mary Margaret's cupboard. Blue-flowered pillowcases and yellow-striped sheets were the only things she found that hadn't been trampled by dirty feet. They'd have to do.

After she'd made the bed, Bethanne slouched over to the fridge and tried to think about food, but she was jumpy. She couldn't settle down to cook, not even a TV dinner. Maybe she'd go out to eat. Yeah, that sounded like the right thing.

But when she got to the door, she felt skittish. Stop this, she told herself. Those guys were long gone. They didn't find what they were looking for, and they wouldn't be back. What she needed was a cheeseburger.

Twenty minutes later, she was sitting in her car at the Quik Treet Drive-In, swilling Coke and shoving salty fries down her throat. There's all kinds of comfort food, she realized, happy to find herself feeling better already.

Bethanne savored the soda and realized that for the first time in a long time, she didn't need a drink when things got tough. No alcohol, not even a beer. Just Coke and fries and a cheeseburger. Pretty damn amazing.

Her thoughts went to Eden, home alone eating pork and beans. Or a can of chili. Spooning food into her brother. Changing his diapers. What kind of life was that for a kid? A good kid.

Bethanne sighed. She'd have to do something about that little tiff they'd had. Find a way to make it up to Eden. But without agreeing to the girl's murder theory. That child had more imagination than was good for her. If she wasn't careful, Eden'd go off half-cocked and put herself in danger, chasing after murderers that weren't there.

Bethanne didn't want to talk about the photos either. Eden was far too young to be exposed to that kind of filth. She finished the last of her fries and looked at her watch. After ten. Time to go home.

The "hoo" of a hunting owl sounded overhead. Dark clouds flew across the moon's face like phantoms searching for someone to haunt. Something rustled in the woods behind the parking lot. Bethanne shuddered. Stop it, she chided herself and drove off.

⸻

Bethanne pulled up in front of the garage and felt the willies prickle between her shoulder blades. She'd spent her whole life trying to get things under control and never succeeding. Instead of Mary Margaret's home becoming a sanctuary, it was turning into a font of endless stress. She felt overwhelmed. The hunch about her sister's suicide and Ray-Jean's blackmail, Eden's suspicions of murder. Kiddy porn and now the break-in. She didn't know how much more she could take.

For starters, how long before she'd stop feeling jumpy every time she came home? She made herself get out of the car, jangling her keys, grateful for the automatic outside light that lit stairs and porch. She put a hand to the solid door Clay had ordered. Its sturdy bulk comforted her. Get over it, she thought and turned the handle.

But her nerves still sizzled. She walked over to the kitchenette, opened the only cupboard that hadn't been smashed and stared at the fifth of Wild Turkey. Nearly full. Maybe she'd have just a nip to steady her nerves. She reached for the bottle and remembered how she'd been with a Coke at the drive-in. That'd been a good feeling, like maybe she could get through life without getting blotto every time she got knocked around. She looked at the Wild Turkey again. Okay, maybe not. Not this time, anyway.

Despite the late hour and the carbohydrate-rich food, she didn't feel sleepy. The pile of soiled bed linen beckoned from across the room. Might as well do it now as lie awake in the dark. The cellar's laundry room was only a few yards away, and Clay had insisted she have a key so she could use the facilities.

Bethanne threw the bedclothes and her keys in a plastic basket. She turned off the lights and stepped outside to wait for the satisfying click of the new door's automatic lock. Then she went down the stairs and followed the lighted path along the darkened main house. Winston must have gone to the lake while she was at the drive-in.

The creaking of the cellar door sent her scurrying into the shadow of a perfectly pruned boxwood. Her heart was beating so wildly she could hear it reverberate inside her head. Were they back? Were they trying to break into the main house? Why hadn't she brought her new flip-phone? She should call the police.

A familiar silver head rose above the cellar door. Bethanne nearly called out, but something told her to be quiet, to stay where she was. Winston continued up the steps, carrying two file boxes stacked one on top of the other.

⌒

It surely took a lot to get Cruz to sleep that night. Seemed like he could feel all the thoughts tumbling round inside of me, and that made him jittery too. I kept rubbing his back, and he finally drifted off. Then I set there on the sofa bed watching the TV. But my mind was a million miles away. Even if it was the University Channel.

That's the kind of TV I like, programs that teach you something about the world. Momma always says I'm gonna wear out my head with shows like that, and Ray-Jean used to make fun of me watching such high-brow stuff. Well, I didn't care. I was home alone, and I could watch what I liked.

Anyhow, I had the TV on, but I wasn't paying no attention, cause my brain was full of Bethanne and the break-in. I was still feeling sore about our fight. Couldn't figure out what was going on. Why'd Bethanne come on so strong and turn away from me like that? And how was we gonna make it up? Act like it never happened or talk it out?

If there hadn't been no break-in, none of this woulda happened. I still felt like there was more to it than Bethanne wanted to say. And that Mr. Gravesly was surely upset about something more'n a couple kids breaking in for the fun of it. Seemed like, deep down, he had something to hide.

Finally, I couldn't take all those thoughts chasing theirselves round and round. So I got my new notebook and writ down everything I knew so far. Then I put in all my suspicions and all the questions buzzing inside my head. By the time I was done, I'd filled up pages and pages.

Just like Miss Bailey said I should. She was always after me to keep a journal. That's what she called it. Wanted me to write things that happened and what I thought about 'em. Seemed like nothing much ever happened to me til Ray-Jean died, so I never kept no journal afore. Now I was overwhelmed with stuff, I just had to write it all down.

Anyhow, once I got done, I felt a whole lot better. Closed up my notebook and clipped the pen to the cover. Then I let go of all that and watched this man showing how there's this tribe in Africa called the Masai. Their young men have to prove theirselves by killing a lion with only a spear. That was just about the bravest thing I ever heard of.

The boxwood's cat-urine smell nearly choked Bethanne. But she stayed put. No way she'd let Winston know she was watching.

He turned away and walked down the driveway. Bethanne looked past him to find his black Range Rover parked in the deep shadow of an oak tree, facing the street. Winston heaved the boxes inside and returned to the cellar. Out he came with more cartons. Bethanne was so close she could hear him grunt with the effort of balancing the weight and bolting the cellar door.

This didn't make sense. Winston wouldn't be carrying stuff out to the lake house at this hour. Everything had already been organized before the family moved in. Where the hell was he going?

Winston put the last of the boxes in the SUV and looked back toward the garage apartment. Bethanne looked too and saw darkened windows. It'd seem like she'd already gone to bed. He let out an audible sigh, got in the car and drove off.

This was too much to let slide. Bethanne ran to her own car, dropped the laundry basket in the back seat, grabbed her keys and took off after Winston's Range Rover. This late at night, there were no other cars on the street, and she could easily follow its tail lights.

When they got downtown, the traffic was even lighter. Winston drove past the courthouse with its shiny new sign proclaiming "Fresh Hope for Lewiston Town Center. Apply for a Grant Now!" Was Winston taking those boxes to his office? But he continued on his careful way, obeying traffic lights and stop signs, past darkened store fronts and barricaded parking lots, all the way through town until he arrived at the gate of a chain-link fence.

Bethanne lowered her head to read the sign shining above the six-foot barrier. "Ralph's Rentals. Open 24/7." The lot had lamps here and there on the perimeter, so she had a dim view of what was inside—rows and rows of garage-like doors in different colors, each securing a storage unit.

Winston got out, rang a bell and spoke through an intercom. A guard came to the office window and waved. The gate slid open on rubber wheels, and Winston drove inside.

Now what was she going to do? No way Bethanne could get inside, and there sure wasn't any cover to hide her sneaking over to see what Winston was up to. The best she could do was cruise around the facility.

Fortunately, Ralph's Rentals filled the whole block, and she could see down each row as she passed. Winston had entered the fourth row from the gate. Bethanne drove to the other end of the row, where the guard in the office couldn't see.

She didn't want to call attention to herself, so she only paused long enough to see Winston opening the padlock of an orange door about halfway down the row. It was pretty clear he was going to put his boxes inside. Winston started to turn back to his Range Rover, and Bethanne drove off so he wouldn't see her hovering.

Don't leap to conclusions, she told herself. But a man didn't wait until the dark of night to take boxes to a storage-rental unless he had something to hide.

So what was Winston concealing? Were those the same boxes that had been in the apartment? Had someone broken-in to steal them? Were they full of kiddy porn?

Bethanne braked for a red light and recognized she was rushing to judgment before she had all the facts. She'd only seen the one photo where the boxes had been. Yes, there'd been ashes of dirty pictures at the lake house, but they were far from Winston's cellar. She recalled Winston talking about his father doing favors for a bootlegger. Winston probably did some shady deals himself, and the boxes could hold incriminating evidence.

She sighed. All this was just conjecture. What she needed was proof. Especially with Winston being buddies with the Police Chief.

The light changed, and she drove on through a night darkened by questions with no answers.

11

THAT BETHANNE IS as full of surprises as them big plastic eggs they sell at the Busy Bee afore Easter. We never got any, but I saw one broke open where it fell on the floor at the market. Full of little trinkets and candy and stuff. Anyway, the morning after our fight, she drove up to the trailer and asked me if I could get away for some fun.

"How'd you find me?" I said.

She grinned. "Turned into Happy Hours Trailer Park and started asking. Everybody knows you."

Momma was out in the kitchen, fixing herself breakfast after working a double shift at the mill. She come out to meet Bethanne, and I introduced her as the lady whose money I found. Luckily, they got off that topic real quick. Those two women took such a shine to each other, they was on a first-name basis in no time. Momma invited Bethanne in for a cup of coffee, and afore long they was exchanging stories about their men running off.

I set there with my mouth open, listening to "Corrine this" and "Bethanne that" like they was old friends. Finally they finished their gabbing, and I got to take off with Bethanne. That old car sure was running good now Buck had fixed it up. I asked her where we was going, and she just smiled. "Wait and see."

We pulled up at the G-Mart, and I was thinking there wasn't nothing special about that. But there was more to it than I realized. Bethanne marched me inside and over to the bathing suit section. Then she made me try some on and show her how they fit. I was kinda embarrassed til she said, "You lost some weight." I looked in the mirror and I surely had. How about that? All them goings-on was taking my mind off food.

"Missus, I don't need no bathing suit," I said.

"Yes, you do. I'm going to teach you to swim."

And that was that. Bethanne bought me the green one we both liked. And a beach towel to match. Drove me to the county swimming pool and talked me into the shallow end. Took some talking too. I was all shaky after the last time I was in the water, even if now it was clear and only come up to my waist.

Well, Bethanne got me to hold onto the side of the pool and kick my legs for a while. That wasn't so bad. Kinda fun, in fact. Next come the hard part. Putting my face down in the water and breathing out. Then turning my head to the side and taking a breath. Over and over. I surely didn't wanna, but she kept after me, showing me how, and finally I just had to be brave and do it.

Then she told me to lean back in the water, let my feet float and hold onto her hands. She was gonna pull me round the pool.

"No way," I said.

"Every way," she said. "What if you fall in the water again, and I'm not there to save you?"

She had a point, so I laid back, holding onto her hands for dear life, and afore long, I was shooting through the water, waves all round. I got the taste of chlorine in my mouth and the burn of it up my nose, but I was feeling pretty proud of myself in the end. Didn't even care if some of them girls was making fun of me.

I'm not gonna go on and on about every step she took, but Bethanne got me swimming all on my own in just a couple hours. Oh, I didn't swim as good as most of the kids there, but I could get across the pool. And I knew how to make my arms and legs work together. And I could float. No way I was ever gonna need her to save me again.

Wasn't that a great way to get back to being friends? And that's not the half of it. Bethanne had another surprise for me.

—

"That's enough for today," Bethanne said. "Let's get something to eat." She led Eden to the pool's concession stand, then on to picnic tables shaded by maple trees growing on the other side of the fenced boundary.

They sat awhile in silence, eating hot dogs and enjoying each other's company. A breeze fluttered the broad leaves high above, and a bumblebee landed amid initials carved through twenty summers in the table's gray wood.

Bethanne brushed a hand at the insect and watched its black-veined wings carry it off. Why couldn't she just brush away her worries like that? Wave a hand, and they'd all be gone.

A big blob of relish and mustard fell off Eden's hot dog onto her suit, and Bethanne handed her a fresh paper napkin to wipe it off. "You'll have to wash your suit when you get home," she said. "Even without that smear. The chlorine'll bleach your suit. I'm hoping we can swim all summer."

Eden nodded, struggling to smile and chew at the same time. "Me too," she managed to get out past the wad in her jaw.

Bethanne looked at Eden's pinkening skin and hoped the girl wasn't in for a sunburn. They'd have to be careful about that until she got some tan. Bethanne tried to swallow, but it felt like her throat had forgotten how. "I owe you an apology."

Eden's mouth and eyes opened like she was astonished. Bethanne hurried on. "Something happened last night that made me realize you're right. There's more to what happened than we knew."

She looked around at the crowded tables. "Come on, let's go for a drive, and I'll tell you all about it."

They changed into their clothes, and Bethanne drove across town, telling Eden how she'd seen Winston hide his file boxes in the storage facility. She didn't want to talk with her young friend about all her suspicions, so she just mentioned that maybe Winston had got involved in some legal deals he didn't want anyone to know about.

Bethanne parked across the street from Ralph's Rentals. "There it is."

Eden craned her neck, taking it all in, the high fence, the gate with its intercom, the office with a window overlooking the entrance. "Bethanne," she said, "let's go inside."

When Eden finally called her by her first name, it seemed like the most natural thing in the world to Bethanne. Despite all the differences that might separate them, they'd come through a lot together. And there was bound to be even more before they figured out what was going on.

"Recon," that's what they call it. I saw that in one of them terrible action movies Ray-Jean took me to. Full of blood and guts all over the place. But the useful thing I remember is that they had to go on a recon mission aforehand. And that's what I wanted us to do, get inside that storage place and see how things was.

"You pretend you wanna rent one of them units," I said to Bethanne, "and maybe we can find out how to get into Mr. Gravesly's and have us a peek."

Bethanne looked at me like I was some wild child down from the hills. She nodded and got outta the car, me following along like I was her niece or something.

Well, she talked to the man real nice, and he was surely eager for her to see how wonderful his storage place was. He walked us up and down, showing us the differnt sizes and all. This tarry smell rose up from all the asphalt under our feet. You know how it is when the hot sun hits a job that ain't been done too good.

Bethanne musta felt like she'd had enough of slogging through that sticky asphalt, cause she stopped him afore long and said, "How can I be sure no one'll get into mine?"

He allowed as how she'd use her own padlock. Then no one else could have the key. Wasn't that the pits? We'd have to get the key from Mr. Gravesly. Or else find out the code, if he had that kind. Or else break the lock. I started thinking about how Buck had some bolt cutters.

"Oh, look," I said. "The doors is all differnt colors. Do you have any orange ones? That's my very favorite color."

I was scared he was gonna get suspicious but he musta thought I was just some silly kid, cause he smiled and said there was an orange one in every row. So I scampered on down the row where

Mr. Gravesly's unit was, like I just couldn't control myself having to touch one.

But really I was checking out his lock. He musta bought that thing at the Dollar Store. Even I could see it wasn't one of them tamper-proof jobs. No combination dial. All we needed was his key.

"Here," the man shouted. "That one's taken. I'll show you another orange one." He took us over to a differnt row, and I tried to make out like I was thrilled to bits just to be there.

Meanwhile, I was looking all round for closed circuit TV like they have at the banks. But I didn't see none. 'Cept at the gate, so they'd know who was there without having to step outside the office. Looked to me like they was more interested in letting people in than keeping them out.

Course the fence was high, and there was three strands of barbed wire on top, but if you got way far away from the office, there wasn't gonna be nobody to see you go over. Best of all, there was this big old tree with a big old branch hanging all the way over the barbed wire where we needed it to be.

And that's how you do recon.

12

"Ain't no help for it. We gotta break in." Eden grinned. "Buck's got some bolt cutters."

Bethanne looked across the Datsun's faded interior at her young friend, remembering their first encounter in the cellar. How did this little scaredy cat turn into such a tiger? "No, we don't." She started the motor and headed away from Ralph's Rentals.

Eden folded her arms across her chest and nodded emphatically. "If we wanna know what's in them boxes afore we go jumping to conclusions, we do."

No way Bethanne was going to let Eden climb over the fence and use bolt cutters on that lock. "First, let's try to get Winston's key and then see if we can bluff our way in."

Eden's voice turned scornful. "How you gonna get that key? He's not gonna leave it laying round like a piece of junk. He'll keep it way down deep in his pocket."

"You remember how I got the lake house key from a hook near the back door? There's a whole lot of keys hanging there. I'll bet he's got a duplicate. Even if he sleeps with the original under his pillow."

Eden made a face of disbelief but kept her own counsel. Bethanne didn't push it, driving on without another word. When she turned into Happy Hours Trailer Park and started down the dirt road, she could smell the dust the tires raised. It coated the trees like someone had misted them with that spray-on color Robbie Ray had used to give his ducktail highlights onstage.

Bethanne pulled up in front of Eden's trailer. Dust kicked up by the tires swirled around and into the car windows. She coughed and gave the topic one more try. "Winston's bound to keep a duplicate key somewhere."

"I don't wanna argue with you," Eden said, "but you ain't gonna find that key hanging by no back door, and that's a fact. I'm gonna see if Buck can help us." She opened the car door and got out.

Patience, Bethanne counseled herself. She'd been that impulsive once. "Hold on. Give me a chance to try it my way. Let's not break in until we have to."

Just cause I agreed to let Bethanne try her way first didn't mean I wasn't gonna start getting ready to put my own plan into action. Once Momma was gone and Cruz fed, I called up Buck and asked him how'd he like to help me out.

"Anything for you, little buddy," he said.

"You still got them bolt cutters?"

His voice got all cautious-like. "What you want with a pair of bolt cutters?"

That made me feel I better be careful. So I said, "Well, I may not need 'em at all. But just in case I do, I wanted to make sure you still had yours."

"Eden, what's this about?"

"Nothing yet. Let's just wait and see. If I need to use them bolt cutters, I'll tell you everything. How'd that be?"

"Make it a promise."

I was all ready to say whatever he wanted. Then he said, "Don't promise if you don't mean it. I'm going to hold you to it."

I surely didn't feel no smile coming down the line. I never heard Buck be so cold. How come grownups always think kids got dumb ideas? It was pretty clear I was gonna have to work on Buck just like I was gonna have to work on Bethanne, if we was ever to see the inside of that storage space.

"Sure thing, Buck. I promise."

I hung up the phone and set there looking at the empty TV screen. Wondering if I was turning into a little con artist like Ray-Jean. That pulled me up some. Seemed like I was starting to see Ray-Jean in all kinda new lights. She wasn't only the bravest girl ever went to Lewiston Junior High anymore.

⌒

Saturday night finally came, and Winston was out at the lake with the rest of the family. Bethanne could search for his padlock key. She opened the back door and turned off the alarm.

She still had house keys from when Mary Margaret was alive and Bethanne had slept in one of the empty bedrooms. Lucinda had demanded she give the keys to Winston when she moved into the chauffeur's apartment, but Clay had countered that it would be good for Bethanne to keep them in case of fire or other emergency. Way to go, Clay.

The full moon lit up a wooden board with keys hanging on rows of hooks. She quickly scanned them. Keys for the garage doors and a big one to fit the giant padlock on the shed where the riding lawn mower was stowed. Extra house and car keys. But no key for the small padlock Eden had seen at Ralph's Rentals.

Damn, this was going to be harder than she'd hoped. Bethanne was determined not to fall back on Eden's break-in plan.

She needed a cigarette to help her think, but that was a non-starter. She had every right to be in the main house—she could always say she'd heard a noise and gone to investigate after her break-in. Even so, she wanted to get in and out as quick as possible to avoid the snoopy neighbors telling Winston what she'd done.

The thought of a cigarette reminded her of the one she'd smoked in Winston's study the day he sneered at her about Mary Margaret not having anything to leave her. He might not want to hang his precious key in the back hallway, but he'd feel safe leaving it in his lair. No one was supposed to go in there without his invitation.

Bethanne pushed open the swinging door beside the double staircase and toed a rubber stop underneath to keep it that way. The door was underneath the junction of the narrow steps going down to the kitchen from the second floor and the grand stairs descending to the foyer. She hurried to the front hall and started to place a hand on the study's doorknob. Then she stopped. What if Winston kept it locked while he was gone?

A scraping noise out back made her start, and she turned toward the porch door. It was standing open, moonlight streaming onto the kitchen's black-and-white tile. She held her breath and listened for the sound to repeat. What was it? Shoes grazing against the step? A mouse scurrying across the porch? A tree branch scratching against its roof?

The sound came again, and she tiptoed back down the hall and into the kitchen, keeping out of the moonlight. She looked through the window, across the back porch and out into the yard. Shadows moved within shadows. She strained to see, but no man-shape separated from the frothy bushes blowing in the wind.

Bethanne shivered, and a tiny laugh escaped her lips. Calm down. Nobody there.

She locked the back door and turned on the light. What if the neighbors did notice? She'd already figured out what she was going to say. She dashed back down the hall and turned the study door handle. Unlocked, thank God. She'd been spooking herself about nothing.

Moonlight spilled through the panes behind the desk, calling her to shut the drapes. She crossed to the window and saw Mary Margaret's lily pond shimmering in the pale light. A hedge masked the house next door, but you never knew when someone might happen by.

She pulled the drape cords on the side window and the bay at the front, then turned on the desk lamp. Its dark green hood cast a beam downward. She tried the desk drawers, none of them locked, and found only supplies of embossed stationery and envelopes, pens, pencils, thumb tacks, clips of various sizes and files of household receipts.

Shit. Didn't Winston have the sense to keep a spare key somewhere?

She sat down in the desk chair and looked across the room. An antique highboy looked back, its rows of drawers beckoning. She tried each one. All slid open except the middle drawer. It was locked.

But it was the kind of catch that Bethanne had easily opened since she was a kid. She looked around for a nail file, always the

110

best choice for jimmying those locks, and spied a thin letter opener instead.

A few steps to the desk and back, a slip of the letter opener into the keyhole, a wiggle, a waggle, a little pressure just so, and the drawer was open. The light from the desk lamp was dim, but she could make out a muddle of string and broken candlesticks, rusty scissors and ancient pen nibs, used twisty ties and brittle rubber bands. And a red lacquer box with a Chinese scene carved in the lid.

The box had a small keyhole, and Bethanne was prepared for another effort at lock-tampering, but it opened easily. She felt like crying. Inside, nestled on a piece of black felt, was a brand new padlock key.

How come it's okay for Bethanne to break into Mr. Gravesly's drawer, but it's not okay for me to use bolt cutters on his padlock? That's what I was thinking while I set in the Arby's across the street and watched her talk to the guy at Ralph's Rentals.

We waited til Tuesday to try that key that Bethanne found. Wanted to make sure Mr. Gravesly'd be at his law office and not just happen by.

I was smarting about not having one little bitty part of the action. But we'd decided it'd be better if she went alone in case the two of us together would spark the memory of the guy on duty. I had to accept that was right, even if I didn't like it. Turned out it wasn't necessary, cause it was a differnt guy from when we been there afore, but you can't be too careful about a thing like that.

Anyhow, I set there trying to make my root beer last and watching the two of 'em talking back and forth. Looked like she wasn't getting nowhere, and I was surely feeling righteous, just like I knew I would all along. I could feel them bolt cutters in my hands, and I was raring to go.

—

"Ma'am, I'm sorry, but I can't let you go near Mr. Gravesly's storage unit without me having his say-so." Ralph's man stood firm, his mouth a hard line.

Bethanne concentrated on keeping her cool. "But I've got the key right here."

"Yes ma'am, I can see that, and I'm sure he give it to you, but I still can't let you use it without some word from him."

She lit a cigarette. "Well, he never said a thing to me about that. All I know is he's in a hurry for me to get his papers."

The man let his face and posture soften a bit. "Tell you what we can do. Let's call Mr Gravesly. If he gives me the go-ahead, then you can open that unit right up."

Bethanne felt her knees go weak. "No! I mean, I don't want to embarrass him."

She inhaled slowly to calm her nerves. "You probably heard his wife was killed in an accident awhile ago." Ralph's man nodded, and Bethanne continued. "He's got so much on his mind, he probably forgot I had to bring his authorization along with the key. I'll go back and mention it in a way that won't make him feel bad."

The man tilted his head and looked at her sideways.

Bethanne threw him her best smile. "Sorry to disturb you. Back soon."

She drove around the block, picked up Eden in the Arby's parking lot and related what had happened. Eden's response set her teeth on edge.

"Bethanne, I'm sorry, but I told you so."

13

WE HEADED OVER TO Buck's house right after we left that rental place. It was way too hot and humid to be outside, so Buck invited us to set in his living room. He had a new Sears and Roebuck air conditioner in the window, and the ruckus just added to my pain. I was getting the worst headache of my life trying to persuade Bethanne that we had to take them bolt cutters with us.

Bethanne had a cold beer in one hand and a cigarette in the other. "We don't need the bolt cutters if we've got the key."

"But we don't know it's the right key," Buck said. I could tell he was ready right then and there. Big change from when I first talked to him over the phone about them bolt cutters. But once he heard the whole story, he knew we had to find out what was in them boxes. Looked like he almost couldn't wait for nightfall.

Felt like I was getting somewhere, with him on my side. Just then Vicki come in from the kitchen. That's Buck's girlfriend. She was carrying their son, Chance, along with his bottle. "What're you-all talking about?"

Buck tried to cut me off, but I was busting to get it out. "We're gonna break into Ralph's Rentals."

"Oh no you're not. Buck's already done enough time."

"Time?" Bethanne felt her own memories come back to haunt her. That shoplifting charge hadn't kept her behind bars for long, but it was long enough. "You mean Buck's done jail time?"

Vicki sat down in a shiny polyester chair and gave Chance his bottle. "Thirty days in the county jail. Assault and battery."

Buck grinned. "Aw, I only knocked that guy around a little. Besides, he deserved it." He set his beer can on a laminated table trying to look like wood.

No need for a coaster, Bethanne noted, thinking about Mary Margaret's concerns over her antique furniture. She felt more at home in Buck's old clapboard house than she ever would in Winston's mansion.

Vicki's frown held fondness in it. "Yeah, he surely did. But that don't mean I'm gonna let you do it again."

Bethanne glanced back and forth at Eden and Buck's family. "I'm lost here. Mind filling me in?"

Chance burped, and the odor of half-digested milk mingled with the room's smell of beer.

Vicki gazed at her son. "Well, we was over to The Keg, and this old boy tried to get me to drink some beer. I was carrying Buck's baby," she patted her tummy, "so I told him no."

Buck looped his long, dirty-blond hair behind his ears. " But he wouldn't take no for an answer. That's when I come back from the head. Popped him a couple times just to teach him some manners."

Vicki's smile was lovely to behold. "I was filled with pride, honey, you looking after me like that." She glanced at Bethanne. "But that old boy broke his arm when he hit the floor. Him being a welder, put him outta work for six weeks. So Buck went to jail."

Bethanne gulped down her beer. Getting into Winston's storage unit was looking less and less likely.

—~

I knew we had to get Buck off to hisself. So soon as it was decent, I said we'd better be getting on home.

Buck said he'd walk us out to the car, like I knew he would. Vicki was busy burping Chance on her shoulder, so she just waved.

Once we got outside, I started whispering to Bethanne. "We gotta do this careful. We gotta take the key *and* the bolt cutters. But it can't be tonight. I need time to find someone to look after Cruz."

Bethanne fairly hissed like a snake. "You can't go. You're too young."

"And you're too old," I said. "Ain't no way you can get over that fence."

Buck seemed to see we was getting a little hot, and that was the truth in both senses of the word. As soon as we got outside, sweat broke out all over my body, and I could see it shining on Bethanne's face and arms. But we was getting hot with anger too, and he stepped between us.

"Ma'am, she's right. You gotta admit your tree-climbing days is over. Eden's gotta go, cause she knows which door to open."

I commenced to grinning at that, but I soon got my comeuppance.

"On the other hand," he said, "Eden's too small to use them bolt cutters." I took a swing at him, kinda in fun, but he held me off.

Bethanne was shaking her head, but Buck went on. "There's only one way to do it that I can see. You go to the gate and distract the guy on duty. Me and Eden shinny up the tree and over the fence. We try the key, and if that don't work, I'll bust it open with the bolt cutters."

Her mouth pulled all tight like it was trying to reach her ears. "Well, you better take something to cut open the boxes. They're taped shut."

Buck give us a wicked grin and hauled out the fanciest pocketknife I ever did see, red on the outside and ten tools on the inside.

A couple of nights later, Bethanne sat in her car at the corner of Ralph's Rentals. She looked at her watch. Twenty-five after twelve. Soon she'd drive to the gate and offer up a little distraction.

She wasn't happy about it, but she'd had to give in to Eden and Buck. How else were they going to get a peek inside Winston's boxes?

They'd all agreed that Winston's secrets might have something to do with Mary Margaret and Ray-Jean's deaths. Bethanne had been careful to mention only her suspicions about legal hanky-panky. She hadn't wanted to talk about connecting the ashes of burned photos in the lake house with Mae reporting that Mary Margaret had returned from there with puffy, red eyes.

What if Mary Margaret had discovered those photos and burned them? She could have realized that Winston was addicted to kiddy porn. Would she have threatened to leave him? Was Winston worried the whole rotten story might get out if she left? Could he have killed Mary Margaret and persuaded the Police Chief to help him cover it up? If so, then Ray-Jean just happened to be in a tampered car.

A miserable weight forced Bethanne's chin to her chest. It was too depressing to contemplate. Mary Margaret willing to spend her life savings to spare Winston the embarrassment of her secret and Winston ready to murder his wife to protect his own.

Bethanne shivered even though the night seemed as hot and humid as the day. Knowing what was in those boxes could tell her if she was jumping to conclusions. Eden and Buck had come up with the only way that seemed like it could work. How much longer before they'd be ready?

She turned her gaze to the side street. Buck was up the tree, knotting a rope over a limb so he and Eden could get back over the fence once they'd checked the boxes.

Bethanne felt bad about using Buck when he'd already been in jail. And she felt worse about having Eden involved and keeping her out so late. She even felt sorry for Cruz, but that was a difficulty she'd been able to solve. She'd used a little money from Ray-Jean's coffee can to hire one of the girls from the trailer park to babysit. Eden knew her and said she was reliable.

Just then, Buck hauled Eden up to the lowest tree branch. Even from this far, Bethanne could see her beaming like this was the most fun a girl could have. Bethanne reacted with an amused snort and wagged her head back and forth. Then she started her engine and rolled toward the gate.

Buck lowered me to the ground, then come down the rope hisself. Next thing, we was running to the right row and the orange door. I had the key zipped up in my pocket. I grinned at Buck when I got it out, and he grinned back. I could see he was enjoying hisself as much as I was. Even if we never could tell Momma and Vicki about it.

I tried to put the key in the lock, but it wouldn't go. Figured maybe I wasn't doing it right, so I handed the key over to Buck, and he give it a try. But he wasn't no better at it than I was. Hot damn, time for the bolt cutters.

Buck got a grip with them cutters on the curved piece that goes into the lock. Then he give 'em a good, sharp jerk. He's surely got some muscles, what with working out while he was in jail and doing all that physical stuff with cars. But he didn't need them muscles with that cheap old lock. Had it open in less than a second. I pulled the lock out and laid it on the ground.

Then I bent down to open the door, and that's when I made my mistake. I turned the handle and let go. That door flew up and hit the frame with a noise like to wake the whole neighborhood, if anybody'd been living there. Which they wasn't.

Buck grabbed my hand. "Little buddy, we're in for it now."

But we didn't run right away. We was paralyzed with staring into Mr. Gravesly's storage place.

~~

Being a sloppy drunk was something Bethanne knew a lot about, so she hung on the gate, waved a pint and kept asking directions to Jerry's house. Of course the guy had no idea. The more he tried to get her to leave, the more she kept insisting. "Come on, you know where he lives. Everybody knows Jerry."

Thank God this was still another guy. Did Ralph have his whole family on the payroll?

A crash rang out from the direction of Winston's storage unit, and Bethanne knew it was all over. "Okay, you old party pooper. See if I ever let Jerry invite you again."

The guy didn't wait to hear her parting shot. He took off running, drawing a gun she hadn't noticed before.

Bethanne leaped in her car and tore around the block. The car's headlights showed Eden already in the tree and Buck going up the rope hand over hand.

"Jump, Eden, jump," he yelled.

Eden's teeth glistened in a grimace, but she let go and dropped to the ground.

Bethanne winced when Eden's ankle flopped over as it took her full weight. Bethanne already had the gas pedal down as far as it would go, but she pushed even harder.

Ralph's midnight man rounded the corner of the row Eden and Buck had just left, waving his gun and hollering, "Stop, or I'll shoot."

Buck swung down from the tree and got Eden's arm over his shoulder. He lifted her to her feet just as Bethanne drove up.

The guard took a legs-apart stance and raised his gun, one hand under the other to steady it. A flash exploded, and Bethanne jumped. Then she realized it was heat lightning. For a moment, she'd thought it was the blast from the gun. She looked at the guard. He was pausing for breath.

Buck threw Eden in the backseat and jumped in after her. "Ma'am, ain't nothing behind that door 'cept a couple dust bunnies."

14

Bethanne hunkered down in her chair, sipped her beer and pretended to gaze out at the lake. She'd come for the weekly Sunday barbecue and ended up with a bonus. But she didn't want Clay or his sister to notice how much attention she was paying to what Lucinda had to say.

"It was the weirdest thing. Daddy said Ralph called to report there was something strange going on with his storage unit. Some funny-looking woman and a kid showed up asking a lot of questions about how safe the units were. Then the woman came back with a key and wanted to get in Daddy's space, but she couldn't show any authorization."

Bethanne almost strangled on the acrid smoke drifting from Clay's French cigarette. Shit, Ralph's men had put two and two together, even if there had been different guys on duty each time.

Clay flipped another burger on the fieldstone barbecue. "Big deal. How could anyone get Dad's key? And of course they're not going to let somebody in without Dad's say-so."

Lucinda finished tossing the salad and put it in the middle of the picnic table. "That's not the point." Her voice held a hint of exasperation. "Who were they, and why did they want to get into Daddy's storage?"

Bethanne followed Clay's glance toward the lake. Winston was demonstrating to his grandchildren how he could swim underwater farther than anybody in the family.

Clay's eyes tightened for a moment. "Did Dad look at the tape?"

The smell of burning grease turned Bethanne's stomach. The tape? That camera wasn't just to let staff see who was at the gate without getting up to look out the window? It was taping her? Double shit.

Lucinda waved away a wasp trying to get under the relish lid. "Yeah, but it's pretty grainy, and they were smart enough to keep their heads down. He couldn't get a clear view of either one of them."

Bethanne gulped her beer. Thank you, Jesus, thank you.

Clay started putting the burgers on a platter. "What's he got in there anyway?"

Lucinda's head jerked toward her brother, and she bit her lip. "How should I know?"

"Wonder why he's renting space. He could store the stuff in the cellar. Probably most of it's not worth keeping. Bet I could go through it and toss half of it out."

"Well, somebody thinks it's valuable. After Ralph phoned Daddy, they came back and broke into his unit. Not just the woman and the girl. Some guy too. It was too dark for the guard to make out the color and make of the car." Lucinda smirked. "But thanks to the light over the license plate, he got the last three digits."

Bethanne tried not to gasp. Oh God. She looked at her car, afraid the plates would be in full view. She let her pent-up air out slowly. She'd parked in the shade of a spirea bush, and its drooping branches covered the license tag.

Her eyes swung to the dock, where Winston and the kids were

toweling off. What would happen when she drove away? Would Winston notice the numbers? Would he tell the police? Could she keep Eden and Buck out of it? Maybe it was time to stop all this nosing around.

Clay put the platter on the table and shouted toward the dock. "Come and get it!" Then he turned to Lucinda and gave her his full attention. "So what did they take?"

"That's what I've been trying to tell you. Daddy and Mr. Jeffries moved all his stuff right after Ralph called. Before the break-in. Put it in Mr. Jeffries' barn."

Bethanne couldn't help herself. Who was this Jeffries, and where was his barn?

⌒

That Bethanne had some funny ideas about friendship. It ain't just about picking out clothes together and learning how to swim. There's the part about through thick and thin too.

Me and Buck was stuck to her sofa Monday morning, listening to what she'd heard at the Graveslys' cookout. She hadn't wanted to go at first, but me and Buck said it might turn out to be a good way to learn something. And we was right, wasn't we? Still, it was pretty scary finding out me and her been taped.

And they had some of the numbers on Bethanne's license plate. She surely was smart to wait for nightfall afore driving off. She just slipped away, and no one paid her no never-mind. 'Cept that Clay, and he only called out, "Bye." Seems to me she's almost invisible to them folks. No way to treat kin, even if they ain't blood.

When Bethanne got done telling everything, she said, "That's the end of the line for you two."

"No way," I said. "We started this together, and we're gonna finish it together."

Bethanne put out her cigarette like there was some nasty bug under it she wanted to squash. "I can't let you do that. It's not just the video and my license number. You got hurt. A man chased you with a gun."

"My ankle's fine now," I said. "Didn't hurt more'n a day. And that dumb guard watches too much TV. Standing there like he was in some cop show. Ain't that right, Buck?"

He shook his head. "He was doing all the right things, little buddy. Took the right stance, took a breath to steady his aim."

That punched some of the starch outta me, but I wasn't gonna give up yet. "Where's the phone book?"

Bethanne looked at me kinda peculiar. "What do you need it for?"

"Gonna find out who this Jeffries is."

"Eden," she said, "you're not in this anymore. It's too dangerous. Besides, there must be scores of Jeffries living around here."

I got up and headed for the stand where I could see the phone book. "How else you gonna find out who Jeffries is? You gonna camp out by their poker game and hope they announce their full names and addresses? Get real."

"I don't care for that tone, little buddy," Buck said, and I had to say I was sorry to be so disrespectful.

"You're not in it either, Buck," Bethanne said.

"Yes ma'am, I am. Ain't nobody gonna nearly shoot us and me walk away."

She opened her mouth to say something, but he held up his hand. "We're all in this, whether we like it or not. Eden's right. We gotta finish it."

I come back with the phonebook and set down in the middle of the sofa. That musty smell was all gone, so Bethanne musta sprayed it with that deodorant stuff you can get for furniture. Anyhow, I commenced to reading. "James…Jason…Jeebles… What kind of name is that?" Course no one answered such a stupid question, but I noticed Bethanne come over and set on my other side. She put her finger in the middle of the page. "Jeffries."

Knock me over if she wasn't right. There musta been forty Jeffries if there was one. You never saw so many first names. There was even seven Jeffries named John, each one with a differnt middle initial. I was getting eyestrain just looking at 'em all.

Then I heard Bethanne huff, and she slid her finger down to one line. "Peter B. Jeffries," I read out, "Photographer."

"That's the one," she said.

⟿

Bethanne couldn't help but smile when Eden stretched her neck, head down, and looked up. Was she copying some move she'd seen on TV?

"Scuse me," Eden said, "but how you know this Jeffries is the right one?"

Bethanne thought about the picture of the boy lying naked in the sheets and the burned shadows of photos at the lake house. Maybe she could talk about this with Buck, but with a thirteen year-old girl? Yet she had to say something about why she'd picked the photographer. Keep it short and to the point, she decided. "I think all this has something to do with child pornography."

"That's disgusting," Buck said.

"You mean like dirty pictures of kids?" Eden said, and Bethanne tried to think how to answer.

"That Marlene Thompson works for some photographer," Eden went on. "Maybe it's Jeffries."

Bethanne was at a total loss for words, but Buck was more than ready. "Who's this Marlene? And how well do you know her?"

Eden sat tall, defiant. "She lives in a trailer down aways from ours. Works part-time for the trailer park and part-time for this photographer."

Buck took Eden by the shoulders. "You stay away from this guy, you hear? There's a lotta sick bastards in this world, and I don't want you nowhere near 'em."

Bethanne finally found her voice. "Buck's right. If this Jeffries is who I think he is, we have to keep you away from him."

Eden looked back and forth at her friend and her cousin. "What if I just ask Marlene the name of the man she works for?"

15

Bethanne looked in the courthouse's mirrored column and patted her hair. She'd just had it done at the Cut-n-Curl, hoping to look more respectable. The beauty shop's receptionist hadn't wanted to give her an appointment on such short notice, but Bethanne had persuaded the owner to fit her in. She couldn't bear to wait more than a day after she and Eden had tentatively identified Jeffries as Winston's helper.

Butterflies winged around her stomach, reminding her of the last time she'd been inside a courthouse. If she hadn't been drunk, she'd never have put up a fight when they caught her shoplifting. Thank God the Public Defender got her off. Said it was a first offense and she wasn't herself because her husband had just run away with another woman. Well, here she was, risking jail time again, breaking and entering not only Winston's storage unit, but probably Jeffries' barn too.

The scent of fresh varnish led her to the elaborately carved wooden banister of the marble staircase and up to the second floor. She paused before the Records door. She had no idea how the system worked to get the information she needed, but she did know it was somehow available to the public. She squared her shoulders and lifted her head. Just get on with it, she told herself, you have a right to know.

Bethanne entered with what she hoped was a confidant smile for the saggy-faced clerk seated behind a counter. "Hi, I need to find the exact location of a property…"

The clerk interrupted, raising a bright red manicure to point at a table in the corner. "Over there. Use the computer."

Bethanne felt way out of her depth. "Uh, sorry, I never did learn how to use one of those things." She offered a lopsided smile, hoping an admission of weakness would be ingratiating. "Too old to learn now, I guess."

The clerk sighed and put red-tipped fingers to her computer keyboard. "Okay." Her voice clearly showed her aggravation. "Tell me what you know about this property."

Bethanne wanted a cigarette in the worst way. She looked at the "No Smoking" sign over the file cabinets behind the clerk and let out her own sigh. She was going to have to get through this without the help of nicotine. "It's a barn outside of town. Somebody told me it might be for sale. Peter B. Jeffries?"

She watched the exasperated woman type. Hoping to win over the clerk, she waved her newly purchased steno pad and smiled again. "Got a notebook to write it all down."

The clerk rolled her eyes. "Not necessary." She picked up a sheet of paper as it fell from the printer. "Here's a printout. Address and map." Then she rose, turned her back and walked over to the file cabinets.

"I sure do thank you," Bethanne called after her, folding the paper and putting it in the steno pad.

The clerk just shrugged and walked on.

I was pushing the chips and dip at Marlene, trying to get her in the mood to talk. Even if Buck and Bethanne told me to hold off. Sometimes you know you just gotta go ahead and do what's right. That's why I got old Marlene over to the trailer park's picnic area the very next day after we found out about that Jeffries guy.

We was setting at the center table next to an oil barrel split in half with a grill on top to make a barbecue. In the late morning, when nearly all the grownups was at work or sleeping after their shifts, it was the perfect place to get Marlene alone. Shady too, under them trees, even if they was all dusty. We sure needed us some rain.

Marlene was stuck on how the kids made fun of her at the pool, and I was saying I knew what she meant cause I been there too, and some of them girls surely can be mean. I kept sipping my Coke and trying to figure out how I was gonna get her to talk about that photographer.

"You know what I done?" she said. "I pulled the cash outta my wallet, and I told them girls that when they could get that much money just for keeping quiet, I'd listen to 'em."

"What d'ya mean, keeping quiet?"

She flipped that long, straight hair of hers. Makes you wonder if she's part Indian. Lotta folks round here is. "Well, I know some secrets, of course," she said. "Like old man Gravesly. I know you been hanging round with some of his family, but he could be in for a heap of trouble."

My heart rose up, but I tried not to let her see. Sprayed some Cheese Whip on a Ritz cracker and handed it to her "Like what?"

She smiled across the table at me. "Mr. J's got something on him."

"That the photographer you work for?"

She nodded, so smug you'd think she'd been crowned Queen of

the Forest Festival. "You'd be surprised all the things he's got going for him. Says I'm the best help he ever had. He counts on me, he surely does."

"What's the 'J' stand for?"

"Jeffries. He surely is one enterprising man." She grinned. "Believe you me, I could tell some tales. But I gotta be faithful to Mr. J."

I was all ready to talk her outta that notion when a police car pulled up, and the cop who was at Bethanne's break-in got out. He pointed at me and said, "Missy, I want to talk to you."

⸺

Bethanne hurried away from the County Clerk's office, holding her steno pad to her chest and her head down. She didn't want anyone to see the exultation in her face. She still had a long way to go, but she was getting closer to figuring out what was going on.

"What're you doing here?" The voice was belligerant, demanding.

Bethanne looked up, and her smile vanished. It was Winston.

He stood in front of her, close, blocking her path. "What're you doing here?" he repeated.

"Ah…" Bethanne dug deep. "Well, I…I saw an abandoned cottage and thought maybe I could buy it and fix it up."

"Really?" Sarcasm drenched his voice.

"Yeah." Bethanne felt herself on firmer ground. "Wanted to find out who owned it."

Passersby were gawking at the palpable tension between the two. Winston took her arm and steered her into a corner. "What makes you think I'd enjoy having you live around here? And how're you going to buy a cottage and fix it up anyway?

Bethanne shrugged her arm out of his grasp. "You're forgetting the money Mary Margaret left me. And I'm looking for a job."

He sneered. "A job? Who'd hire a lush like you?"

Anger climbed up from Bethanne's gut and swelled her chest. If what she suspected was true, what gave this porn-monger the right to be so high and mighty? "Maybe you haven't noticed, Winston, but I don't hit the bottle like I used to. Not since Mary Margaret went off the dock. Made me realize I got to take my life into my own hands."

"Snoopy little hands too. Been out to Ralph's Rentals?"

Bethanne felt like a rabbit was thumping inside her chest, but she managed to shake her head.

"Oh yeah, I saw that tape," he said. "Maybe I can't prove it, but that woman sure looked a lot like you, and the kid reminded me of that girl who was in your apartment." Winston leaned over Bethanne, his breath heating her face. "You better keep those snoopy hands out of my business."

You never saw nobody scoot away faster than Marlene did when that cop got outta his car. "Bye" was all she said, and she was gone.

The cop straddled the bench and parked his scrawny butt where Marlene had been. He stuck a finger in the plastic tub of bean dip and licked it. Fingernail all black like he'd hit it with a hammer or something. "So Eden, how come you was casing Mr. Gravesly's house?"

My jaw musta nearly hit the table. "What're you talking about? I was visiting Miz Swanson, like she told you."

"I ain't talking about that night. I'm talking about how the neighbors saw you before that, standing out front of the house and taking it all in."

I felt sweat start to dribble down the middle of my chest and hoped it wasn't breaking out on my face too. He was going way back, afore I met Bethanne, and trying to connect me to the break-in.

He scooped up some more dip. "Cat got your tongue? Afraid to tell me you was watching the house so you could tell your buddies how to get inside? Couldn't be your cousin Buck's involved, could it?"

Something foul was rising up in my throat, and I took a big swallow of soda to push it back down. The Coke was flat and warm, but it did the trick. Once I did that, I could see the best way was to tell part of the truth. Just not all of it. Like I did afore, when I first met Bethanne.

"You got it all wrong. I was there cause I felt bad about Ray-Jean going off the dock in Miz Gravesly's car. I just needed to see where that lady lived. Sure was a long way from the Happy Hours Trailer Park. I couldn't figure out how them two come to know each other."

He put both elbows on the table and leaned his sweaty face across at me. "We been wondering the same thing. And now we're wondering why you're so cozy with Miz Gravesly's sister."

I give him what I hoped was a nice smile. "We was just comforting each other in our loss."

He stood up and towered over me. Man musta been six-foot-four if he was an inch. "I'll believe that when horses can fly. Meanwhile, I got my eye on you, Missy. Don't do nothing you'll be sorry for."

16

Sunlight shimmered off the pool's blue-tiled border and drilled into Bethanne's aching head. After her courthouse confrontation with Winston, she just wanted to float in the soothing water until evening brought cool relief. But first she had to deal with Eden's enthusiasm.

"I think we better hold off awhile," she said.

"Just cause Mr. Gravesly believes he mighta seen us in that old video? I don't think so." Eden splashed at a chlorine-intoxicated bee floating near. "Where'd you run into him, anyway?"

Bethanne sunk underwater to ease her pounding head. She hadn't told Eden about researching the barn's address and had no intention of doing so now. She didn't want the girl nosing around when Winston was already suspicious.

She lifted her face to keep her hair back and rose until her chin cleared the surface. "Oh, downtown."

"Like on the street? Inside his office?"

"What does it matter where? Winston's suspicious, that's what's important. Let's leave it alone for a while. A couple of weeks won't matter."

"How you know he won't move them boxes again? We gotta find out where that barn is, and we gotta do it now."

Bethanne shielded her pupils from the glare and looked at Eden. The girl may have started out the summer pale as paper, but she was going to end it tan as a biscuit right out of the oven. But Eden could be as exasperating as ever. Bethanne pushed off and swam across the pool, hitting the water as hard as she could. Eden paddled after her.

"I'm getting a headache," Bethanne said. "Let's not talk about it now. What'd you do yesterday?"

Eden practiced her flutter kick. "Aw, you know, just hanging out at the trailer park."

"You staying away from Marlene?"

Eden grinned. "Why don't you teach me to swim underwater? Like how you saved me out at the lake?"

"Take a deep breath," Bethanne said and pushed her under.

I surely was hot by the end of that afternoon at the pool, but it didn't have nothing to do with the weather. Gotta admit, though, every day was more hot and humid than the last. What we needed was some thunderstorms to cool things off, but we wasn't getting none. Even if it was nearly August. The clouds'd build up, and the sheet lightning'd flash, but they'd move on and dump their cooling rain and wind somewhere else.

Anyhow, it wasn't the weather that was making me so hot, it was Bethanne refusing to get on with our investigation. And I could tell she was hiding stuff from me. Guess she thought she was protecting me, but that made me feel like she thought I was a little kid. Well, two can play that game, even if they is friends. I had stuff to hide too. Like how much I had to do with Marlene.

I got back home in time to wave Momma 'bye and give Cruz his juice bottle. I was watching the TV and trying to decide what I wanted for dinner, when Marlene banged on the screen door.

"Hey, Eden. Am I bothering ya?"

I wasn't exactly sure I wanted to talk with her so soon after me and Bethanne nearly had it out at the pool, but Marlene already had the door halfway open. So I naturally had to say, "Come on in," and offer her a can of Coke.

I switched the tube to MTV. Marlene'd never go for all that history stuff. Too bad. They was talking about this big fire nearly destroyed London hunnerds of years ago, and I was hungry for the whole story.

Marlene set there awhile, watching Cherika wiggle her butt up against some guy. "I surely do admire that woman. She's worked hard for what she's got." Marlene swigged from the can. "Just like me. I'm gonna work my tail off til I'm a star."

I could hardly believe my ears. Marlene had about as much talent as one of them sock monkeys they sell at the church bazaar. "I didn't know you could sing."

She shifted round on her cushion like she couldn't get comfortable. "Well, you don't have to sing to be a star. Look at Lacey Young. She started out in porn flicks, and now she's in real TV shows."

Cherika and Lacey Young. That Marlene sure had her some heroes. But I could see maybe this was gonna lead somewhere, so I said, "You thinking about being in porn movies?"

Marlene wore this cheap red lipstick she got down at Brand's drugstore, and when she smiled, it was like some fleshy thing opening up to show its white insides. "Why not? Mr. J says I got the talent."

"How does he know?"

"Don't go telling your momma I told you, but me and Pete is having an affair."

My heart started beating like this machine Buck's got to take off wheel lugs. Battabattabatta, like that. All I could think of to say was, "For real?"

"It's okay. I'm old enough." She winked. "And he's divorced."

"But what does he know about porn movies?"

She give me this soft little smile, like I was some kind of doll baby. "He makes 'em, ya little dope."

I was ready to shout out a big yahoo, but I kept it in. Now I knew what road we was on, I figured I could follow it all the way to Jeffries' barn.

Marlene finished off her Coke. "You're getting me way off the subject. What I really wanted to talk about is that cop who come by yesterday. What'd he want, anyway?"

I never felt so much frustration in my life. Not even when Cruz done his best to keep me from one of my programs. As soon as I got on the road to that barn, Marlene took a detour. And it was a scary one too. Had to find just the right answer. "He was following up on some stuff about Ray-Jean's death."

Marlene's breathed out a big whoosh. "I was afraid he mighta wanted to know if I'd let slip about the things Pete does outside of studio photography."

I felt some hope creep back in "Where does he make his porn movies?"

Marlene seemed to recollect herself. "Have the cops got any leads about how Ray-Jean come to die like that?"

"Didn't say." I walked over to the fridge and got her another Coke. "Does Jeffries make his movies out at his barn? Where is it, anyway?"

I could just taste how surprised Bethanne was gonna be when I come up with the location we needed.

Marlene stiffened up. "Like I said afore, Pete counts on me to keep his secrets."

⌒

Bethanne picked up the damp towel rolled around her swimsuit and got out of the car. She couldn't wait to get inside and turn on the a.c., even if she didn't normally like it. So hot outside the birds were silent, hiding in deep shade until dusk. Even the insects had lost their buzz.

The silence was interrupted by the sound of weeping. Bethanne turned toward the kitchen. Mae stood just inside the screen door, wiping her face with a gingham apron.

"Oh, Miz Bethanne, I'm in a heap of trouble."

Bethanne crossed the porch and felt cool air leaking through the screen. Best not waste Winston's central air conditioning. She went inside, closed the main door and led Mae into the kitchen. "What's the matter?"

Mae's eyes brimmed over again. "I should've gone to secretarial school like I planned. Never meant to be anybody's maid. But I met Jim, and I got pregnant, and here I am."

Bethanne felt confused. All that had been years ago. She put a hand on Mae's plump elbow and steered her to the kitchen table. "And now?"

Mae collapsed into a chair and wailed. "I've been fired. And after working for this family ever since I was young and slim. This never would've happened if Miz Mary Margaret was still alive."

Bethanne pulled up a chair beside her. "Winston fired you?"

"Yes'm. You know how he doesn't like anybody going into his study?"

Bethanne nodded, thinking about her secret foray to find the padlock key.

"Well, when I came in this morning, the study door was wide open. There was the smell of smoke everywhere, cigarette butts and cigar stubs spilling out of the ashtrays. Whiskey slopped on the carpet. If Miz Mary Margaret'd been here, she'd have told me to clean it up. So I did."

Bethanne scrunched her face in consternation. "Did Winston have one of his poker games last night?" Why hadn't she noticed? Was her air conditioner so loud it had covered all this up?

"Don't know. There weren't any cards or chips on the table, but maybe he put them away before he went to bed."

"Why would he put them away and not clean up the rest of it?"

"Well, Mr. Winston's very particular about his poker stuff, but he leaves it to me to clean up the mess. I thought I was doing him a favor, but I guess I should've waited to be asked."

Mae started to cry again. Bethanne patted her pillowy arm and tried to figure out if there was more to this than a housekeeper being too conscientious. "Tell me exactly what happened when he fired you."

Mae wiped her eyes again with her apron. "I was straightening up his desk when he came in. I guess he needed something from his files. Happens all the time. He stores some of his legal papers here, the ones he wants to keep really private."

Bethanne rocked back and forth with impatience. "And?"

"He grabbed up this big manila envelope on top of the desk

and started shouting at me. He was so mad, I was backing up and stammering and trying to get out of there as fast as I could. Mr. Winston followed me into the hall and locked the door behind him. Paid me off then and there and told me to leave."

"All that happened this morning?"

"Yes'm. But I've been hanging around until it was time to go home. I don't know what I'm going to tell Jim." She blinked back tears. "Ever since he lost his fingers in that accident, life's been going downhill. Drawing disability's taking away his manhood. And now we got to deal with this."

Bethanne's attention was still on Winston. "Did you get a good look at the envelope?"

Mae nodded. "Mr. Winston had written across it in black ink. 'Jeffries favors,' it said."

Favors, Bethanne repeated to herself. From Winston to Jeffries, or the other way round? She looked at Mae's teary face and thought about Winston running hot and cold. That's what Mary Margaret had said years ago when they were first married, and she had to get used to Winston's flip-flop emotions. Bethanne smiled. "Winston'll probably be over it by tomorrow and ask you to come back."

"We sure need the money." Mae stood up. "But I don't know if I want to come back. Seems like Mr. Winston might be doing something shady he doesn't want anybody to know about." She sighed. "If that's the case, thank God Miz Mary Margaret's not here to see it."

17

AFTER MARLENE LEFT, I started thinking about how there was more secrets in Lewiston than I ever coulda imagined. That turned me to Ray-Jean sneaking into people's houses and finding what they kept hidden. But she stopped showing me what she found, even though we was best friends.

What if she knew she was in danger and didn't want any of it to slide on over to me? I thought about how I been searching out at the dock for a clue that Ray-Jean mighta left for me to find. But what if she already saw how risky things was afore she went out to the lake? She mighta left a clue for me somewhere else.

I looked out the window at her momma's trailer. I hadn't been over since Ray-Jean died. Made me feel kinda guilty, cause I shoulda been to see Miz Shackleford, even if I did speak to her at the funeral.

It was still daylight out, and Cruz was awake, so I picked him up, locked the door and walked over to her trailer. Ray-Jean's momma was setting outside with a glass of ice tea, and I felt even worse when she got up from that beat-up old plastic chair and give me a big hug.

"Eden, you're a sight for sore eyes. Lemme get you some tea." Nothing would do but she had to step indoors, come back with another glass and go on about everything that was on her mind.

Meanwhile, I was fidgeting inside, waiting for enough time to pass so I could bring up what I come for. She did get my attention, though, when she talked about some lawyer.

"One of them ambulance-chasers come by," she said. "Wanted me to go after the Graveslys for Ray-Jean dying in their car." She blinked real hard. "I was sorely tempted, cause life's been real hard since Dave run off. But I'm not gonna make any money outta my Ray-Jean dying, and that's it."

She blew out a long breath, took in another one and went on to other concerns. Meanwhile, I was thinking about how I seen on the TV that folks are wanting more and more to sue, even when there's no good reason. Miz Shackleford had as good a reason as you can get, but she didn't wanna lower herself. That's something to admire.

Cruz had long gone to sleep in my lap and the lightning bugs had started to come out when I finally got round to asking if Ray-Jean had left anything for me.

Miz Shackleford looked at me kinda funny. "No, sugar. Why would she do that?"

"Oh, I don't know," I said. "Guess I just wanted something to remember her by."

She jumped up. "Well, I can fix that. Saved some keepsakes for you."

Course that made me feel about as no-count as you can be. I only went to see Miz Shackleford cause I wanted something from her. And she was my best friend's momma. I gentled Cruz up onto my shoulder and followed her through the screen door.

She picked up an old shoebox setting on the table. "I couldn't bear to go through Ray-Jean's things til now. I know how much you two was friends, so I wanted you to have these."

We was both in danger of getting all soppy, and I wanted to get outta there in the worst way. So I said, "Thank you, I surely do appreciate it." She seemed to see how much I was feeling, and she just nodded her head. I picked up the box with my free hand and turned to go. Then I thought of something else.

"I don't like to say this," I said, "but Ray-Jean was acting kinda strange afore she died. Like she had something on her mind." Lord, that was another lie, but it was for a good cause. I put down the shoebox and shifted Cruz to the other shoulder. "Did it seem like that to you, or am I just looking for answers where there ain't none?"

Miz Shackleford looked out the screen door toward where the reporters had stood round yammering. "I didn't like to say this afore, but Ray-Jean was having nightmares and talking in her sleep."

Mercy, I thought, this is it. "What'd she say?"

"Kept going on about one secret too far."

⌒

Mae stood up and took off her apron. "I got to be getting home."

Bethanne smiled. "Why don't you just show up tomorrow like nothing happened? Winston's probably already sorry he fired you."

"I hear you, but I've got to think on it some."

"Because you think Winston's involved in something shady?"

Mae nodded and held the yellow-plaid apron against her ample bosom. "Maybe it's time for me to move on before something hits the fan." She gazed off into the distance. "On the bus home, the maids all gossip about what happened during the day. They say white folks around here can't understand why Mr. Winston is always doing favors for this Jeffries."

Bethanne felt like a long-closed door might be opening. "Like what?"

"Like getting a drunk-driving charge reduced to negligence. And defending Jeffries against drug-dealing charges when everybody knows that man sells Ecstasy out his back door. Why does Mr. Winston want to have anything to do with a man like that?"

Bethanne took Mae by the arm. "I don't know, but let's find out. Let's go look at those legal papers he wants to keep so private."

She felt her conscience jabbing about using Mae, but Bethanne didn't wait for her to answer. She kept her hand on Mae's elbow all the way out of the kitchen, down the hall and to the study door. Goose bumps rose up on Bethanne's arms, whether from nerves or the a.c., she couldn't tell.

Mae pulled free. "He keeps those file drawers locked."

"Is there a spare key somewhere?"

"Not that I know of." Mae started down the hall toward the kitchen. "Got to be getting on home."

Bethanne pushed her wavering conscience aside and followed Mae past the main staircase. "I never noticed a file cabinet in Winston's study. Where is it?"

Mae stopped and looked Bethanne straight in the face. "He doesn't like his study to look like an office. The built-in bookcase has double drawers underneath. What looks like two drawers is really one deep one." She continued to the kitchen.

Bethanne kept pace. "Where's the key?"

"None of my business." Mae hung her apron on its peg, picked up her purse, pushed open the back door and hurried down the steps as fast as her swollen ankles would carry her.

I was feeling almost as low as I did when Ray-Jean died. Here she'd been having nightmares, and I didn't even know it. Come to think of it, she had been looking a little tired, but I was so wrapped up in the worry that she had another friend that I never noticed.

When I got back to our trailer, I left the box Miz Shackleford give me on the kitchen table and went to Momma's room. Put Cruz in the crib next to her bed and turned down that noisy a.c. He never woke up, and that made me feel even guiltier, keeping him away from his own covers.

Then I slid a TV dinner into the microwave and got me a Coke. Seemed like I wasn't ready to open that box and handle them keepsakes. Even if there was a clue inside. Set there eating my turkey dinner and staring at the University Channel. But I didn't take in a word they said.

I washed up what little bit there was, opened the living room sofa into a bed like I do every night and got in it with the box. I set there holding it awhile, trying to sort out my feelings. How I missed Ray-Jean, but how far away she seemed already. How I had a new friend who was taking up some of the space where Ray-Jean used to be. How I was beginning to see other sides of her than when we was always together.

And how I really didn't know her as well as I thought I did. What did she mean, one secret too far? Not the black baby. Something else.

Finally, I felt ready to face up to them keepsakes. I opened the shoebox and laid everything out on the bedcovers. A baggie full of marbles we played with when we was little kids. A rock with the prints of sea shells like you find all over these hills. A secret decoder medallion same as the one I used to have. We both got 'em so we could send messages no one else could read. That was a long time ago.

I was hoping for an envelope or a scrap of paper. Maybe she'd used that decoder medallion to write something down. But I was just kidding myself. Ray-Jean never could write very well, so why would she make notes about her secrets? That was something I woulda done, not Ray-Jean.

That made me teary-eyed all over again, and I picked up the medallion to see if that little wheel was still inside, the one you could spin to make differnt codes. Had a hard time getting it open, cause it was all bent outta shape. Finally, the two halves popped apart, and I could see a shiny photo folded up inside where the wheel used to be.

I got Momma's nail file and dug it out. Then I smoothed it open on the table and felt my heart leap. If that picture wasn't kiddy porn, I don't know what was.

⌐⌐

The next morning, Bethanne was hunched by the study door, trying all the keys she'd pulled from every door in the house, hoping one of them would fit. Stood to reason that with a house this big, some of the locks might be the same. If she could get inside, she'd pick open the file door. Then she'd find out if her suspicions were right. There had to be a connection between Winston's favors for Jeffries and Mary Margaret's death.

She shifted her weight on tender knees and looked at her watch. Nine a.m. Only two keys left and no luck so far. Winston'd already gone to the office, and she was alone in the house. But if Mae was going to return to work, she'd be here any minute now. Bethanne wanted to get in and out of the study before that. She picked up the next-to-last key.

Click went the study lock and *click* went the back door. Bethanne spun around and saw Mae standing there, wearing an unusually somber dress of green-and-white seersucker.

Damn. Just what Bethanne didn't need. The only way through was to keep Mae moving. Bethanne scurried down the hall and into the kitchen. "Hi, Mae. Glad you decided to come back. I got Winston's door open. Let's see if we can find those files."

Mae rocked from front foot to back like she couldn't make up her mind which direction to run. "Miz Bethanne, you're going to get me in even more trouble. What if Mr. Winston comes home to get something?"

Bethanne grinned. "We'll hear his car in time, put the files back, shut his door and run out to the kitchen. What if all the talk about Winston doing something fishy is just gossip? Wouldn't you like to know?"

"That doesn't mean I'm willing to risk him getting mad all over again."

"He won't get mad if he doesn't know. Come on. If we're going to do it, we've got to get to it fast." She took Mae by the arm and pulled her toward the studio door.

"It's those drawers there, right?" Bethanne said. "Not the highboy." No need to tell Mae she'd already been snooping in there.

Mae just nodded, frozen on the threshold.

Bethanne got the letter opener, ready to jimmy another lock.

Mae rushed to the window. "I hear Mr Winston's car."

"Just a minute." Bethanne got down on her aching knees and looked at the lock cleverly concealed in the drawer's carving. She felt a swell of elation. Even if she had to leave the study now, she could easily come back and open the drawer. That lock could never keep out anybody really determined.

"It's not Mr. Winston." Mae bustled down the foyer. "Somebody else's coming to the front door."

Bethanne sat back on her heels and inserted the tip of the letter opener in the lock.

The bell rang, and Bethanne could hear Mae's voice saying Mr. Winston had already left for the office.

Bethanne got up, went over to the window and peeked through the net curtains. A tall man with thinning hair seemed to be insisting on something.

"Best try at the office," Mae's voice said. The door shut, and the man went down the steps and back to his wine-red Lexus.

As Bethanne turned from the window, her view shifted to the bookcase's top shelf. Would Winston be so stupid as to put the drawer key in that big enamel vase?

She was dragging a chair over when Mae returned. "Miz Bethanne, we got to get out of here."

Bethanne climbed up on the chair and slid a hand into the vase. "Who was that?"

"Mr. Jeffries."

Bethanne stopped dead still. "No shit."

Mae came over to steady the chair, but her shaky hands only made it wobble. "Wanted to see Mr. Winston in the worst way. I sent him off to the office."

Bethanne winced. She could have started the ball rolling with Jeffries, but instead she was up here with her hand in the cookie jar.

Her fingers touched something square, thin and plastic. Disappointment pushed away hope. What the hell was it? She raised her eyebrows at Mae and pulled out a DVD case. "Kids," the label said. In Winston's handwriting.

18

That dirty picture settled it. That was the one secret too far. Somehow Ray-Jean had found the photo and used it to blackmail Miz Gravesly even more than she did over having a black baby.

My best friend'd been murdered, and I was determined to find out who did it and why. Seemed like it coulda been any of 'em— Miz Gravesly committing suicide and taking Ray-Jean with her. Her husband killing 'em both. Or Jeffries. If he was making kiddy porn, he sure didn't need that to come out in the open. Even the next generation of Graveslys mighta killed 'em. Stood to reason they'd wanna protect the family reputation as much as their parents would.

I set up late drinking Coke and reviewing everything I'd written in that notebook Bethanne give me. Looking for clues and patterns, cause I knew they had to be there. I finally got to sleep after midnight, but I was back up at seven-thirty. Wanted to call Marlene afore Momma got home.

Marlene was just waking up, and that was to my advantage. Didn't want her being too sharp.

"Marlene," I said, "I been up half the night worrying you gonna get yourself into trouble helping that Jeffries make porn movies."

Figured the best way to get what I wanted was to start with a little show of concern.

This big yawn come over the phone, and Marlene said, "Don't you worry about me none. I know what I'm doing. Besides, Pete's looking out for me."

I couldn't help but smile to myself. So far, so good. "But what if he's into other stuff you don't know about?"

Marlene's voice got a little more awake, but she didn't stiffen up like last time we talked. "Like what? I know everything there is to know about Pete's doings."

"What if he's making kiddy porn too?"

"I been all over that barn. After he shoots some of them scenes, he gets all hot and bothered." I could hear her grinning down the phone. "We get to it right in the bed where he's been shooting." Marlene seemed to recollect herself, and her voice got too sharp for comfort. "The only porn Pete's making is the adult kind."

Just then Momma come through the door, so I said, "Well, I'll try not to worry." Then I hung up.

Course Momma wanted to know who that was, so I made up some tale about a girl at school wanting to tell me about a rumor we'd have to take Geometry in the fall. Momma asked how come this girl was calling so early. I said cause Judy never could wait to repeat gossip, and that seemed to satisfy her. But I was just about to drown in the guilt of lying to Momma so often.

That made me wonder how much I was gonna have to lie to Bethanne or whether I should tell her I found out Jeffries for sure made dirty movies in his barn.

Bethanne held the DVD and watched Mae raise a fat-dimpled hand to wipe her face. "I'm in enough trouble as it is," Mae said. "I don't want to look at that thing." She turned on her heel and disappeared.

In a few moments, Bethanne heard the crash of the pantry door, followed by a pail being filled with water. She stuck her head out of the study and saw Mae attacking the back hallway's black-and-white tile with a wet mop. Mae looked up, saw Bethanne and closed the door between the kitchen and the front of the house.

Okay, if Mae didn't want to get involved, that was easy to understand. But Bethanne felt like she didn't have anything to lose herself. She didn't care anymore about Winston's warning at the Courthouse. Winston's shenanigans were tied in with Mary Margaret's death, and she was determined to figure it out.

She stuck the DVD in the player, turned on the TV and sat back on the Persian rug to watch. It wasn't long before a jerky hand panned the camera to Clay and Lucinda's kids playing in the backyard pool. They were laughing and splashing each other. The camera zoomed in and out on each child, lingering on wet skin and rosebud mouths.

Lucinda's Tad stuck his tongue out at the camera, and Winston's hand came fuzzily into the frame, motioning the kids to do something. What was he saying? Bethanne turned the sound up as far as it would go, but Winston's voice was garbled.

All the kids lined up with their backs to the camera and looked over their shoulders. Tad seemed to say something, and they all pulled their pants down and mooned the camera.

Bethanne felt her breakfast rise into her throat. She swallowed hard to get the burn back down. Was Winston really so sick as to make kiddy porn of his own grandchildren?

A pair of navy shorts rushed into the frame, and the camera tilted up to reveal Lucinda walking toward Winston with her hand out.

"Where'd you get that?" Lucinda's voice startled Bethanne. For a moment, she thought it was on the DVD. Then she realized Lucinda's voice was coming from the hall.

Bethanne pivoted and saw Lucinda standing in the study doorway, hands on hips, anger mottling her face. "I told Daddy to delete this from the camera, or I'd smash it. But instead he made a DVD."

Oh shit. Bethanne pushed herself upright with a hand on one knee. "What're you doing here?"

Lucinda advanced on the DVD player. "Daddy sent me to patch things up with Mae." She pushed the reject button and grabbed the disc. "Where'd you find this? Why're you watching it?"

Bethanne forced a smile. "I saw the title. Thought it was a home video."

Lucinda shoved the DVD into its plastic sleeve. "Daddy got a little carried away. He always did like to provoke the kids into doing something naughty." She tried to laugh, but it came out false. "He didn't realize how a stranger might see this." She gave Bethanne a pointed look.

"I'm not a stranger. I'm your aunt."

Winston's daughter came close and bent down to look Bethanne in the face. "Doesn't matter who you are. This wasn't for your eyes or anybody else's."

After I talked to Marlene on the phone, the day wore on, me cogitating about all she'd let drop plus how I was becoming something I didn't wanna be. Lying to Momma. Not telling Bethanne everything I knew.

I stared into the bathroom mirror, expecting to see something differnt. Turned my head back and forth, peered into my eyes. I still looked like my old self. But I didn't feel that way.

Evening come, and Momma went off to work her shift. I put Cruz to sleep and set in front of the TV, watching the University Channel, like I most usually do. This lady professor was reading some old poetry about honor. I thought it was about the soppiest stuff I ever heard, but I somehow saw through it and the mirror and my face to what I ought to do.

~

Bethanne couldn't get to sleep, worrying whether Mary Margaret's grandchildren were in jeopardy from Winston's obsession. As happened so often when her sister came to mind, her fingers strayed to Mary Margaret's filigreed bracelet. She hadn't taken it off from the day she'd slipped it on her arm.

What to do about this latest proof of Winston's foul preoccupation? No way she could talk with Lucinda. His daughter seemed to be in denial. At best. Surely she wasn't protecting her father?

Bethanne sat up, turned on the light and lit a cigarette. Maybe she could talk with Clay. Did he know about the DVD? What did he think about it? Would he tell her it was a harmless grandfather's prank?

Maybe she should go to the police. But with what? She didn't have any proof. Clay had burned the photo she'd found in the apartment. Lucinda had confiscated the DVD. The ashes in the lake house fireplace were long gone. Besides, the Police Chief was Winston's buddy.

She had to get proof. Then she could go to the State Police. Winston couldn't have them in his pocket too.

The air conditioner's racket kept intruding on her thoughts. She stubbed out her cigarette, got up, turned it off and opened a couple windows. A breeze circled the room. Back in bed, she punched her pillow into another configuration and tried to come up with a plan to put Winston away. He'd moved his boxes into Jeffries' barn. Somehow, she had to get in there, find the proof and take it to the cops. The right cops.

She lay there a long time coming up with schemes and rejecting each one until finally she fell into fitful dreams.

It was five a.m., barely daylight, when the sound of frantic knocking at the main house woke her. Bethanne got up and tiptoed to the window overlooking Winston's back door. The porch roof hid the visitor's upper body, but she could still see from the khaki pants and chunky Rockports that it was a man. Then the door opened, and a pair of pajama legs and slippers stepped onto the threshold.

Even though the window was ajar, Bethanne couldn't hear what the two men were whispering. Her frustration climbed when both pairs of feet went inside, followed by the closing door. She snorted with aggravation. Who was it? What was so important that he had to rush to Winston at this hour?

Bethanne grabbed a pair of jeans and slipped them under her

sleep-T. She snatched up her keys, then creeped down the stairs and across the driveway to the kitchen window. Slowly, slowly, she inched up until she could peek inside.

Winston's pajama-clad backside was leaning against the sink below the window. Facing him and gesticulating wildly was the man who'd come looking for Winston yesterday. Jeffries.

Dammit. She had to find out what was going on, but the window was closed and the central air conditioning going full blast. What the hell could she do? Her hands shook in vexation, and the rattling of her keys gave the answer.

Bethanne ran down the driveway, crossed the front porch, opened the front door and tiptoed inside. The door separating the wide front hall from the narrower back corridor was closed, but she could hear the murmur of male voices behind it. She sidled up to the door and opened it a crack.

"It's not like I'm asking you for the moon," said a nasal tenor, clearly not Winston's baritone. "I only want you to say we were together last night. Just in case anyone asks."

"Jesus, Jeffries. What kind of trouble have you got yourself into this time?"

Bethanne turned her head to hear better. Jeffries needed another favor. What kind of sway did he have over Winston?

"Come on," Jeffries said. "I was bonking that kid who works for me, and I don't want Joellen to find out."

"You got a live-in girl friend and a piece on the side." Winston sounded exasperated. "If you can't handle your women, don't come running to me."

"Winston, old buddy, we got us a deal, and I'm going to hold you to it til death us do part."

19

THE SNACK BAR'S PICNIC area seemed dark after the sunlight exploding off the pool. But the maple trees' shade was almost as hot and certainly as humid. Bethanne wondered how she'd have made it this far through the summer without water's restorative grace. After what she'd heard pass between Winston and Jeffries that morning, she'd definitely needed the relief of a long swim.

She led Eden to the most isolated table and looked around to make sure no one was near.

"I need to tell you something…"

"I wanna talk to you…"

Bethanne laughed. She and Eden had said almost the same thing at the same time. Eden hunched her shoulders and grinned back.

"You first," Bethanne said.

"No, you."

Bethanne sopped her hot dog in the paper plate's spilled chili sauce and onions. "I've been keeping back some things that happened."

Eden nodded. "Me too. And I figure we mustn't do that."

Bethanne smiled. Nice to be on the same wavelength.

"Miz Shackleford give me a box of keepsakes," Eden continued. "Stuff that used to be Ray-Jean's. I found a dirty picture hidden inside an old decoder medallion we used to play with when we was little. That photo showed kids doing things they'd never think to do by theirselves."

Bethanne felt her eyes widen. "Kiddy porn everywhere we look."

"That's not all. Miz Shackleford said Ray-Jean was having nightmares, talking about going one secret too far." A dark cloud drifted overhead, bringing a gust of wind. Eden pulled her beach towel around her damp body. "Remember when the cops was at your apartment after the break-in? And somebody said there'd been one afore that?"

"That's right. When I was cleaning up the apartment and moving in. Clay found the bathroom window broken open."

Eden grinned. "There you go. Ray-Jean sneaked in, found some dirty pictures and upped the ante on the blackmail. I figure she was killed for sure, and maybe this Jeffries done it."

Bethanne shook her head. "We can't be sure of anything right now." She shuddered. "I'm starting to think it might have been Winston."

"Kill his own wife? I don't think so. It's gotta be Jeffries. Everything points to him. I been talking to Marlene, and she told me he's into all kinda stuff besides his photography business. Maybe Ray-Jean found that out too, and told your sister. So they both had to go."

"Jeffries isn't going to kill somebody over a little Ecstasy. I heard he's been selling it all over town."

"So that's where the kids been getting it. Jean Marie Coffindaffer almost died from Ecstasy. How'd you find out it was Jeffries selling it?"

Bethanne paused, not wanting to expose Mae.

Eden rushed on. "Never mind. That's not all Jeffries is doing.

He's making porn movies out at his barn. Marlene told me that too."

"Kiddy porn?"

"Nope. Just the adult kind. Least that's what Marlene says. Wants to be a porn star herself."

"Winston's been doing a lot of favors for Jeffries. Got him off DUI and drug-selling charges. Jeffries must have some kind of hold over him."

"Maybe he feeds Mr. Gravesly kiddy porn. If he's in the business, he can probably get all kinds. Saves Mr. Gravesly from being found out."

Bethanne felt her gorge rising. "Winston's been making his own porn movies. At least, that's what I think I saw. A DVD of his grandkids mooning the camera."

Eden looked like she was going to be sick. "That's way too freaky."

"Jeffries showed up at Winston's house early this morning. Said he needed an alibi for last night. Claimed he was having sex with the girl who works for him and didn't want his live-in sweetie to know."

"Marlene was bragging about having an affair with Jeffries."

"He seemed way too agitated for it to be just a little sex on the side."

"I could talk with Marlene again. She said they do it out at Jeffries' barn. We gotta find out where that is."

Bethanne cleared her throat. The pool's chlorine seemed to burn all the way to her lungs. "I went to the Courthouse and looked up the barn's address."

Thunder boomed nearby, and the wind picked up.

Eden frowned. Her breath came out in huffs. "When? Why didn't you tell me? You don't trust me?"

Bethanne reached over to pat her arm. "I was afraid for both of us. That was when I ran into Winston, and he threatened me about the video at Ralph's Rentals." She shook her head. "But we know way too much to stop now."

Eden leaned across the table. "We gotta get in that barn. I'll bet I can talk Marlene into taking me out there."

Lightning sizzled across the sky.

Bethanne couldn't keep the worry out of her voice. "Forget it. That's just too dangerous."

⸏

We finally got us a thunderstorm that afternoon, and a good thing too. It didn't just cool things off, it stopped me and Bethanne from having another fight. She drove me home right away with the rain coming down like shotgun pellets. So noisy, we didn't even try to talk over the racket on the car roof.

That almost-fight got me to thinking while we was driving. Honor was turning out to be a lot harder than I thought after I heard that lady reading poetry on the TV. Bethanne was trying to protect me, I realized that. But did honor mean I should protect her too? Like from not knowing about that cop coming to warn me at the trailer park? It was pretty clear from that big break-in at Bethanne's apartment that she had some reason for not wanting to deal with the police. So maybe I shouldn't tell her about the cop coming to my place.

And what about getting into Jeffries' barn to get the proof we needed? I didn't have no doubt that having the barn's address wasn't good enough. One of us had to go in there first and do a little recon. Bethanne didn't have no way to get in that barn, but I did.

Seemed to me that honor meant I should pay attention to Bethanne's cautions, but then I should go ahead and do what I thought was right. Even if it meant not telling her, cause she'd worry. In spite of sorting out all them ideas about honor, I had to wonder if I was still a little con artist. Only this time, was I conning myself?

Anyhow, when I got home, I rung up Marlene and asked if she needed any help straightening up the barn after one of them porn scenes. Said I sure could use a little money of my own.

I knew Marlene all right. She jumped at the chance to get outta doing the scut work. Said she'd talk sweet Pete—thought I'd barf when she called him that—into giving me a chance.

That Saturday afternoon, Jeffries picked me and Marlene up at the trailer park and drove us to his barn. Had this swanky wine-colored car. "Lexus" it said on the trunk. Never saw one of 'em afore, 'cept on the TV. Musta cost him a bundle, and that's for sure. Crime surely does pay. I give real close attention to where he was driving, so me and Bethanne could go back in the dark of night.

Another thunderstorm was coming in, and the air was heavy. Made my head feel full and tight. But maybe that was nerves.

From the outside, it was just an ordinary barn. Tin roof, Mail Pouch Tobacco paint job nearly faded away. But inside, it didn't look like no barn at all. Jeffries had rigged these pink satin curtains all along one wall and wrapping around to cover most of two more. There was big lights slung from the rafters, and smaller ones clipped to stands so he could move 'em round. Over to the side was a rack full of all kinds of dress-up stuff. He had a bathroom in one corner where the curtains didn't reach, and the mirror had lights all round it, just like you see on the TV. And that whole barn was air-conditioned. I surely never saw that afore—who'd wanna air-condition a barn? But when you come to think about it, that wasn't really a barn no more. It was a studio, like out in Hollywood.

Best of all, the whole place smelled like vanilla. As soon as we got there, Jeffries went round lighting these big perfumed candles, and afore long we was surrounded by the scent of Christmas cookies.

I was plain stupefied. The whole thing wasn't sleazy at all. Even if there was a big brass bed all lit up, right in the middle of the floor. And a video camera aimed straight at it.

Jeffries offered us some beer from the fridge. He had this dinky little kitchen with a hot plate and a sink over against the partition that set off the bathroom. Marlene took a beer, but I asked if he had any Coke. He give me the nicest smile and said, "Sure thing." I felt sorta off-balance, cause I was expecting him to be a lot differnt, kinda slick and dirty. But he acted like a real gentleman, even to a trailer-trash kid like me.

I have to admit, though, that I was put off by him dying his hair this unreal, sooty black color. And he was dumb enough to comb what little bit there was up over the top of his head, like it was really gonna cover up his bald patch. Why do men do that? They think nobody's got eyes to see with?

Anyhow, we set round what he called his office—a couple armchairs and a desk against the wall that didn't have no curtains—drinking our drinks and talking. I made it clear I was there just to talk about helping out after the sexy stuff was over and done with.

Jeffries said he been thinking Marlene was wasted on that cleaning-up work, but I seemed a little young. I come back with that's why it was such a good idea. I was too young to get a real job, and he didn't wanna bring in somebody who didn't have a stake in keeping their mouth shut.

Marlene chimed in and vouched for me. He smiled and said he'd give it a try. That made me feel a lot better, and I started to looking around, trying to figure out what me and Bethanne should concentrate on when we come back together.

The whole thing seemed so easy. Over in the corner opposite the bathroom was a big bookcase full of DVDs. Next to a closet that wasn't even locked. His file cabinets wasn't locked neither. The bar and lock for 'em was off to one side like he just couldn't be bothered. Right beside 'em was a stack of cardboard boxes that coulda been Mr. Gravesly's. Marlene's sweet Pete didn't know the meaning of security.

After a while, Jeffries lifted his tall, skinny self outta his chair and went to get us some more drinks. Marlene strolled over to this CD player and turned on some music. It was kind of dreamy and had a good beat at the same time, and she started dancing. Swaying back and forth, tossing her long hair, lifting her arms so her boobs stood out against her tight T-shirt. Jeffries come back, nodding his head in time with the music. He handed us our drinks and smiled encouragement to Marlene.

I took a big gulp of my Coke and wondered if I'd seen everything I needed to see.

"Sure is hot in here," Marlene said, and afore I knew it, she had her top off. Her boobs was pushed up by this lacy bra that didn't leave nothing to the imagination. "Come on, Eden," she said, "let's try on some of them costumes."

Jeffries lit this fat cigar and just set in his fake leather desk chair, nodding and smiling.

Outside, the thunder begun to rumbling, and I could feel it inside my head. I looked from one to the other, and all I wanted to do was get outta there as fast as I could. "What time is it?" I said. Ain't that lame? But it was all I could think of to say.

Marlene held a slinky green number next to her body. "Ain't this just the prettiest color? Goes with my eyes." Next thing, she had her jeans off and was wriggling that dress past the tiny triangle of her panties.

My throat was so tight I thought I was gonna choke. I finished off that Coke in one swig and said, "I'm really sorry, but I gotta get home in time to take care of Cruz afore Momma leaves for her shift."

That was the truth, and Marlene knew it. Her face turned all serious. Then she give Jeffries this fluttery look. "Why don't you take Eden home and then come back?" She swayed her hips at him. "We could rehearse what I can do with this green dress."

He wasn't happy about it, but he stubbed out his cigar and drove me to the trailer super fast, like he wanted to get there and back afore the rain hit.

The whole time I was thinking I didn't have no idea what Marlene thought she was up to, coming onto Jeffries in that dress while I was there. But at least she had the brains to see it was no good. Even so, it felt like some kinda close call to me.

Bethanne peeked through her open window, watching Winston's poker buddies arrive. Since the family had moved out to the lake, Winston hadn't been hosting his regular sessions every Saturday. So what was different about this Saturday?

She held the little digital camera at the ready. She'd bought the simplest one she could find at the G-Mart, hoping she had the brains to take some decent photos when she got the chance. Then she'd show them to the State Police.

Jeffries got out of his car, waving a DVD. "Got something brand new for you. Just shot this afternoon, and so hot it'll steam up your bifocals."

He grinned at the Police Chief. "I'll bet you never saw a green dress do this." Hastings laughed and clapped him on the shoulder. They all went inside and closed the kitchen door.

Behanne pocketed the camera. The thunderstorm had just passed, leaving the air electric-clean. There'd been enough light to get a photo of Jeffries waving the DVD at Hastings, but without the automatic flash going off and attracting their attention.

She needed to show everyone watching the porn video with Winston. How was she ever going to do that? Central air conditioning meant no chance of the study window being open. The drapes were drawn too. Going inside and sneaking down the hall again was just too dangerous with any of those men likely to come out at any time.

Bethanne decided to get a beer and give the whole thing some thought. She left the lights and the a.c. off and sat by the open window. Down below, she could see the flickering light of Winston's TV on the beige drapes.

She was on her fourth beer and as many cigarettes when the light changed to the steady yellow of Winston's floor lamps. Most of the men left right away, some of them slipping DVDs into their pockets as if they were ashamed to be seen.

But Hastings' metallic gold Escalade and Jeffries' Lexus remained in the parking space between house and garage. Shadows started walking back and forth against the study drapes like somebody was too agitated to sit. What the hell was going on now?

Bethanne put out her cigarette and stepped out on the porch for a better look. The shadows were still jittering. She pictured the layout of the house, and a plan of action tottered through her beery brain. She could sneak in through the kitchen, up the back stairs and onto the landing just above the study door. If that door was open, she might hear something.

20

I got home just in time, cause I started feeling woozy all over. Jeffries zoomed off in his fancy car, not even looking back. Good thing, or he'da seen me stumbling up my trailer steps.

Momma saw right away something was wrong when I staggered through the door. Wanted to know what was the matter.

"Think I musta et or drunk something didn't agree with me," I said. But I knew what it was. It was that Coke.

Bethanne was right. That was one dangerous man, and I didn't wanna have no more to do with him. Not directly, anyway.

Momma offered to stay home, but I knew she needed the Saturday night overtime pay. So I said all I needed was a little Alka-Selzer, and I'd be fine. Drunk one down while she watched me and made out like I was feeling better than I was.

After she left for a double shift, I went in the bathroom and made myself throw up. Then I brewed a cup of strong tea and sipped it with some soda crackers. I set there, trying to get better and thinking I was gonna put that sucker in jail if it was the last thing I ever did.

Bethanne stood on the stair landing and looked down at the light streaming through the study's open door. At least two men seemed to be on their feet and pacing.

"What the hell were you thinking of?" came Winston's voice. "That's the girl who's been snooping around with my sister-in-law. Out at Ralph's Rentals."

"How was I to know?" Bethanne recognized Jeffries' tenor. "I never saw Ralph's damn tape."

"And you can just stop selling that filth in my house," Winston said.

There was a smile in Jeffries' voice. "Just a little new product, that's all."

"Shut up, both of you," came the Police Chief's deep voice. "Between the two of you, we're in a helluva mess."

"But Billy," Winston said, "It's not my fau…"

"I'll tell you one thing," Hastings interrupted. "You better do something about your goddam sister-in-law, or I'll take her out myself."

Bethanne grabbed her stomach and stepped back into the shadows. Oh Jesus. Oh shit. What was she going to do?

Once Sunday morning rolled round, I was feeling a lot better. So when Momma come home from the mill, I decided it was time to face up to Bethanne and tell her what happened out at Jeffries' barn.

I had to wait ages for the bus, cause there wasn't a lotta maids going out to that neighborhood on a Sunday morning. When I got there, it was past ten o'clock and hot enough to fry an egg on the sidewalk. Ray-Jean's granny used to say that, and I never really knew what she meant til that morning.

I moseyed up the steps to Bethanne's apartment and knocked on the door. But she didn't answer, so I run back down and peeked in the garage. Her faded old Datsun was the only car inside. I figured Gravesly must be out at the lake, and Bethanne overslept.

It was too hot for all that running, so I took my time going back up the steps to spy through the crack between the window curtains. There was Bethanne falling off the sofa, a whisky bottle on the floor and her mouth wide open, catching flies.

I pounded on the window and shouted her name She never even stirred So I decided to see if I could break in the way Ray-Jean did all those weeks ago. Good thing I was losing weight, cause I shinnied up that tree, jimmied open that bathroom window, marched right over to Bethanne and give her a good shake.

Boy, was she pissed. Both ways. Pissed-mad at me for waking her up, and pissed-drunk from all that booze. There was three or four empty beer cans in addition to the fifth of Wild Turkey. She musta tied one on the best she could.

"Bethanne," I said, "You gotta get you some help. You been laying off the booze, but now you fell so far off the wagon you'll never get back without the AA. They done my momma a world of good, and they can do the same for you."

"Fuck the AA," she said. "They can't save me from being killed."

Bethanne never swore in front of me afore, so I figured there had to be more to it than I realized.

"What d'ya mean, getting killed?" I said, and she told me about Gravesly and Jeffries arguing and the Police Chief threatening to take her out.

By then she was setting up and drinking the ice water I brung her from the fridge, and I figured I better tell her about me going out to Jeffries' barn. Told it fast, so she wouldn't have a chance to break in and tell me how I been courting danger.

Told her all about them satin curtains and vanilla candles, Marlene putting on that green dress and me wanting to go home. I didn't wanna tell her about that Coke being drugged, but she got it outta me just the same. That got her to worrying so bad I felt myself covered in guilt.

But I was mad too. Madder'n I ever been since I was born. Mad at Jeffries for fooling me like that. Madder at Marlene cause she musta been in the know somehow. And maddest of all at myself for being such a stupid little kid.

"Bethanne," I said, "we gotta speed things up. We can't let 'em get away with this. Let's get the proof and go to the State Police."

⚊⚊

Bethanne pulled up at the lake house and took another swig from the thermos of instant coffee Eden had made for her.

"You gotta go out to the lake like nothing happened." That's what Eden had said, and she'd been right. Bethanne had to continue with the normal Sunday afternoon as if she hadn't heard anything the night before. But she was upset about what Jeffries had done to Eden. And she'd rather take a beating than see Winston again.

She rotated the rearview mirror so she could get a look at herself and wished she hadn't. A second set of bags under her eyes. Face even more wrinkled from all the alcohol she'd drunk. Hair still damp from the shower Eden had pushed her under. Jesus, she was a mess, inside and out.

Shame crept up her face like a hot tide. Eden had found her passed out. Eden had cleaned her up, sobered her up and told her what to do. Eden. A young girl shouldn't have to deal with a drunk like that. Even if they were friends. Even if Eden's mother was a recovering alcoholic.

Bethanne scrunched her nose and shook her head. Regardless of what Eden said, she didn't need the AA. She just had to exert a little self-discipline like she'd been doing. Say no to booze. Only have a beer now and then.

She looked out the open window at the kids running along the dock. The planks were so hot they scampered on tip-toe. Like she used to do when she was small, trying to make as little contact as possible with the scorching wood.

Clay was already in the water. He saw her and waved. "Aunt Bee. Come on in!"

Maybe that was just what she needed. A nice swim in the cool lake to help her get it together. She grabbed her suit and towel and opened the car door.

—

Once I got Bethanne on her way to the lake, I went back home, cause I had a lot to do to get ready for us breaking into the barn the next night. Monday was gonna be Momma's day off. Seems like them bosses change the days off to suit theirselves. Ain't got nothing to do with what the workers need. But this time, it was gonna work out for me. Momma was going to be to home tomorrow night, so I'd be free to get away. I'd already told her me and Bethanne was going to the movies, and she thought it was just fine that I was gonna get a little fun in life.

When I got home, I found Momma setting outside with Cruz wearing nothing but his diapers and sucking on his bottle of water. We had an old air conditioner in that trailer, but Momma liked to save money whenever she could by setting out in the shade of them high old trees. She had a Coke so cold the can was frosty and dripping on the outside. But it didn't seem to help, cause the sweat was still shining all over her body.

"Hey, dearheart," she said. "Get yourself a soda and come set. It's boiling in there."

She was dead right, so I took a Coke from the fridge and pulled my notebook out from under the sofa. Wanted to make a drawing of everything I remembered about Jeffries' barn, inside and out.

I set down in the other plastic chair and started making a diagram of the outside. Where to park Bethanne's car so nobody passing by could see it. How Jeffries' road come off the main road and where his gate was. Even put in his old vegetable garden so we wouldn't fall over it in the dark.

Momma wiped Cruz's sweaty face with a tissue. "What're you drawing? Lemme see." She took the notebook outta my hands afore I could stop her.

"Just getting ready for art class next year. Miz Franklin said we was gonna start making birds-eye views of places round town, and I wanted to see if I could do it now." I was trying not to squirm, cause I didn't want Momma to get suspicious. But is sure sounded clumsy to me.

"So where's this, then? Don't look like no place I ever saw."

That was my chance. "It don't? Guess I must not be doing it right." I reached for my notebook. "Here, let me try something else." I turned the page and started drawing the county swimming pool.

Momma got up, careful of Cruz, and peered over my shoulder. "That's a lot better. I can recognize that right away." She set down again and smiled over at me. "Maybe you're finding you got yourself a talent. Maybe you're starting on your career right here and now."

—

Bethanne jackknifed down into the cool lake and swam underwater a few strokes. She broke surface and headed for the wooden raft anchored thirty yards out in the lake. Her entire respiratory system was stinging by the time she climbed up the ladder, but the exercise was doing her good.

She lay down on the wooden planks and let the sun dry her off. The water dripping from her body cooled the wood just enough to make it comforting after the cold currents running through the lake. She could hear the kids shouting over by the shore, where Clay and Lucinda were keeping tabs on them, but their noise was too remote to be bothersome. The float rocked gently, and the sun turned her closed lids a deep coral. A hawk screeched from his circles high above, while the scent of wild roses drifted across the water.

A piercing whistle woke her "Aunt Bee! Time to eat. Come and get it."

She sat up and shook her head to clear it. She must have dozed off. Her skin felt tight, and she touched a fingertip to her thigh. A yellowish spot blanched against the reddening skin. You idiot, she thought and dived into the water.

Just as her head came above the surface, something grabbed her ankle and yanked her back down. She'd been starting to take a breath, and water rushed in, burning her nose and throat. She felt her body being whirled around, like the game she used to play long ago with the other kids at the public pool. But this was no game, and whoever had hold of her was no kid.

Bethanne kicked out as hard as she could, lashing with her legs to get loose. Her free foot struck something soft, and she felt the grip let go of her ankle. She was too far under the dark water to see anything, and she felt disoriented. Which way was up?

She twisted and looked wildly around. Where was the light? Where was the surface? She looked down at her feet and realized she was really looking up. They were silhouetted against a greenish glimmer. The light seemed so far away, and she had no air at all.

No, no, no, no, no. It wasn't going to end this way. She was going to find out why Mary Margaret died. She was going to get those dirty old men and make them pay.

She started pushing with her arms and legs up toward the light. But it didn't seem to get any closer.

Her lungs begged her to open her mouth and pull in air. Her head hurt, and her ears ached. How deep was she? *Breathe*, said her lungs. *No*, said her brain. *Kick. Kick. Kick.*

Something grabbed her across her chest. Bethanne knew she didn't have the strength to fight anymore, even though her hands tried to pry the thing loose. It held on and hauled her through the water.

Dear God, what a stupid way to go.

21

BETHANNE WOKE UP COUGHING and heaving, lying on the dock with Clay applying CPR. She could taste his vile French cigarettes on her lips where he'd been giving her mouth-to-mouth.

Clay sat back on his heels and grinned. "Thought you were a goner for sure. What happened?"

Lucinda towered over them, her wet hair dripping on Bethanne's chest. "That's easy. She's obviously hungover. Never should have gone swimming in that cold lake. She got a cramp, and she went under."

Bethanne tried to speak, but she still couldn't breathe properly. She squinted up at Lucinda, lean and mean in her T-backed racing suit. What a bitch.

Clay frowned at his sister. "Doesn't matter how it happened." He turned a smiling face to Bethanne. "The main thing is I saw her go down and got to her in time."

Lucinda turned toward the house. "Enough of this. The burgers are burning."

Clay held out a hand. "Can you stand? We should get you into the shade."

Bethanne sat up and felt like the world was ending. She tried to clear her head, to remember what had happened, but everything was jumbled up inside.

Clay scooped her into his arms and carried her toward the house like she was one of his children. The muscles in his arms felt hard against her back and legs. How strong was he? Strong enough to pull her under, for sure. But then why save her? Besides, Clay didn't have any reason to drown her.

He set her down next to Winston, huddling under a towel and looking distinctly uncomfortable.

Bethanne stared at Winston's tight jaw and his hands white-knuckled in his lap. She remembered her foot striking something soft. Had she kicked Winston in the nuts?

~~

I nearly fell off the G-Mart bench when Bethanne told me how she nearly drowned the day afore. We was having lunch and planning our attack on Jeffries' barn that night. I was ready with my drawing of the layout, but what she said brought me up short.

I mean, at least one of them Graveslys was a natural-born killer. Bethanne kept arguing it was probably just a warning. And probably from Mr. Gravesly, cause of what the Police Chief said. But I come back strong with my own argument. Maybe it was Mr. Gravesly, or maybe they was all in it. Everybody was wet from the lake. Whoever it was, they wasn't just trying to scare Bethanne, they was trying to drown her.

I could see Bethanne was getting upset, what with me not agreeing with her, and I realized I didn't really need to win this quarrel. I just had to figure out how to keep Bethanne safe and still get the proof we needed.

"Bethanne," I said, "we gotta keep you away from them Graveslys til this is all over. We're gonna spend the afternoon at the trailer, and then we'll drive out to Jeffries' barn when it gets dark."

Bethanne looked through the Datsun's windshield at the narrow country road striped by moon-shadows of overhanging trees. A porcupine lumbered out of the woods, its erect quills piercing the night. The animal froze for a moment, then shambled back into the safety of the darkness. The smell of hog manure came through the open windows to gag her.

She glanced at Eden, leaning forward and peering at the road. Ever since they'd left the trailer park, her young friend had concentrated on finding her way back to a place she'd visited only once in daylight. Eden had murmured that it all looked different at night, but she'd still given confident and precise directions each time they'd had to turn from one lane into another.

Headlights swept across Bethanne's vision from the rearview mirror as a vehicle came up fast behind. The thought that it might be Jeffries darted through her mind and departed just as quickly. A rusty old Ford pickup swerved around and rushed on. Clearly not Jeffries' red Lexus. Her reaction made her wonder why she wasn't nervous about breaking into his barn. It wasn't that she was numb. It was as if fear and worry didn't exist. Instead, she was filled with the sense that she and Eden were somehow coming into their own.

A grin lit Bethanne's face.

"What you smiling so big for?" Eden asked.

"It feels like the two of us are turning into a couple of gutsy dames."

Eden grinned back and pointed at a faint dirt track. "Pull in here and leave the car behind them bushes."

Bethanne reached over and got a flashlight out of the glove compartment. "We'll need this when we get inside. Don't want to turn the lights on and advertise what we're doing."

"Okay, but hold it down low."

Eden led the way to a wide wooden gate chained with a lock and climbed over. Then she helped Bethanne to the other side. A chain-link fence stretched out on both sides. Eden took the lead again, down the dirt track toward the barn, their way lit by the half-moon.

The series of thunderstorms had cut the humidity and made it easier to move without suffering. But Bethanne could still hear herself panting and realized she was more nervous than she'd thought. She caught up with Eden and looked at her face in the moonlight. That girl would find getting washed away in a flood interesting.

An owl hooted, and Bethanne smelled the comforting scent of new-mown grass. They passed a vegetable garden like Eden had drawn on her map. The girl picked up a sharpened tomato stake lying on the ground and used it as a walking stick.

Neither of them said a word. Probably no one around, but why draw attention to themselves, just in case? The only sounds Bethanne could hear were the normal ones of a summer night—crickets, tree frogs, that same owl hunting for his supper. They rounded a bend, and there was the barn, its tin roof shining in the night. Bethanne smiled. What was she afraid of?

A black shape hurtled around the barn, low to the ground and snarling. Moonlight bounced off sharp teeth and flying saliva.

"Run, Eden, run!" Bethanne shouted and reached for the girl's arm. But it wasn't there.

⸺

I seen that big old dog heading right for us, and I knew I was gonna find out something about myself for sure. Ever since I seen them Masai hunt lions on the TV, I been speculating whether I was brave enough to do what they done.

Now's the time, I told myself. I run forward a couple steps to draw that old dog's attention. Then I knelt down and pushed the butt of the stake in the ground. I took a deep breath and held up the sharp point. Seemed like Bethanne was shouting something, but I didn't have time to pay her no mind.

"Hey," I yelled, "Come here, dog!"

And he did, he come for me like he was gonna rip my throat out. And dear Lord, I was so scared I nearly peed. But I held on. I held on, and I pointed that stake right at that dog's chest when he jumped high to come down on me from above.

⸺

Bethanne screamed as the Rottweiler let out a hideous growl and fell on Eden. What had she done? Brought this child out into the night to be killed. Nothing, nothing was worth that.

"You fool, you God-damned fool," she cursed herself and ran toward the dog's heaving body. She could hear Eden groaning. Thank God she was still alive.

Then Bethanne realized the dog was moaning too. She looked down and saw a stake run clear through his body. What the hell? It was the tomato stake Eden had been carrying.

Bethanne grabbed the stake and levered the dog off Eden. A terrible cry ripped from its throat, but its eyes were beginning to glaze over.

She knelt beside the girl. Eden was covered in blood from her neck to her legs. Even her face was smeared with it. She was clearly unconscious, but at least she wasn't dead.

Bethanne felt for a pulse under Eden's jaw. Her throat seemed intact, and her heart was beating fast and strong.

Bethanne didn't know what to do. If Eden was seriously injured, it might kill her to move her. She reached in her purse for her flip-phone, then stopped. If she called 911, she'd have to explain what they were doing out here. But Eden's life was at risk, so she started pushing the buttons.

Eden's eyes opened. "Guess I'm just as brave as Ray-Jean after all."

Bethanne knelt in the dew-wet grass beside a dead dog and a half-alive girl, her hand cradling Eden's bloody cheek, and sobbed.

22

I STARED UP AT Bethanne trying to wipe her eyes and dial 911 at the same time. Told her I wasn't hurt none and set up to prove it. She cancelled the call afore they answered and turned on her flashlight to give me the once-over.

"See?" I said, "It ain't my blood. It's that old dog's."

She seemed to have a frog in her throat and kept clearing it over and over. All the time telling me to take my shirt off so she could see how bad hurt I was. But then we realized all the ruckus was bringing the neighbors outta their house.

"That you, Jeffries?" somebody called from aways off.

We was out in the country, so nobody lived real near. But they was near enough. We could see a couple flashlights jerking as folks run across the fields.

"Bethanne," I said, "we gotta get outta here right now and check me over later."

So we run fast as we could go back to her car. I was starting to discover I wasn't nearly in perfect shape. Hurt all over, and that's a fact. But I didn't tell Bethanne nothing. I wanted her to concentrate on getting us away afore them folks got to us.

She had an old beach towel in the back of the car, and she wrapped me up good in that, so I wouldn't get blood on the seat. Good thing we parked the car aways from Jeffries' gate, cause the neighbors couldn't see Bethanne start the engine and pull away. She left the lights off til we was far down the road.

We drove round for a while, trying to figure out where to go. I couldn't go back to the trailer and let Momma see me covered in blood. But we didn't wanna go to Bethanne's, cause we was afraid it wasn't safe there.

Finally, we couldn't think of no place else to go, so we ended up in her apartment after all. We was both spooked going up her stairs, but the main house was dark, and there wasn't no other cars round the place, so maybe we was all right. First thing we done was pull the curtains so nobody could see inside.

Bethanne told me to take a shower and put on her robe while she washed my clothes. I done what she said, and I saw why I was so sore. I had a big bruise on my bum where I fell back when that old dog jumped me. And two marks on my chest where his paws hit. Good thing I didn't have no boobs to speak of. He'da hurt me bad for sure.

But the biggest wonder was that he didn't lay a tooth on me. No bite marks anywhere. Guess that stake went right through his heart and put him in shock, so he couldn't be bothered to snap them terrible jaws. Least not nowhere on my body.

Later on, we set at Bethanne's little square table, waiting for my clothes to finish in the drier and drinking hot cocoa. May seem kinda strange that we was drinking something so wintry when it was middle of summer, but I think we both needed the comfort of it. I never saw nobody make hot cocoa like that afore, heating up the milk and stirring in sugar and that Hershey's powder. Me and Momma always just added boiling water to the store-bought mix we got down to the Busy Bee.

Anyhow, I took a long slurp and smiled over at Bethanne. It pleased me to see her getting through all this without needing to hit the bottle. Maybe we'd turned another corner as far as that was concerned.

"What're you thinking about?" I said.

"I'm totally stumped about what to do next."

"Me too," I said. "But don't you worry none. We'll figure it out. We always do."

By the time Bethanne dropped Eden off at her trailer, she and Eden had made up a story to tell her mother about going to the movies. Kept it short and sweet, saying Bethanne had to get on back home.

As she drove away, Bethanne started thinking about how little money she had left. After what had happened that night at Jeffries' barn, she'd feel safer in a motel, but she couldn't afford it. Not even for a couple nights at a no-tell kind of place. The money from Ray-Jean's coffee can had to last until she could get her inheritance.

The best she could do was go back to her apartment and lock the car in the garage so it wouldn't show. But she still felt more vulnerable than ever before, even more than that time Robbie Ray got drunk and came looking for her with a knife. She'd known he'd never use it, that all she needed do was give him a little loving, and he'd calm down like he always did.

But this was different. As soon as the neighbors saw what had happened at the barn, they'd call Jeffries. Wouldn't be long before he got Winston involved. Chief Hastings too. Then what? Would they come for her?

She hurried inside, bolted the door and put a chair under the handle as an extra precaution. Then she checked all the windows, especially the vulnerable one in the bathroom.

Bethanne was wide awake even though she felt so tired she barely had the strength to undress. She took a hot shower before going to bed, but she couldn't sleep. Her brain replayed the horrors of that night over and over. The spit flying from the dog's mouth. Eden covered in blood. The neighbors' flashlights trying to find them. The run through the night to the car. Her legs feeling too old to get away.

The hours kept changing on her digital alarm clock, but still she couldn't sleep. She'd left the air conditioner off, so the noise wouldn't signal she was there. With the windows closed, she felt like she'd suffocate. She stripped off her sweat-soaked sleep-T and lay naked on the bottom sheet. Every wrinkle was a trial to the fear-heightened sensitivity of her skin.

Bethanne thought about taking a drink to calm her nerves and get to sleep. But she'd made Eden a promise about laying off the booze. The girl had risked her life for Bethanne. The least she could do was keep that promise.

Finally, mental and physical fatigue took over, and she began to drift off. Outside, the eastern sky was just starting to get gray. She heard a mouse scurrying between the walls and smiled at the thought of its belly full of flower seeds from Mary Margaret's garden.

I surely slept the sleep of the blest. I was so sore, it was all I could do to open up my sofa bed and fall into it. As soon as my head hit the pillow, I was out like a light. So deep asleep when Momma got up, she thought something was wrong.

Course I couldn't tell her a thing about why I was sleeping so sound. I hopped outta bed and fixed us both some breakfast to make up for her finding me like that. Fed Cruz too, so she wouldn't have to do a thing but enjoy the morning after a good night's sleep. Which she almost never got, never being on the day shift and all.

Then I went outside and played with Cruz in the shade while she watched the soaps on the TV. Like I said, Momma's a slave to the soaps. But she rarely gets to watch 'em these days.

After a while, I went back inside and asked Momma if I could take a little money to pick up some things we needed at the Busy Bee. She just nodded and waved, lost in whichever soap was on at the time. I put Cruz in his baby stroller and took him along. Figured it was nice for him to have a little ride. Momma got that stroller about third- or fourth-hand, so it took some doing, but we made it.

I was standing in the checkout line when my heart froze.

"You hear what happened out to Jeffries' barn?" the clerk said.

"Who'd go and do a thing like that to a poor, dumb animal?" said the customer in front.

Right then and there, I got totally interested in the rack of them cheap tabloids. Normally, I can't abide all that stuff about being abducted by aliens and what movie star got caught with somebody else's wife. But I didn't want nobody asking if I knew about Jeffries' dog, cause I was afraid my face'd show the truth.

"Wake up! I know you're in there. I saw your car in the garage. Come on over to the door."

Bethanne sat up with a start. They were here. They'd found her. She looked at the door's window, blocked by the giant shadow pounding so hard the frame shook. Her focus jumped all over the room. How was she going to get away?

"Miz Bethanne, you sick? It's Mae. Open up."

Bethanne's panic turned to chagrin. She hadn't even heard the voice was female. She'd only heard the words. Mae. Mae wasn't going to hurt her. She wrapped the unused top sheet around her naked body, moved the chair and opened the door.

Mae stood there with hands on hips, their awesome width accentuated by a swirling print in red, pink and white. "What's the matter with you? It's ten o'clock in the morning. You okay?"

Bethanne nodded.

"Well, that's good. I got a lot to do. Fried chicken. Mashed potatoes. Jello salad with shredded carrots. No idea what I'm going to make for dessert." She smiled. "Mr. Winston called. Guess I'm back in his good graces. He's coming home for lunch, and he wants you to join him."

Bethanne went in the bathroom and threw up.

23

Bethanne watched Winston push back from his empty plate and touch a mini-flamethrower to his pipe. "That Mae sure knows how to make a peach pie," he said. "Sorry you didn't have much of an appetite."

She licked her lips. Winston would never have dared smoke in the dining room when Mary Margaret was alive.

His smile seemed forced. "Glad you came, though. We need to talk."

She'd spent the whole meal trying to convince herself she was safe as long as Mae was out in the kitchen. Now she needed a cigarette to calm her nerves. She lit up and concentrated on holding her hands steady.

Winson blew out a gusher of smoke. "I can see now I got off on the wrong foot with you, Bethanne. I should've known better than to treat Mary Margaret's sister like that."

Inwardly, Bethanne shuddered. Like what? Trying to drown her? The overly sweet smell of his tobacco was nauseating.

He leaned his elbows on Mary Margaret's embroidered cloth, pipe cupped in one hand. "Pete Jeffries came to see me this morning."

Her stomach bounced, and she felt like she was going to heave any second. She gripped the seat of the mahogany chair to get a hold on her emotions.

Winston held her gaze. "He told me what happened to his dog. The neighbors saw a woman and a girl running away."

He paused as if to let her respond, but Bethanne couldn't get her throat working right.

"You don't realize what you're doing," he continued. "You're putting the whole family at risk. Maybe you don't care about me, but you're fond of Clay. You don't want to see him hurt."

Bethanne swallowed hard. Clay? What did he have to do with this?

Winston tilted even farther forward and softened his voice. "You're getting yourself in a whole lot of trouble. And the girl too. Jeffries never should've doped her. That was just plain stupid, and I told him so. But don't you go compounding all the wrong that's been done. Leave well enough alone."

Bethanne's eyes darted around the exotic birds and flowers on the wallpaper behind Winston's head. She was mystified. Winston seemed to be pleading with her. She felt her stomach calm. Now it was her turn to lean forward and put elbows on the table. "What's really going on here?"

Winston sat back. "I'm going to make you a deal. You quit all this messing in other people's affairs, and I'll talk some sense into..." His lips worked in and out as he seemed to seek the words. "...into everybody. I never realized it would go this far." His lips worked again, and his eyes blinked rapidly, like they were going to spill over. "I'll put a stop to it, and everything'll be okay."

Bethanne took a long drag on her cigarette and looked across the table at Winston. He looked scared enough to shit his pants.

~~

I got me and Cruz back home without having to talk to nobody about Jeffries' dog. Fixed us some lunch and put Cruz down for a nap in the crib next to Momma's bed. She was taking her afternoon sleep, getting ready for her shift, and that was okay by me. I needed some time to think.

Momma had the a.c. on, but the trailer smelled stuffy, so I got a Coke and went outside. There was a little bit of a breeze moving through the trees, and I went over to the picnic tables where the shade was deepest.

Seemed like me and Bethanne couldn't get nowhere forward with tracing down the clues of why her sister and Ray-Jean died. The whole thing just got more and more complicated, and we was blocked at every turn.

I finished off my Coke and lay down on the bench. The sun was sending little points of light through the trees like they was fairies coming down to help me. But for the life of me, I couldn't feel myself helped.

I musta dozed off in the heat, cause the next thing I knew, Marlene was standing over me and calling out my name.

I shot up like an arrow headed for her heart. Threw all my weight into shoving her right in her prideful chest. "Get outta my sight. You set me up at that barn. What was you two trying to pull, anyhow?

She nearly fell, but she tried to smile. "I was only coming over to apologize. I never shoulda done what I did."

It was all I could do not to slap her disgusting face. "Well, you did," I said.

She was still trying to smile, but it come out all lopsided. "Wasn't no harm done. You went home, and Pete made a video of me playing with that green dress."

I was so hot under the collar, I wanted to shout. But I knew there was lots of ears round, so I kept my voice low. And mean. "I don't care about you and that old dress. What was you gonna do if I stuck round?"

Marlene rubbed her sandal back and forth in the dust. "Dunno. Guess Pete had an idea for some girl-on-girl action."

She purely took my breath away, but I got it back pretty quick. "Kiddy porn, you mean. What was you gonna do? Trick me into doing something dirty?" It made me wanna barf, just to think about it. They was ready to ruin my life. I woulda never met the boy of my dreams and shared that first time with him.

She shrugged, and a twisted bra strap fell outta her tank top. "Aw, we was just gonna play dress-up, like kids with their mommas' clothes." She smiled at me. "It wasn't gonna be very sexy. Not like what I done with that green dress."

I was struggling to keep calm and figure out how I could turn this to me and Bethanne's favor. "But you told me Jeffries don't do kiddy porn."

"Well…" She looked to the left of me, and she looked to the right of me, but she couldn't look me in the face. "I was kinda surprised when he brought up the two of us doing that. But Pete said he had to branch out into stuff that would really pay. Said I'd be surprised there was even folks in town who'd lay out big money if they could get it on the sly."

Oh boy, I was thinking. Folks in town? Like who?

Marlene went on, "After he left to take you home, I snooped around in those file cabinets, and sure enough, I found some."

Deep inside, something started dancing. I knew if I could get my hands on that kiddy porn, me and Bethanne could send them scumbags to jail. And maybe we'd find out what all this had to do with Ray-Jean dying in Miz Gravesly's car.

I give her the most wide-eyed look. It sure felt false to me, but she didn't seem to notice. "I never seen none."

"Eden, you need to do some growing up." She looked over her shoulder in the direction of her trailer. "Come on, I'll show ya what I found."

Off we went, me just busting to tell Bethanne how I saved the day after all.

—

Bethanne stood on her porch and made sure Winston was leaving. She could hardly wait to tell Eden about his latest little game. She dialed the trailer's number. The phone rang on and on. Finally, her mother answered.

"Hi, Corrine. It's Bethanne."

"Who? Oh. Beg your pardon. Not awake yet." A yawn distorted the next words. "Eden's not here. Gone back to the store, maybe. She's a good girl, that Eden, always running errands afore I even ask her."

Bethanne felt deflated. "Sorry to trouble you."

"No trouble at all. Why don't you call back in an hour? Eden'll be home soon."

Bethanne tried to keep busy while she waited, but it was hard-going. When she dialed again, Corrine was fully awake.

"Dunno what's keeping Eden. Shoulda been home by now."

Bethanne struggled to calm the concern rising in her chest. Was that Winston's game? Keep her busy while somebody went after Eden? "Did she go to the store for sure?"

"Dunno. She went this morning. Maybe she forgot something." Cruz started crying in the background, and Corinne said, "Scuse me a minute."

Bethanne felt like she couldn't wait even half that. Her heart began to race, and nothing she did could slow it down. After what seemed like ages, she heard the rattle of Corrine's receiver being picked up.

"Listen, why don't you come over for a cup of coffee? We can wait for Eden together."

What else could she do? "Great idea. I'll bring some doughnuts."

Bethanne swung by Fredlock's and picked up a half-dozen cinnamon-sugar. It was just going on three when she arrived at the Happy Hours Trailer Park.

Eden's mother met her at the door, Cruz on one hip and her hand on the other. "I'm getting real worried now. It's not like Eden to stay away like this."

Bethanne stood before the cement-block stoop, sweating and trying to think. "What about Marlene? Could Eden be over at her trailer?"

Corrine grimaced. "That white trash? Eden wouldn't have a thing to do with her."

Bethanne didn't know what to say. How was she going to find Marlene's trailer without telling Corrine her daughter had gone off with the older girl before? "Still, it might be worth a try. Eden mentioned her name to me awhile back."

Corrine's nose twitched, and the corners of her mouth fell. But she started down the cement blocks. "Come on, then."

She stomped along the dirt lane, Cruz howling in her arms. Bethanne followed, feeling like she needed a good howl herself.

Eden's mother stepped under the sagging awning of a rusty trailer, then paused to jiggle her son and croon. When he ceased crying, she knocked on the door. And knocked again. And again.

Bethanne moved to a window and looked through a torn curtain. Then another window, and another until she'd looked through them all. There wasn't a soul inside.

24

I woke up more confused than I ever been in my whole life. This dirty burlap smell was all the way round my head. I could see the loose weave and feel the scratchiness of it. What was I doing tied up inside a burlap bag that come all the way down to my hips?

And bouncing in the backseat of somebody's car? I could hear voices talking in the front. Who was they? I tried to listen, but just then the car stopped, and they did too. Talking, I mean.

Anyhow, a car door opened, somebody got out and then come back after a few seconds. We drove on a bit, and the whole thing repeated. Seemed like we musta passed through a gate.

Then it hit me. I was in the backseat of Jeffrie's swanky car, and we was on the way to his barn.

I was ready to curse that Marlene with every word I knew. And knew a bunch of 'em, even if Momma woulda whipped me for saying 'em. You can't live in a trailer park without hearing that kind of cursing day and night.

But my brain took over my anger, and I started thinking as fast as I could. We was gonna arrive at the barn any minute. What was I gonna do? Pretend to be still knocked out? What'd they use, anyhow? My head didn't feel sore, so they musta doped me again. I didn't remember eating or drinking anything at Marlene's trailer, but then I couldn't rightly remember what did happen. Anyhow, I swore I'd never take another thing to eat or drink from either of their hands.

Corrine poured the last of the coffee into Bethanne's cup. "We already waited pert' near an hour. I got to get to work. On the early shift tonight. I used up all my sick days, and I'm not due for no more vacation time til Christmas."

Bethanne rubbed her pounding temples. They were sitting inside Corrine's trailer with the a.c. going full blast to keep the heat and humidity at bay. But the rackety sound and musty smell of the ancient air conditioner was feeding her headache. "It's too soon to call the police," she said. "Eden's only been gone a few hours. They won't do a thing until a lot more time has passed." She didn't want to tell Corrine about Chief Hastings being up to his neck in whatever was happening.

"What do we do in the meantime? Just get on with our lives?"

Bethanne nodded and wished she didn't have to.

Corrine looked down at the baby in her lap. "What about Cruz? I can't leave him alone, and I can't afford a sitter. I save up during summer, when Eden's outta school, so we can have a sitter in winter."

Bethanne held out her arms. "That's easy. I'll watch him, and I'll wait for Eden. You go to work."

Course it wasn't no surprise when they hauled me into the barn and took off that burlap sack. It was Marlene and Jeffries all right.

I tried to look like I wasn't scared. But my whole insides was fluttering like I swallowed one of them moths that beats her wings against the light til she don't have no strength left.

Jeffries pushed me down into an armchair. I didn't even blink when a broken spring poked into my backside. Wasn't gonna give him the satisfaction.

I looked round the room like I was really interested to see how it was gonna be this time. And truth to tell, it come across all differnt to me. Them satin curtains was sagging, and they had stains on 'em here and there. I could see scratches on the bedpost and smell something stale and nasty, like maybe a rat had died under the floorboards where they couldn't get at it to clean up.

Jeffries lit one of his stinky old cigars and squinted down at me through the smoke. "Well, Miss Smartypants, you got yourself in the shit now."

Marlene come over and tugged on his sleeve. "What're you gonna do, Pete?"

He shook her off. "That's for me to know and you to find out."

The way Jeffries talked to Marlene set me to wondering how come she was so sweet on him. Or was she playing him to get ahead in show biz? Some kinda blind ambition, if that was the case. Anyhow, she went over to the other armchair and plopped herself down.

Jeffries stood smirking over me. "I told Winston I was going to shoot you gals and him too, if he didn't put a stop to you and that old bitch nosing around. Winston likes to keep me happy, said he was going to talk with her." He winked. "I just picked you up for insurance."

I set up and looked at Marlene. She was slouched back in her chair, chewing on her thick lips. Wasn't gonna get no help from her, that was for sure. Only thing I could do was act tough til I could think of a way out. "Who you figure's gonna pay off your policy?"

Jeffries stuck his cigar between his teeth, took hold of my shirt with both hands and shook me. "Don't get smart with me. I oughta kill you for what you did to my dog." He slapped me so hard my ears rung.

"Didn't know I had a guard dog, did you?" he snarled. "You think I'd be dumb enough to leave all this stuff unprotected? I hope he scared the shit out of you."

I tried to keep back the tears cause I didn't want him to see how weak I was, but it was no use. My nose started running, and my eyes too.

Jeffries smiled. "Stop sniveling. I'm not going to kill you. I need you alive for what I got planned."

Bethanne sat on one of the plastic chairs outside the trailer, rocking Cruz in her arms and trying to think. She didn't know which was worse—the racket and smell of the air conditioner inside or the hot, soggy atmosphere outside. Her head felt like it was full of molasses. She forced questions through her clogged brain.

Had Jeffries snatched Eden? Should she drive out to the barn? If Eden was there, would her arrival put the girl in greater jeopardy? Would Jeffries kidnap her too? Besides, what was she going to do with Cruz if she went gallivanting through the night, trying to find Eden?

Dear God, she needed a drink. And a cigarette. She went inside and looked for a beer in the fridge. Just Coke and iced tea. Then she remembered Eden saying her mother had joined AA. Maybe the lack of booze was a good thing after all. She needed to keep her head clear. But she could at least put Cruz in his crib and go back outside for a smoke.

Bethanne was reaching for her purse and a Kool when her flip-phone rang. She grabbed the purse and went out so the noise wouldn't wake Cruz.

"Got a young lady here says her name is Eden."

Bethanne's head snapped to attention. "What have you done to her, you bastard? If you've hurt her, I'll…"

Jeffries snickered "Well, well, aren't you the mother hen? If you want to keep Eden safe, pack up and get out of town. Once you're gone, I'll let her go."

Stall, she told herself, stall. "How do I know you've really got Eden? Let me talk to her."

"Sure thing."

The line went dead for a few moments, then Eden came on. "Don't you worry none. I'm not even tied up. He's afraid…"

Jeffries' voice came back on the line. "I'm not afraid of this little girl. Nor you, either. Don't try to come out to the barn. I got a shotgun, and I won't hesitate to use it on the both of you. Just get out of town. Marlene's going to be watching to make sure you do."

The phone went dead, and Bethanne realized her legs were wobbling. She sat down and cradled her terror like a crystal vase that could shatter and break her heart.

25

After my ears stopped ringing, I started speculating about the logistics of the thing. I learned that on the University Channel too. You always gotta think about the logistics when you're planning something important.

I was looking at that shotgun leaning next to Jeffries' desk and wondering if Marlene was gonna take Jeffries' car to go watch Bethanne. That'd leave him on foot. Maybe I could go to the bathroom, sneak out the window and get a head start. Then maybe his long, skinny legs couldn't catch up, even if I was short and fat. Besides, I wasn't fat as I used to be, and I been swimming a lot, so I had me some stamina.

Course that Jeffries was way ahead of me. Just like he'd been most of the time so far. He reached in his pocket and pulled out some keys. "Here, Marlene, you take the Vespa and get on over to that woman's apartment. And take the other cell phone too. I want you to keep reporting in." He held up a new finger each time he added to the list. "When you arrive. If she's there. What she's doing. When she leaves."

He sneered at me. "You notice I didn't say, 'If she leaves.' That woman is going to get out of town to save your life."

Right then I'da give almost anything to soap that smirk off his face. But all I could do was pray to God my chance would come.

He turned back to Marlene. "What're you standing around here for? Get on the road, girl."

Marlene looked like she wanted to get outta town herself, but she grabbed the keys and the cell phone and took off.

Jeffries set down in his desk chair, puffed on his cigar and blew out a smoke-ring of satisfaction. Just like him to have a chair like that, covered in brown plastic trying to look like real leather. That man didn't have a genuine bone in his body.

Outside, I heard Marlene zip off on the motorbike.

"Got that red Vespa to impress the kids when I'm…" Jeffries seemed to recollect himself and change the subject. "I let Marlene ride it as a reward for being a good girl, doing what I tell her. You could have ridden it too, but you had to go and be a smartass."

I meant to get back some of the nerve I lost when he hit me. "What if she gets caught sneaking round them rich folks' house?"

He leaned back and crossed a bony ankle onto the other knee, showing two inches of dead-white, flaky skin above his droopy sock. "Won't matter a bit. I got friends in high places."

—

Cruz began to cry, and Bethanne's attention was dragged from Eden to her brother. She went in, picked the baby up and walked the floor, trying to calm him and herself too.

The trailer consisted of a bedroom at one end and a living room at the other. In between were a tiny bathroom and a kitchenette. Not much room to walk up and down, but it was enough. Cruz went to sleep, and Bethanne saw what she had to do.

She put him back in bed while she gathered up what she needed. An old cardboard box she could rig up as a carry-cot. A can of baby formula, one of his bottles, some baby food, a box of Pampers. And a plastic rattle that looked like it had been through several families before it got to Cruz.

She left a note for Corrine. Then she loaded baby and supplies into the Datsun and drove away into the gathering dusk.

I'm ashamed to say I jumped when Jeffries' phone rang. Here I was trying to put on a big act, and a little bitty phone showed me to be the pathetic thing I was.

He tapped the screen. "Yeah?…Okay, so you're there…what's happening?"

I was worried I wouldn't the able to follow what Marlene was saying, but it turned out Jeffries made it easy for me.

"Use your brains," he said. "Go look in the window. See if she's packed up or not."

He put the phone to his chest and looked at me. "No car. Windows dark. Maybe your friend's left town already."

That made me sink so low in my spirits, I didn't know what to do. Surely Bethanne wasn't gonna leave me all by myself. She had to have a plan. But I didn't have one, so how could she?

Jeffries put the phone back to his ear and listened for a while. Then a big gust come outta his mouth like he was so full of exasperation, he couldn't hold it in. "I said look in the window, Marlene. What do you see?…What do you mean, 'Nothing'? Like everything's packed up and gone?" He smoothed them few sooty hairs over his bald spot and listened some more.

Then he turned to me. "Looks like your friend isn't home. But all her stuff's still there." His lip curled like it was trying to touch his nose. "Maybe she's so worried, she just left everything behind."

I set up straight and put on a face I didn't feel. "Well, that just shows how you don't know Bethanne. She'll do the right thing, I know she will."

Jeffries stopped paying attention to me about halfway through what I was saying. He put the phone up close to his ear and then give Marlene orders like he was a drill sergeant. "Get the hell off the porch and hide. Watch her every move and tell me what happens."

He tapped the phone to turn it off and give me a look that said he was on top of the world. "Your friend just pulled into the driveway. Must've been out when I called. Now we'll see some action."

I stayed setting up straight like I wasn't worried. But that moth was still beating her wings all over my insides.

⌁

Bethanne left Cruz fast asleep in his box and ran up the stairs to her apartment. She turned on all the lights and opened all the curtains in case Marlene was watching.

She pulled her suitcase out of the closet, threw in some clothes and cosmetics, banged it shut and dashed down to the car to stow it in the trunk. Back up the stairs to fill a box with stuff so it would look like she was leaving. She looked at the fridge, thinking she ought to eat something to give her strength. But her stomach was too nervous to hold down even a cracker. She turned off the lights, closed the curtains and locked the door.

Was Marlene out there? No sign of her, but Bethanne had to

count on the girl being near and reporting back to Jeffries that she was on her way out of town.

⌒

Jeffries got up from his plastic-leather chair and went over to one of them super-automatic coffee-makers. "You want a cup? Help keep us alert while we wait for Marlene to say your friend's gone for good."

No way I was gonna drink nothing of his, but I told him so as nice as I could. I was beginning to realize there was more I needed to know. "What's gonna happen to me once Bethanne's gone?"

He put in one of them coffee-pods. "You're going to keep your mouth shut, or I'm going to burn down your trailer. With you and your baby brother in it."

The way he said it made it more scary than just the words theirselves. Like he was talking about going fishing. Or shopping. Like it was the most natural and obvious thing in the world.

That's when the moth died, and my insides didn't feel nothing but cold and empty.

⌒

Bethanne took the main route out of town, glancing in her rearview mirror now and then to see if she was being followed. Her mouth was dry, and her eyes hurt from headlights grazing them when vehicles pulled out to pass or turn into another road. None of them seemed to be tracking her.

She lit a cigarette from the glowing dashboard lighter and dragged smoke into her grateful lungs. The familiar sensation didn't help a lot, but it helped some.

She peeked at the mirror. Was that a single headlight following? A pedinkle, they'd called them when she was a kid, a car with one lamp out. She turned onto the Interstate ramp and sighed with relief when the single light stayed on the surface road.

26

THAT MARLENE COME THROUGH the door grinning like she just won the Porn Award. If they got such a thing. They must. The TV's so full of award shows, you gotta wonder what's next. All-American Plumber? Best performance by a trucker? Best new forklift operator?

Course I can make fun of it now, but I wasn't making fun of my situation then. I was setting in that chair, worrying about what Bethanne was doing and whether Jeffries was gonna let me go or not.

Jeffries jumped up so fast, he spilled his coffee. "You saw her leave for sure?"

Marlene strutted into Jeffries' office, swaying her hips and sticking out her bouncing boobs. "Got on the freeway and took off. Musta been doing ninety."

He let out a rebel yell and turned round to me. "Now we got to take care of you, Miss Smartypants."

⸺

Bethanne pulled into the service area twenty miles down the highway and looked for a beige pickup with a full crew cab. It was still relatively early, and the parking lot was jam-packed, the vehicles' drivers inside filling their faces with double fries and giant burgers. The smell of over-used fryer oil snaked through her open windows.

She drove to the rear and found Buck, dressed in camouflage and holding the next space empty for her. She parked and looked over at Vicki, sitting in the truck's front seat with Chance in her arms.

Bethanne got out of her car. "Vicki, I'm sorry to get Buck involved, but I didn't know what else to do."

Vicki smiled. "Don't you worry none about that. This is a whole lot differnt than breaking into Ralph's Rentals."

Bethanne glanced at Buck. He was pulling his long hair into a stubby ponytail. His head moved ever so faintly in a negative signal.

"That guy grabbed our Eden," Vicki continued, "and my man is gonna get her back."

Bethanne nodded at Buck to show she understood to keep quiet about what happened at Winson's storage facility. Then she walked to the passenger side of her car and lifted Cruz, box and all. Buck followed and picked up the rest of the baby's things.

Vicki got out and helped stow the two babies in the rear seat of the truck. "Now you three show up for breakfast, ya hear? I'll make us some biscuits and gravy."

Buck opened the driver's door so she could get in. "Wouldn't miss it for the world." He turned toward the truck's cargo area. "Hold on a sec, sugar." He hoisted a long canvas case and put it on Bethanne's back seat.

Bethanne felt little lizard claws run up her spine. "What's that?"

"Rifle. Thought about bringing a shotgun."

She shook her head. "I don't think we ought to…"

Buck got out a tin of snuff and put a pinch in his lip. "You said Jeffries got a shotgun."

Vicki sat in the truck, head rotating from one speaker to the other. Every time Buck spoke, she nodded her head in agreement.

"Well..." Bethanne thought for a moment. "Maybe you're right. He's not going to do what we want just because we say so."

Buck spit a brown stream onto the tarmac. "If Jeffries got a shotgun, I thought maybe I need something long-range."

Bethanne frowned. "You think he might hear us coming? We can park away from the barn and go in on foot."

His head jerked up. "You keep saying 'we.' You're not going nowhere near that barn."

Bethanne crossed her arms over her chest and stuck out her chin. "If I don't go, you don't go. I'm the only one knows where the barn is."

Buck stood there, staring at Bethanne, his jaw muscles knotting. "Okay, but I'm taking the rifle. Thirty-aught-six. Oughta do the trick."

Vicki leaned over and grinned at Bethanne. "Buck's the best shot in Lewis County."

—

I knew I had to make the most of Marlene's news, so I stood up like I been there visiting. "Okay, you can let me go now."

Jeffries pushed me back down in the chair. "Not so fast. You're staying the night. In case your friend tries to double back."

My mind was working overtime trying to figure a way out. "What about my baby brother? I need to be watching him."

I was surprised when Marlene spoke up for me. "You remember, Pete. Eden watches Cruz while her momma pulls the night shift."

"Marlene," he said, "if you ever want to work for me again, you'll keep your thoughts to yourself." That took all the wind outta her puffed-up chest. She slunk over to her chair and set down like a hunting dog been smacked for barking at the wrong time.

He grinned at me. "Your momma surely solved that problem hours ago. Either she's watching him herself or she found somebody to do it for her. Either way, no one's coming after you til tomorrow."

He went over to his desk and pulled out a pair of handcuffs "I got these for the porn flicks. Never knew I'd need 'em for real." He jerked me up and dragged me over to the brass bedstead.

Then he tossed the handcuffs to Marlene. "Get out of that chair and make yourself useful. Cuff her ankle to the bedpost."

I started to put up a fight, kicking out at Marlene. I wanted to hurt her in the worst way. But Jeffries picked up the shotgun, and I knew there wasn't no point in going on like that.

"Glad you see the advantage of settling down," he said and nodded at Marlene to continue. "Time to celebrate. I'll go get us something to eat and a couple six packs." He looked down at me, and this spiteful smirk come over his face. "Then maybe we can have us some fun."

The way he said that—like maybe he was back to thinking about making a video of me and Marlene—sunk me into the deepest misery. It wasn't just cause I was worried about what he had in store for me. That look made me realize I had to accept the idea that maybe Bethanne wasn't coming to save me after all.

≈

Bethanne parked the car behind the bushes where Eden had told her to leave it the last time. Buck got out and walked to the rear of the car. Bethanne took a deep breath to calm her nerves, then followed him.

Buck lifted his rifle out of the trunk and looked Bethanne over. "If you're going with me, you gotta do something about that white blouse. Ain't you got anything else you can put on?"

Bethanne studied his camouflage and saw what he meant. She had on jeans and dark sneakers, but her blouse was so light it could be seen a hundred yards away. Even if the moon wasn't full. She picked up her suitcase. "Turn your back."

She changed into a black shirt with long sleeves and covered her hair with a navy bandana for good measure. Her skin felt confined, and she started to sweat, but she'd have to put up with it. "How's this?"

Buck turned around and nodded his approval. "Looks like just the thing for catching bastards."

Bethanne smiled. "And getting Eden back."

"You ever been hunting at night?"

She shook her head. She'd never been hunting at all.

Buck pulled a tin out of his pocket, opened it and started smearing something dark on her face.

27

I COME TO APPRECIATE pretty quick there wasn't no point in staying down in the mouth forever. Wasn't nobody gonna help me but myself. So soon as Jeffries left, I started working on Marlene. Figured now was my only chance to get free. Told her that old handcuff was biting into my ankle something fierce.

And it was too. She put it on the same ankle I hurt at Ralph's Rentals. Marlene come over, and she could see for herself that my leg was swelling up round that cuff.

"You gotta let me loose," I said. "What if I get gangrene and die?"

Trust Marlene to be so dumb she couldn't see what a whopper I was feeding her. Well, she may have been dumb, and she surely was ambitious, but she wasn't mean. Not like Jeffries. She went over to the desk and got the key.

I was all ready to knock her down and run off into the night when she come back with another set of cuffs. She fastened one end to my wrist and the other to hers. Then she unlocked the cuff on my ankle. Pretty smart for dumb old Marlene.

"Come on," she said and pulled me toward a door on the far side of the barn. I was digging in my heels and hollering, but it didn't do no good. Afore I knew it, I was unhooked from Marlene and locked in a pitch-black closet.

⸻

Bethanne and Buck scrambled over the gate and ran down the rutted dirt track. Buck was in the lead, motioning for her to keep low to the ground. The air was so thick with humidity, she felt like she was struggling through steam, and her back hurt from running bent over.

Just as they got in sight of the barn, Buck pulled her behind some bushes and held his finger to his lips. She got down behind him just in time. A car bumped by, coming from the main road, a man at the wheel. Buck asked a question with a look, but she shook her head and hunched her shoulders. In the dark and without a good view, she didn't know if it was Jeffries or not.

Bethanne squatted against a tree and tried to get her breath. She'd been swimming a lot with Eden, but she still wasn't in the kind of shape Buck was. She was beginning to wonder if it was such a good idea for her to come after all.

Over near the barn, a dove cooed like someone moaning for help.

She craned her neck to see around Buck. The man got out of the car and went inside. The dome light in the car was off, so she still couldn't see enough. Was Jeffries alone in the barn, or did he just get some reinforcement?

⸻

I couldn't figure out why there wasn't no light coming round the rim of that closet door. Jeffries musta used that stuff you can buy down at Haymaker's to seal it. I felt all round the door, trying to find a light switch, but there wasn't none anywhere. Finally I had to be content with keeping my ear to the door—flimsy old thing made of pressboard. Coulda busted right through if only I'd had a hammer. Wasn't long afore Jeffries come back, and I heard Marlene telling how she locked me in the closet.

Wham! Jeffries threw open the door, cussing a blue streak at Marlene for being so stupid. But when he saw me cowering against the back wall, he laughed and shoved a takeout box at me. "Here. Miss Smartypants, have yourself some fried chicken."

Then he shut the door, but not afore I seen there was a light bulb with a cord up on the ceiling.

⁓

Bethanne groaned when Buck motioned her to bend over again and scoot along behind him. How much more of this could her back take?

Mick Jagger's voice boomed from the barn about how he couldn't get no satisfaction. Off in the distance, thunder seemed to pound in rhythm with the music. Bethanne had to smile. If all went according to plan, that would be Jeffries' swan song.

They darted under one of the barn windows and slowly raised themselves until they could peek inside. All they got for their trouble was light shining through some pink curtains hanging from a ceiling-track a couple of feet away. A sliver of light shone under the curtains, and there appeared to be somebody moving in time to the music.

They trailed around the barn from one window to another, but each one was blocked by the long curtains. Maybe Bethanne had never been hunting, but it was obvious you had to see your prey before you could pounce.

I set down on the closet floor and started on that greasy chicken. I know I said I wouldn't take nothing to eat or drink from their hands again, but I was hungry, and that's the truth. Nerves, probably, but I told myself I was gonna need my strength to break outta there when the time come. Anyhow, I figured the chicken was OK, cause it was still warm in the box, so how'd Jeffries have time to dope it?

On the other side of the door, Marlene and Jeffries was having theirselves a party. They had a CD playing this old-time song as loud as it would go, and I could hear Jeffries saying, "Yeah, baby, yeah. You sure know how to turn me on." Had to be that fool Marlene dancing for him again. Seemed like no matter how bad he treated her, she was willing to do anything to make him happy.

If they was that far into what they was doing, I figured I could turn on the ceiling light and take a look round that closet. Only stood to reason if their light couldn't shine in, mine couldn't shine out. Maybe I could find something to bust open the door with.

I stood up and gently waved my hands above my head til I hit the light cord. When I pulled it, I could see shelves round three sides of that closet. And every shelf was full of old shoe boxes. Well, I didn't have nothing else to do, so I started opening 'em up and looking inside.

I clapped a hand over my mouth to keep from crying out. Them boxes was full of pills, red ones and blue ones, lots of colors, all fastened up in little plastic baggies. Musta been hunnerds of 'em.

I remembered Bethanne telling me about Jeffries selling Ecstasy to the kids. There was a whole lot more drugs than just Ecstasy in them boxes. Here was more proof to put that sucker away, if only I could get outta that closet and outta that barn and take some of them baggies with me.

Bethanne was about as mad as she'd ever been. Buck had pushed her back from the one window with a view inside. What made him think she couldn't take seeing whatever he'd spotted? He had no idea what she'd had to deal with before she met him.

Buck didn't give her a chance to say any of this. He held the rifle in one hand and used the other to pull a hunting knife out of a sheath strapped to his leg. Then he started running for the front of the barn.

She looked at the window and then at his back. Take a peek inside or follow him again? She hated having to follow, but she didn't want to be left behind if there was going to be some action.

She picked up a fallen tree branch, broke off the side shoots and raced after Buck.

The shelves of that closet went all the way up to the ceiling, and the only way to find out what was up there was to climb. So I put one foot on one side and one foot on the other. Figured I'd go up like a mountain climber inside a big old crack in the rock. Seen that on the TV too.

But I didn't think about the fact I was climbing up rickety shelves instead of something rock-hard. I no more'n got up to the third shelf, afore the whole bunch of 'em come tumbling down, and me with 'em.

I was setting on the floor of that closet, surrounded by piles of pills and the smell of fried chicken when the door slammed open. Jeffries stood there, shaking like a leaf and purple in the face. He looked so funny, I thought I was gonna laugh.

Then he started running for the shotgun, and I figured it wasn't so funny after all. I tried to get up and outta that closet, but one of them fallen shelves had pinned my foot in a corner. Hurt pretty good too, cause it was the same ankle I wrecked at Ralph's and the same one swelled up from the cuff.

Thoughts of Momma and Cruz come to me like angels trying to save me, but them visions didn't do no good. Jeffries was running across the barn, his long legs eating up the floorboards, his hands getting that shotgun ready for me. Just like he threatened afore. I couldn't see no way out, and my stomach took a big heave. I tried hard to hold it back, but I up and barfed that greasy chicken all down my front.

The next thing I done, I didn't wanna. These big old tears started running down my face. I wanted to be brave. But thinking about Momma and Cruz, puking myself like a baby, I just couldn't help it.

28

BLAM! THE BARN DOOR flew open, just like that. The hot, damp air poured in, and I twisted round so I could look outta the closet. What did I see but Cousin Buck in a crouch, rifle in one hand and big old hunting knife in the other. And dearest Lord, Bethanne was right behind him, holding a club like she was gonna hit a home run with Jeffries' head. Made me think of Ray-Jean's action movies, the way they both had dark clothes and dark stuff on their faces. Felt like the cavalry arrived just in the knick of time.

I looked back at Jeffries and thought I was gonna throw up all over again. He was swinging his shotgun round toward Buck, and my heart started pounding at the thought of what all that shot would do to the only grown man in our family.

But Buck hadn't been hunting all his life for nothing. He didn't even pause, just threw that hunting knife in one smooth motion like he was aiming at a target instead of a man. Jeffries dropped to the floor, and the knife missed him. But that give Buck the time he needed.

He flew through the air like one of them Chinese kung-fu guys and kicked the shotgun outta Jeffries' hands. But Jeffries rolled over and got on his feet. Then the two of 'em went at it. Buck was younger and stronger, but Jeffries was taller, so they was pretty well matched.

Up and down they thrashed, both of 'em holding onto Buck's rifle like their lives depended on it. And I guess it did. Either Buck was gonna get the rifle and shoot Jeffries, or the other way round.

I plumb forgot Bethanne was there, til she come up behind Jeffries and pulled back her club to give him a good whack.

Just then the two men fell into the curtains, and the pink satin come spilling down all over 'em. Bethanne had already started to swing, and it was too late to stop. The club hit somebody, and I heard him go "Oof." Like the air got knocked outta him.

Bethanne bent over and started pulling the curtains off 'em. I saw her wince, and I wondered if she'd hurt herself when she hit whoever it was.

One of them two men was really struggling, but the other one was pretty much quiet. I just about stopped breathing with the worry of which one was which.

Then a half-bald head come out from under the curtain on the far side. Afore I could shout a word of warning, Jeffries was sprinting for the door. All that long hair he normally combed over the top of his head was flopping alongside his ear. I almost laughed, but then I realized Buck musta been the one Bethanne hit. I looked back and there she was, unwrapping him from that dirty pink satin.

Bethanne heard Jeffries' car start up and move away. She looked out the door. Heat lightning dimmed his retreating tail lights. "God damn it."

But there was nothing she could do to stop him with Buck lying there with his eyes clenched, Eden pinned in a closet and Marlene mewling behind a chair. Bethanne smiled over at Eden. "Hang on, I'm coming. But I got to help Buck first."

Eden nodded. "I been here awhile. Little longer won't hurt none. You take care of Buck."

Bethanne's gaze fell on Marlene. The girl seemed to be coming out of some kind of stupor. "Marlene, you got yourself nearly buried in trouble, but it's not too late to dig out. Go get Eden loose."

Bethanne lay Buck's head down on a wad of satin and went over to the sink in the makeshift kitchen. She wet a stained dishtowel and put it on Buck's forehead. He opened his eyes, but they didn't seem like they were fully focused yet.

She watched Eden limp toward her with Marlene's support. "How bad is it? Can you make it back to the car?"

Eden appeared to be trying to smile, but it came off more like a grimace. "Piece of cake," she said, "but first we gotta get the evidence." Bethanne grinned back. That girl had more grit than she'd ever imagined.

Eden glared at Marlene. "Where's the kiddy porn?"

Marlene looked like she didn't know whether to cooperate or run, so Bethanne gave her a nudge. "Remember what I said about redeeming yourself? Get it and get it now."

Buck heaved himself up into a sitting position and unbuttoned his shirt. A purple bruise bloomed right below his ribs. Bethanne must've knocked the wind out of him.

"Oh Jesus," Bethanne said. "I'm so sorry."

He shook his head and tried to smile. "I tell you, Missus, you pack one helluva whollop. I'll remember that next time I need somebody to back me up in a bar fight."

She smiled back. " Well, I've been in a couple, but you better take to heart what Vicki said. You're not going to be in any more bar fights."

—

Well, that Marlene finally realized she'd better help us. What else could she do? Jeffries done took off without giving her a thought. She poked round the file cabinet til she found a DVD and a folder of photos. I bet Jeffries was gonna be sorry he ever left that thing unlocked.

In the meantime, I told Bethanne to look in the closet, and she let out a whoop when she saw all them pills. Buck popped the kiddy porn and some pills in a box he found lying against the wall and grinned. "This here's more'n enough to put Jeffries away til he's an old man."

We was just about ready to go, but there was no way we could leave yet, what with me being covered in puke. Is there anything smells worse than putrefying barf? I could see everybody's nose scrunching up, and I knew mine was exactly the same.

Me and Marlene rummaged through the costumes til we found something I could put on without causing too much comment. No sequins, no slit skirt, no see-through. Just a short pleated skirt and sailor blouse with an emblem on the collar. Seemed kind of funny to me that Jeffries had that kind of stuff in with the sexy clothes. But Buck said some men had fantasies about schoolgirls, and I had to take his word for it.

I cleaned up in the bathroom and put on that outfit, while Buck and Bethanne got the black stuff off their faces the best they could with some of Jeffries' paper towels. I told 'em them schoolgirl duds felt so strange I didn't want Vicki or nobody else to see me in 'em. Bethanne said she had some clothes in her car, but nothing that would work for me. Said I could borrow some shorts and a T-shirt of hers back at the apartment, so we took off. I felt like I still smelled bad, but nobody said nothing, so maybe it was just my imagination.

I set in the front seat with Bethanne, both of us talking at once and trying to catch up with the news each of us had to tell. I asked right away about Cruz and Momma. Bethanne said Momma was awful worried about me, but I knew I couldn't bother her at the mill. We'd just have to wait til she finished her shift.

Meanwhile, Buck was calling Vicki, telling her we all got out safe and not to fret. Then he slumped down in the back and got all quiet. I figured he was probably feeling bad about Jeffries getting away, and we was gonna have to deal with that when we got to Bethanne's.

The whole time, Marlene was setting in the backseat with Buck, not saying a word. That was fine by me. I think I'da climbed back and slapped her face if she even opened her mouth.

Good thing it was round midnight by the time we got to Bethanne's. The neighbors woulda called the cops for sure, what with the way we looked and Buck hardly able to move without groaning.

Bethanne pulled up beside the garage. Afore any of us could open a door, Marlene was outta the car and running back toward the street.

Buck cursed and started running after her, but I could see how bad his chest was hurting him, so I took after the two of 'em.

Sheet lightning showed Marlene cutting left into that rose garden, same one I snuck through the day I first met Bethanne in the cellar. Guess Marlene thought she could squeeze through where he couldn't. And she was right. Buck was too bulky to get between them thorny branches. But I wasn't. I jumped in right behind her. I was getting slashed right and left by all them thorns, but there was no way I was gonna let her get away.

I could hear Buck running on down the driveway, groaning with every breath and ready to head Marlene off if she turned back that way.

Meanwhile, Bethanne turned on her porch light, and I could see I was gaining on Marlene. She may've been getting a lot of exercise dancing for Jeffries, but she sure couldn't run, and that's the truth.

I was almost to Marlene when she stopped dead in her tracks and started making this whimpering sound. I slammed into her and knocked her to the ground. That's when I realized we was beside the lily pond, and some man's feet was sticking right up outta the water, toes caught on a little concrete wall.

29

FROM HER APARTMENT PORCH, Bethanne looked past the two girls sprawled on the ground and saw the man's body floating face-down among the lilies.

"Buck," she shouted, "come back and take that brick path to the pond." She ran down the stairs, feeling each step jar her sore back. What the hell was going on? Who was it?

Marlene's voice had risen to a wail, and Bethanne could hear Eden trying to calm her down. She saw Buck turn into the path she'd meant, and she took another from the rear of Mary Margaret's rose garden. Her back was hurting so bad from being bent over all that time at the barn, she had to put both hands on her hips to ease the suffering.

Thunder rumbled all around, and she looked up at the sky. The last thing they needed right now was rain.

She lowered her eyes to the lily pond and saw Buck pulling the body out of the water by the heels. Eden and Marlene were rising to their feet.

The neighbor's outside lights came on, and a man's voice called out. "I don't know who you are or what you're doing, but I called the police. Don't try anything stupid. They're on their way."

Bethanne kept moving down the path toward the pond. "It's Bethanne Swanson, Mary Margaret's sister."

"Well, you can tell that to the police," the man said and banged his window shut.

The sound of a siren reached the pond as Bethanne arrived. Buck had just got the body out, and he was standing over it, a hand clutched to his bruised midriff, trying to stifle a groan. The body lay stomach-down on the grass. A smell of rotting vegetation rose from the muddy hair. Bethanne stared at the tan back showing through the sopping shirt and the wet chinos plastered to thin legs. She looked at Eden, Buck and Marklene. They all had the same question on their faces. The same one she was asking, although she feared she already knew the answer.

Buck turned the body over.

Bethanne's knees went weak, and she plopped down on the ground. "Sweet Jesus, it's Winston."

⌒

I heard that siren, and I knew we had to think fast. This was gonna be the police, and Chief Hastings was their boss. We couldn't trust 'em an inch.

Buck was way ahead of me. "They'll wanna know why we're here."

"We just come back from the drive-in," I said. "You know, the one they re-opened over on the Moorestown road."

Marlene started to bolt, but Buck reached out a hand and grabbed her arm. "Hold on. You're part of this story too. You got it?"

She nodded and stood there, her head hung down like a cat caught out in the rain.

I stooped down beside Bethanne. "You hear what we said? Can you tell that story?"

She looked over at me. "Yeah, but we'll have to know what was playing."

Marlene's head come up, and a grin tiptoed across her face. "That's easy. *March of the Ghouls*. With a bunch of actors nobody ever heard of."

Trust Marlene to know all about the flicks.

Well, by then the cop car was turning into the driveway, and there wasn't nothing we could do 'cept tell our story and stick to it. Halfway through, I remembered the proof against Jeffries and Buck's rifle was both in Bethanne's trunk. What if the cops wanted to search her car?

But they was too busy taking down our stories and calling for the experts and getting Chief Hastings outta bed. I thought I was in the middle of one of them TV shows Ray-Jean always liked—that crime scene investigation stuff. But then I thought about how this was for real, and it definitely wasn't entertaining.

The storm passed by, bringing no relief. The air seemed to weigh Bethanne down in the delicate metal chair Buck had brought from Mary Margaret's French bistro set. Dear God, would this night never end? And now the Police Chief was on his way, the same one who'd threatened to do something about her and Eden snooping if Winston didn't take care of it himself.

She sat there, trying to get her brain to work while the police continued their investigation of the scene. Murder or suicide? She had a hard time accepting either one. Why would Winston kill himself?

And if he did, why do it in Mary Margaret's pond? But if somebody killed him, who did it? Jeffries was on the lam, and the Police Chief had been in bed. Who else was there?

Her mind raced all around, finally stopping at the fact that no one had called Winston's family. That realization brought shame to further dampen her already soggy spirits. Why hadn't she thought about that before? With a sigh, she went back to the car, got her flip-phone and called Clay about another parent lost.

He couldn't believe it either.

Seemed like that Tuesday night was gonna go on and on. The police was done talking with me, but there was no way they was gonna be finished with everything for a long time. None of us was supposed to leave yet, so I set on the back porch of the main house with Buck and Marlene, worrying about Bethanne. She looked like somebody hit her with a two-by-four, and she wasn't never gonna recover.

When she got up from that twisty metal chair, she walked toward the car like an old woman. She never really was an old woman afore. Older, yeah, but not old.

After Bethanne got off the phone, I went over to her and give her a big hug. "You ain't alone in this, you know. We been through a lot together, and we'll get through this too."

Her cheeks, her eyes, everything about her face was hollow. "Clay's going to call Lucinda, and then he's coming over." She turned toward her apartment stairs. "Guess I better make us some coffee."

Bethanne was measuring grounds into the coffee-maker when she heard feet running up her stairs. The screen door burst open, and Lucinda pounded in. "You couldn't leave well enough alone, could you? Now Daddy's dead, and it's all your fault."

Shit. Bethanne didn't feel ready to cope with Lucinda being a total bitch. Her back knotted in a spasm, and she reached behind to push her fingers into the pain. "What're you talking about?"

Lucinda strode forward, fists clenched at her sides. "You think Daddy was helping Jeffries because he wanted to?"

Sarcasm took hold before Bethanne could stop it. "What else?"

"Jeffries had a hold over him. He made Daddy host those porn evenings so he could try out his DVDs on an audience before putting them up for sale on the website."

Bethanne felt like she was running to catch up. "Jeffries had a website?"

Lucinda's jaw knotted, and her lips parted to reveal teeth tightly clamped together. She looked like a rabid dog.

Bethanne took a step back. "Hold? What hold?"

"I saw what he did."

"Who?"

"Jeffries."

"Jeffries did something wrong? How did that give him a hold over Winston?"

"No, you idiot. Daddy did something wrong, and Jeffries took a picture of it."

Bethanne felt like she was finally getting close. "You saw Jeffries photograph something that Winston did."

"Yes." Lucinda folded her arms across her chest, holding in whatever she knew.

Bethanne rubbed her face and tried to think what to do. "I could use a beer." She headed for the fridge. "How about you?"

Lucinda slumped against the kitchen counter. "Clay'll be here soon."

Bethanne popped the tops on two beers and handed one to Lucinda. Bethanne took a big swig and watched the younger woman. Better not mention Winston again. That might shut Lucinda up. "What was in Jeffries' photo?"

Lucinda threw her head back and gulped her beer. "It was on the father-son camping trip. I was jealous, so I stowed away in the back of the station wagon. When they got out to greet everybody, I sneaked out of the car and hid."

"That's how you saw Jeffries."

"Yeah. He was there with Pete Junior. They were all having fun roasting hot dogs, and I was out in the cold eating bologna."

"You were back in the woods, watching."

"I stayed there all night with just a sleeping bag." Lucinda looked across the room and scowled. "Sure can learn a lot in the Girl Scouts."

"What'd you see?"

"After everybody went to bed, Jeffries slunk out of his tent with a thirty-five millimeter camera. They were pretty big in those days, and it was easy for me to see what he had in his hands. He went over to Dad and Clay's pup tent and stuck the camera through the flap."

Lucinda's jaw was working, and she gritted her teeth again. "I slipped up as close as I dared. Didn't want them to see me."

Bethanne prodded as gently as possible. "Could you look into the tent?"

"No, but whatever it was, Daddy came out and knocked Jeffries down. I nearly cheered when I saw him do that. But Jeffries got up and smiled. I could see his teeth shining in the moonlight."

"He smiled?" Bethanne prompted.

"And said now Daddy had to do whatever Jeffries wanted or he'd tell."

"Did Clay come out of the tent?"

"No, but I could hear him crying."

30

I WANTED TO BE with Bethanne in the worst way. She seemed so down, like she was whipped. But I figured if Gravesly's son and daughter was coming, it might be best if they was all alone together. So I stayed where I was back on the kitchen porch with Marlene and Buck, listening to the tree frogs and feeling my brain slide from one fret to another.

I could hear the gawkers making noise out front, but the cops had them plastic tapes up making a boundary they couldn't cross. Them busybodies couldn't get even a glimpse of us out back of the house.

It was a comfort to me to have Buck near. I could tell he was hurting, but it seemed like the pain'd calmed down some, so that was a blessing. But Marlene was nothing but a worry. She kept shifting round, all nervous like she was gonna run. Or talk. I kept wondering if she was gonna hold up til all this was over.

Then I started to worrying about Momma. It was way past midnight, and her shift was over. Bethanne told me she'd left a note, but Momma'd still be filled with dread for all of us. I didn't wanna call her, cause she'd want the whole story, and I couldn't tell her with all them cops round. I scooched closer to Buck and whispered how I was feeling.

He give me a gentle smile. "Don't worry, little buddy. I'll call Vicki and have her call your Momma. She can come over to our house and wait for us." And he was as good as his word, getting out his cell phone right then and letting Vicki know what to do without the cops realizing what he was talking about.

Just then Chief Hastings pulled up in this metallic gold SUV. My face musta showed my reaction, cause Buck said, "Cadillac Escalade," and shook his head. How a man on a police salary could afford such a car was a mystery to me.

Anyhow, I watched Hastings swagger over to talk to his boys. That's what he called 'em, even though every one of 'em was thirty if he was a day. And at least one of 'em was pushing retirement.

It's not just that he kept calling 'em his boys. Everything about him said he was the king and they was just peasants. I caught a couple of 'em giving each other a look behind his back, and it was easy to see they thought about as much of him as I did.

He didn't have on his uniform, neither. I know he was called out in the middle of the night, but you'd think he'd put on his uniform for official business. Not him. Had on some kinda designer jeans and this pretty shirt, all pressed and starched. He always was a snappy dresser. Course the effect was starting to get ruined by the hint of a soft belly, but he was working on that. Had this exercycle in his office. That's what I heard at the trailer park, anyway.

After a while, he caught sight of us and sashayed over. "Well, well. Buck Perrine. Didn't know you were out of jail."

I watched Buck knuckle under to that grand-feeling pig, and it broke my heart. That's what happens when you do time. The police'll never let you forget it, even if you spend the rest of your life holding down a job and going to church on Sunday.

Then Hastings turned round like he'd just seen me and Marlene. "You-all still here? We got your contact info. Best you get on home now." He bent over and winked at us like we was too cheap for words. "But don't you leave town now, you hear?"

Made me sick, worrying about Hastings recognizing my schoolgirl outfit from one of Jeffries' porn flicks, but he was too full of hisself to pay attention to what some trailer-trash girl was wearing.

His voice and his body got all hard when he stood up. He give Buck a nasty look. "That goes double for you, Perrine. You stick close to home."

Hastings' mean laugh followed him all the way back to his boys.

~~

Bethanne tried not to shudder. Lucinda's story made her realize there were two more suspects. Lucinda could have killed her father in order to keep the family secrets. Even if she was a daddy's girl. The family reputation might mean more to her. On the other hand, Clay could've taken revenge on Winston for what he'd done to him as a boy.

She jumped when she heard the Police Chief call out down below. "Clay. Thanks for coming. Sorry for your loss."

Clay mumbled something, and then Hastings' voice echoed through the night. "Lucinda's up in the apartment. Why don't you go give her a little consolation, and I'll join you-all just as soon as I get the rest of my boys' reports."

Lucinda rushed what she had to say before anyone else arrived. "Clay doesn't remember a thing about that night. He's totally blocked it, and that's for the best."

Clay's footsteps sounded like he was dragging himself up the steps. Bethanne had a clear vision of the photo of the naked boy with "CG 81" on the back. Did that stand for "Clay Gravesly, 1981"? Did Jeffries get young Clay to pose for him? With Winston's knowledge and consent? The thought sickened Bethanne. But then she had one even worse. What if Winston had taken the picture?

~

Didn't matter what that old Police Chief said, we naturally stuck round. I even got up to do a little recon. Figured Mr. Gravesly surely been murdered, and I wanted to see if there was any marks on the body. Or any signs of a struggle. But they had him in a body bag by the time I got there, and so many feet had walked round that pond, it was just one muddy mess.

So I snuck back to Buck and Marlene. "How we gonna get home?"

Buck shook his head. "Don't know. Sure don't wanna ride home in no police car. Scare Vicki half to death."

Marlene spoke up. "Why don't you call her to come and get us?"

I give her a look that said just how dumb I thought she was. "Use your head. What makes you think Vicki's gonna bring two sleeping babies out into the night? And besides, she's waiting for Momma to come over."

Buck raised an eyebrow. "S'pose Bethanne'd let us use her car?"

But I was thinking about Bethanne going with us, so I said. "Let's wait til things calm down some, and we'll ask her. Be nice if she could come eat biscuits and gravy too."

~

Bethanne had just served coffee to Lucinda and Clay when Hastings pushed open the screen door. "Mind if I come in?" She held back a scowl when he paraded through the door without her say-so.

He looked at the steaming mugs. "Could do with some of that myself."

She forced her aching back out of the chair, consciously chose the cracked mug and poured him a coffee. What an ass he was. But a dangerous ass. He'd wanted her out of the picture before all this. What now?

Hastings helped himself to the remaining chair, slurped his coffee and beamed at Lucinda and Clay. "My heart goes out to you, it surely does. Losing both parents like this." He shook his head as if the whole thing was incomprehensible. "Two fatal accidents in as many months."

Relief washed through Bethanne when Hastings' attention lingered on Winston's children. She wasn't sure she could keep her thoughts from showing. What did he mean, "accidents"? Was he trying to pull off another cover-up?

"I know how anxious you must be to have this all settled," Hastings continued. "I'm going to release the body just as soon as I can get the paperwork done. Don't think we need an autopsy. Cause of death is obvious."

Bethanne looked at Clay and Lucinda. He seemed in shock, but she was nodding like she was getting what she wanted.

Hastings finished his coffee. "Clay, why don't you come down with me, and we can talk over some details I don't want to bother Lucinda with."

He put an arm around Clay's shoulders and steered him toward the door. Hastings turned back to the two women standing side by side, and Bethanne held her breath. "Lucinda," he said and bowed his head politely. He pointedly turned his back on Bethanne and left without another word.

Lucinda pivoted to her. "See what trouble you've caused? Daddy never meant anybody any harm."

Bethanne's spine was hurting so bad she lost any constraint she might have had. "What about his grandkids? What about his shot of their bare bums? And those DVDs he lets Jeffries show—how do you know they're not kiddy porn?"

Lucinda's face blanched, and her right arm jerked out from her side like she was going to slap Bethanne. But she got her body and her emotions under control. "You don't know what you're talking about. Daddy worships…"

She stopped, bit her lip and corrected herself. "…worshipped children and their innocence. In the nineteenth century, no one would have thought twice about him photographing them in their purity. But nowadays, you and everybody else has a dirty mind. Daddy would never let Jeffries show kiddy porn in his house."

Bethanne gave Lucinda a scornful look and waited to see what else she would say.

Lucinda put her hands on her hips. "Jesus, you're thick. Why do you think I told Clay that story about Daddy seeing the surveillance video at Ralph's Rentals? I wanted you to hear. I wanted you to know you couldn't get away with your silly little games."

Bethanne mirrored Lucinda's posture and spat out her response. "They're not silly little games. Your whole family's been trying to cover up their dirty secrets." She shook her head and let contempt curl her lip. "What make you think you can keep the lid on when both your parents died trying?"

Lucinda laughed. "You threatening me? Do you really believe I'd be scared of you? Who pulled you under at the lake?" She grinned and licked saliva from the corner of her mouth.

Like a mad dog looking to bite, Bethanne thought.

Winston's daughter leaned down until her face was inches from Bethanne's. "Pulled you under enough to give you a warning. Maybe you didn't scare then, but you'd better be scared now."

31

ONCE ALL THEM PEOPLE left, Bethanne changed into a sleeveless blouse and seersucker pants. Said them jeans and heavy shirt was weighing her down.

I put on a pair of her shorts, so Momma wouldn't ask why I had on that funny schoolgirl outfit. Couldn't believe I'd slimmed down that much, but the elastic waist fit me just fine, and so did one of Bethanne's T-shirts.

Then Bethanne drove us over to Buck's. Took Marlene too. Didn't want her sliding off into the night and making trouble.

Momma grabbed ahold of me so tight I couldn't move. She was breathing something fierce, like she couldn't get enough air. I put my head right into that little hollow between her neck and her shoulder, trying hard not to cry. When I looked up, she was blinking away the tears too.

Course Vicki was hugging and kissing Buck, and then she and Momma wanted to hear the whole story.

We went into the kitchen and set down at Buck's round maple table. He surely was pleased to own that piece of furniture. Been in his family for generations, and he got it when his momma died. Buck turned the air conditioner on high, cause some folks sleep with their windows open, and he didn't want nobody hearing what we had to say. The cool air sure felt good after all that standing and sitting round in the heat of an August night.

Vicki'd made us the most delicious biscuits, and we scarfed 'em down as fast as we could get 'em in our mouths. I was licking gravy off my lips and begging for more. Marlene too. Guess them big boobs take a lot of feeding.

Buck kept saying how he really blew it, letting Jeffries get away. But me and Bethanne both praised him real good. He surely was brave busting in there like that, and we wanted Momma and Vicki to know how great we thought he done. Once we was through, Buck was setting taller, and Vicki was smiling at him like he was the grandest hero in history.

Well, we finished telling all about what happened at the barn, then we started on the doings at Graveslys'. By the time we got done, it was nearly five a.m., and outside the window, the sky was starting to get just the littlest bit lighter. I was worried about Momma not getting her sleep. But I wasn't sleepy none, and she didn't seem to be neither. In fact we was all so full of energy, we was ready for the next adventure.

Throughout the whole thing, Marlene didn't say one word. Just set there drinking her coffee and turning her head from one person to the other while they was talking.

All of a sudden, Bethanne leaned across the table and stared right in her face. "Where's Jeffries?"

Marlene scooted down like she wanted to sink under the table, but Bethanne's gaze held her up. Marlene's eyes flew to the ceiling. "How would I know?"

"Because you know him really well," Bethanne said. "He uses you for sex, and he brags to you about his secrets."

⌒

Bethanne knew she was taking a chance, but she remembered Jeffries coming to Winston's backdoor and talking about his live-in girlfriend. She watched Marlene's glance flit around the room like she was looking for a way out.

Buck was sitting near the door, and he casually put a foot halfway up the frame, blocking the exit.

Bethanne's back pain had relaxed, and she was warming to her task. She reached across the table and placed a hand on Marlene's forearm. "You know Jeffries lives with his main girlfriend, don't you?"

Marlene gnawed her pouty lips.

"If I'd done all you did for a man like Jeffries," Bethanne said, "and he was so cheap with his appreciation, I'd want to get back at him."

Part of her mind was roaming through her own life. More than one man had done her dirt. She'd always taken it too long and never fought back. The best she'd ever managed was finally to leave.

"He's been using you, Marlene. And when things got rough tonight, he threw you away."

Marlene put her chin in her hands, elbows on the table, head down. "I was planning to replace that bitch, but it didn't do no good. I'm just for relief when he's all hot from making one of his porn flicks."

Buck sat up. "What's her name? Where does she live?"

Marlene pulled back from him and closed her lips in a tight line. Damn, Bethanne thought, just when they were getting somewhere. She lifted the coffee pot from the plastic cloth and poured some more into Marlene's cup. Then she narrowed her eyes at Buck to keep quiet. He nodded.

Bethanne sipped her own coffee. "Been too many guys like that in my own life. You know what I think?" She noted Marlene's eyes slewing toward her. "They get away with too much for too long."

She leaned toward Marlene and whispered, "Maybe it's time for a little payback."

I was about to fall over watching Bethanne play Marlene like that. I knew enough to keep my mouth shut, even if Buck didn't. But when Bethanne talked about payback, I couldn't keep quiet. "You mean go over there now?"

"No, I mean we got everything we need to go to the State Police. We got the DVD and the pills. You and Marlene can both give evidence. And Marlene can tell where she thinks Jeffries is hiding out."

I looked at Marlene, and she was setting real still like she was giving all this the carefullest thought.

Bethanne lit a cigarette. "This isn't a job for us. Let the State Police take over from here."

Buck jumped up. "Hold on, Missus. I can't take this no more. I can't let a man get the best of me and just do nothing. I'm gonna kick his..."

Vicki put a hand on his arm, and he seemed to recollect there was ladies present.

Bethanne offered Buck a Kool, but he shook his head. "You'll be hurting him more than he ever hurt you," she said. "You turn him over to the cops, he's going to jail. When he comes out, he'll be an old man."

Buck's face was all hard with his disagreement, but Bethanne wasn't giving up easy. "I think Jeffries may have killed Winston."

"No shit" come outta my mouth afore I could stop it. Momma give me a look, and I knew I was in for it once we got home.

Bethanne was staring at Buck more intense than I ever saw her. "If Jeffries did kill him, then he's more dangerous than we thought, and we don't want to go up against him."

Buck shrugged. "What's the difference? We went up against him afore."

"A lotta difference," Vicki said. "That was to save Eden."

I give her a big smile, and Bethanne nodded. "Now we just need to get him arrested," she said. "Let the State Police handle the investigation."

Buck crossed his arms over his chest. "And if he gets away? If I was him, I'd be packing up and heading for parts unknown."

Bethanne seemed at a loss for words, so I put my two cents in. "You know what I seen on the TV? Best time to win the day is with a dawn raid."

⌐⌐

Bethanne sat on the front seat of Buck's truck and wondered if she was losing her mind. What was she doing, going against her better judgment? Maybe it wasn't going to be a dawn raid—the sun was already peeping over the horizon—but there surely was going to be some kind of confrontation. She seemed to be the only one at all concerned. Buck was whistling, and Eden was going on about the right tactics once they got to Joellen's.

That was Jeffrie's girlfriend, Joellen Grimes. Marlene had finally given up her name, and Eden had found her address in the phone book. She lived some ten miles away, in a little town called Bealton.

Now Marlene sat in the back, chattering with Eden like the whole thing had been her idea all the time. Bethanne felt like she ought to take some pride in turning Marlene, but things had gone much farther than she'd intended.

Eden's mother and Vicki had joined Bethanne in arguing against anybody going after Jeffries, but they'd given in when they'd seen the fire in Buck's eyes. He was going regardless, all three women finally realized.

Everyone wanted Eden and Marlene to stay at Buck's house. But Eden had pointed out that once the police got Jeffries, she and Marlene would have to give evidence. So it was decided they'd come along and stay in the truck once they arrived.

All this meant Bethanne felt she had to trail along to keep things from getting out of hand, especially if Eden was going. But she wasn't happy about it.

She was starting to worry about an even more complex picture. Could Winston and Mary Margaret have been murdered by the same person? Someone trying to cover up the kiddy porn? But who'd killed them? Jeffries made the best suspect, but not the only one. Chief Hastings had threatened to take Bethanne out only recently. Clearly a man who thought death was a solution.

Then there were the other men at Winston's "poker nights." She recalled seeing some of them sneaking DVDs into their pockets as they left. Maybe Jeffries didn't show kiddy porn in Winston's house, but he might have been selling it in the back hall. Any of those creeps might've killed to keep from having his secret vice exposed.

Buck passed the Bealton town limits, and Bethanne's attention was yanked back to why they were there.

The game plan was to see if Jeffries was at Joellen's. If he was, Buck was going to call the State Police and say Jeffries was holed up in the house with his teenage cousin making kiddy porn. That'd get them there in a hurry, and then Bethanne and company could tell the whole, complicated story. With proof.

And if Jeffries made a move, Buck was ready to ensure it was his last one until the State Police arrived.

They were almost to Joellen's. Bethanne felt her backache returning. And her stomach knotting. Here she was following another man with his macho hanging out. She should have stood up to Buck and insisted they drive to State Police Headquarters with their evidence.

But would the state cops have believed their story about some of Lewiston's finest citizens? A story told by a drunk, a trailer-trash kid, a jailbird and a two-bit porn star? By the time they'd have convinced the cops, Jeffries could have been on his way out of the country.

She watched Buck park the truck across the street from Joellen's shabby bungalow and gave up worrying. Too late now, anyway.

32

I SET THERE IN that truck, jiggling my feet, staring out first one window, then the other. How come I had to stay in the backseat with Marlene? I didn't do nothing wrong. That's all I could think of. Felt like I was gonna bust with how unfair it was.

Bethanne was setting in the front seat, and she wouldn't have none of it. "We shouldn't even be here," she said, "but now we are, I'm making sure nothing happens to you."

I ducked my head and peeked up at the sky turning from dawn to early morning. All the truck windows was down, and I could hear birds whispering. Somewhere a rooster was advertising his manhood. Even though the sun was just barely up, sweat was seeping outta every pore in my body. Sure was gonna be another hot one.

I looked at Bethanne. What had I got that woman into? She didn't wanna come at first, but then she changed her mind. Now here she was at Joellen's, trying to protect me once again.

The truck was full of that greasy smell of oily rags. Buck'd probably tossed 'em on the back floor in case they was ever needed again. I wished Buck was with us, but he'd gone round the house to make sure Jeffries didn't bolt out the back door. He'd already called the State Police as soon as we seen Jeffries' fancy car out front. Now all we had to do was wait for their Smoky Bear hats to show up.

If Joellen wasn't any better than her run-down, itty-bitty old house, Jeffries had surely sunk low in the world. When we was telling our stories at Buck's, Momma said Jeffries used to be somebody in Lewiston. Married this doctor's daughter, had a couple kids, joined the country club. Then something happened, she said. Left his family and started running round. His wife divorced him, and he acted like he didn't even know she was gone.

Midlife crisis, that's what. Learned about that on the TV. Wife got the house, so here he was holed up with some white-trash hottie and about to be in the worst trouble of his life.

And there I was, tired of being cooped up on the sidelines. And tired of Bethanne being so negative. So I just opened the door, got out and run along Buck's dew-slicked path through the grass.

Felt kinda mean, treating Bethanne like that, but there she was, treating me like a little kid again. After all we been through.

⸺

"Shit," Bethanne whispered. Eden was going to get them all killed. But Bethanne couldn't shout for fear of alerting Jeffries. And she couldn't go after Eden either. Someone had to stay in the truck and watch the front of the house.

And Marlene. The girl's hand was sneaking toward her door handle.

Bethanne grabbed Marlene's other wrist. "Don't even think about it." She held on and twisted around to keep watch on Joellen's door.

She needed something, anything to happen. Her back was screaming from holding that contorted position, and she wanted the whole thing to be over. She pictured Jeffries in jail, his only comfort a monthly visit from Joellen.

Was it her imagination, or was the doorknob turning? She blinked. No, the door was opening. Where were the cops? Where was Buck? What could she do?

"Look out, Pete! They're coming for ya." Too late, Bethanne turned back and clapped a hand over Marlene's mouth.

—

When I heard Marlene shout, I wished I was still in that truck. I'da busted her chops. That girl was playing both ends against the middle, and I wanted to show her the consequences in the worst way.

I took off running, but Buck passed me afore I even got to the corner of the house. By the time I run to the front, Jeffries was lugging this big old suitcase toward his car, and Buck was diving through the air. Just like he used to do in high school when he was bringing down the quarterback.

Joellen come flying outta the house with an iron skillet, ready to bop Buck on the head. Well, I couldn't have that, so I jumped on her back like a shell on a turtle. But I wasn't big enough to hold her, and she just kept going.

Next thing I knew, Bethanne's got ahold of Joellen too, and we're wrassling her to the ground. All three of us grunting and sweating so much it was hard to hold on.

First I'm on top, then Joellen, then Bethanne. Clothes all wet from the dew. Joellen cussing and tearing at our hair. Good thing I cut mine all off. I saw her pull out a handful of Bethanne's.

That made Bethanne so mad, she socked Joellen in the jaw. That woman's head snapped back like her neck was made outta rubber, and me and Bethanne managed to both get on top of her at the same time.

Felt like I was on the high dive, finally ready to jump off for the very first time. I looked over at Buck, and he was whaling the daylights outta Jeffries. Had him down with both knees on his shoulders and going to town. Jeffries was trying to put up a fight, but Buck had him pretty well where he wanted him.

Bethanne took off her belt and tied up Joellen's feet. Then she took the shoe laces outta my sneakers and tied her hands. Good thing Bethanne had a web belt and not leather. That's all I could think of. Ain't it funny how your brain works sometimes?

I stayed setting on Joellen in case she got any ideas, and Bethanne hustled back to the truck. I could see Marlene cowering inside, and I wondered why she hadn't took off.

Bethanne brought some rope outta the back of the truck and helped Buck hog-tie Jeffries. That man's face was pretty much a mess, and I was starting to worry the cops was gonna charge Buck with assault and battery again. But I surely was proud of him, even so.

⌐⁻

Bethanne returned to the truck to make sure Marlene hadn't been able to break loose. As soon as she'd seen Jeffries run out of the house, Bethanne had jumped in the back with Marlene and tied her to the hand-hold with one of Buck's oily rags. No way she was going to let that girl keep switching sides.

"Help," Joellen hollered. "Somebody call the police."

Bethanne looked to see if Jeffries was going to shush her, but he seemed too beat up to care. The neighbors were coming out of their houses, so she walked back to where Joellen was lying on the ground, Eden perched on top.

"Somebody already did," Bethanne said. "They're on their way."

Buck grinned. "I'm sure old Pete here…" he nudged Jeffries with his heavy hunting boot. "…would just love to show 'em his DVDs."

He looked at the neighbors drawing near. "Go on home, folks. This jerk's been dealing drugs and making kiddy porn. Now he's gonna pay."

The neighbors pulled back with disgust on their faces. But they waited to see what else was going to happen.

Bethanne sat on the front steps and lit a cigarette. The peeling paint felt rough through the thin cotton of her trousers, but it eased her back to have her bum down and her knees up.

Too old for this kind of thing, she thought. Staying up all night, wrestling younger women to the ground, trying to keep up with a thirteen year-old kid.

She glanced over at Eden. The girl seemed to have grown older in these last few days. And slimmer. All that baby fat was just about gone. Eden sat there triumphant, but her eyes had lost their innocence. Bethanne didn't know whether to laugh or cry.

33

THE STATE POLICE SHOWED up not long after we hogtied Jeffries and Joellen, and we was the heroes of our own stories.

Well, not right away. Course the whole thing looked pretty fishy to the cops. And they wanted to know why we hadn't called the local police. So they took us all into custody while they sorted everything out. And that's how we spent most of the afternoon. But at least they fed us. Sandwiches outta their canteen. Tasted pretty good too.

By the time we showed 'em the DVD and the pills, and Bethanne give 'em the photos she took of who watched them porn flicks, they was starting to believe us. Then Jeffries decided he'd better make a deal, and he named names, including Chief Hastings and a lotta other important men besides. Said he was selling kiddy porn right under Gravesly's nose. But we'll never know the truth of that.

I couldn't help but keep on wondering what I'd been wondering all along. How come them men, with all their wealth and power, had to sink down to having them porn parties once a week at Gravesly's house? Was they missing something in their makeup?

Funny thing was, though, Jeffries swore up and down he didn't kill Gravesly. Said he phoned the man to warn him but never went near him. Only made sense Jeffries'd rather admit to drugs and porn than own up to a murder charge. I purely hated his guts, but I had to admit that I didn't know whether Jeffries done it or not.

Marlene turned tail one more time and offered up everything she knew just as fast as the stenographer could take it down. Trust Marlene to look out for her own self whichever way the wind was blowing. Even if she couldn't write her own statement.

Anyhow, once the State Police realized we done the right thing, they started telling us we done the wrong thing. Taking too much into our own hands. Risking our lives and safety. Beating up the suspect. Shoulda come to 'em afore and let 'em do their jobs. Stuff like that.

But Bethanne stood up to 'em. Said just how much would they believe folks like us if we didn't come with the proof. Specially with us having to lay the blame on Chief Hastings and them other big shots. The Police Commander didn't have no comeback to that, and I realized Bethanne was a treasure more precious than anything Ray-Jean ever found.

Bethanne sat in the interview room's gray metal chair trying to figure out how much to tell the State Police. Would Jeffries say what hold he had over Winston? Would Clay have to face up to what had happened at the father-son camping trip?

Would the State Police investigate Winston's death now? She felt sure he'd been murdered, probably Mary Margaret and Ray-Jean too. Should she tell them her suspicions or just stick to the facts? God, she hated having to talk to them at all.

She looked around the room. Walls in two shades of gray, gray linoleum on the floor, gray furniture. Strong smell of industrial disinfectant. Did the cops go out of their way to make this place as dismal as they could? She was already down in the dumps. She didn't need their help to get more depressed. She took in the "No Smoking" sign and felt her vitals twinge. She needed to get this over with, make her statement and go outside for a cigarette.

The door opened and Trooper Kelly entered. She'd already met him during the preliminaries. She couldn't help noticing his tall, trim form. Was he as smart as he was good-looking?

Trooper Kelly sat down on the other side of the table. "Are you aware that Mr. Gravesly's daughter is rushing to have him cremated?"

⌒⌒

After being up all night and taking Jeffries down and talking to the State Police, we was so beat, all we could do was each of us fall into our own beds and sleep for hours and hours. The next day, Bethanne come by and invited me over to her apartment for lunch. That way, me and her could have us a private talk. On the way, Bethanne told me all about the hurry to cremate Mr. Gravesly.

"Maybe Lucinda killed her father," I said. "But I surely can't see why."

Bethanne come back with Lucinda's story that long ago Jeffries took this compromising—that's what she called it, "compromising"—picture of Mr. Gravesly and his son at a camping trip.

"So maybe Lucinda killed him to protect her brother," I said.

Just then some guy cut Bethanne off at the Gravesly driveway. She honked her horn and shouted, "Son of a bitch!"

That kinda shocked me, cause Bethanne only swore in front of me that one time when she was drunk. But she turned to me right away and begged my pardon. Made me wonder if I was getting more grown up, that she would forget herself like that.

Anyhow, Bethanne said Lucinda was a daddy's girl, so it didn't make no sense she'd kill her father. If she was protecting anybody, she was protecting Mr. Gravesly.

Bethanne no more'n got the car into the space between the house and the garage than the kitchen door banged open, and Gravesly's maid came hustling out. Wiping her hands down her flowered dress like she needed to get something nasty off it.

"Miz Bethanne," she said. "You got to help me. The police are after me to tell them if Mr. Winston had any enemies. And you know how you two didn't get along."

The sickening smell of boxwood drifted across the drive and made Bethanne's head reel. Did Mae think she was a suspect? Bethanne made herself calm down. No jumping to conclusions. Facts first.

She got Mae into the kitchen and asked Eden to pour them all a glass of iced tea from the fridge. She put a firm hand on the housekeeper's shoulder and set her down at the table. "You got to collect yourself, Mae. You don't want the neighbors calling the police again."

Mae gulped her tea. "No'm, I don't. I don't want the police here. But I don't understand how Mr. Winston ended up dead. You-all didn't have another fight, did you?"

"I wasn't anywhere near here from Tuesday afternoon until we found Winston's body after midnight." Bethanne nodded to Eden to sit on the corner stool, so she wouldn't distract Mae. "And there was always somebody with me to prove it."

Mae sighed. "That's truly some good news. I didn't want to point the cops toward Miz Mary Margaret's sister." Her fingers began spinning a cigarette pack on the table like they needed something to do.

Bethanne looked at the pack. Blue. French. Clay's cigarettes. Only one gone. "Where'd those come from?"

Mae regarded the pack, still twirling it on the table top. "After the police left, I walked all over this house, trying to make myself believe that Mr. Winston was gone. Ended up in his study. That was his special place, and I guess I wanted to be near him somehow."

Bethanne tried not to let her impatience show. "Is that where you found the cigarettes?"

Mae nodded. "Been worried about that myself. I know how Mr. Clay likes these French cigarettes. They weren't there when I vacuumed and dusted Tuesday morning." Tears started down Mae's cheeks. "After Mr. Winston asked me to start cleaning his study again."

⌒

I was setting there quiet as a fly on the wall, but it didn't do no good once Mae told about finding them cigarettes. Bethanne give her a kleenex and said what we all needed was something to eat. Then we'd feel better.

Made me mad when Bethanne told me to help Mae fix sandwiches while she went in the study to call Clay and ask him to meet her out at the lake. It wasn't that I minded helping a black woman in the kitchen. Do that all the time out at the church when we're having a social. But Bethanne was trying to cut me outta what was gonna happen. Trying to protect me again, probably. But I wasn't having none, and I was ready to tell her too.

But she never give me a chance. She snuck out the front door, round the house and back to her car. When I heard that motor start up, I run out the kitchen door, but I was too late.

"Son of a bitch!" I shouted. If she can say it, so can I.

⌐⌐

Bright sunbeams shot down through the trees, flashing in Bethanne's eyes and making her squint to see the lake road.

Clay, how could it be Clay? The towheaded boy turned family man. Her little pal, a killer? Impossible. The photo in the apartment and the one Jeffries took on the camping trip reared up to mock her. Was Winston molesting his son all those years ago? And Clay suppressing it until now, when he finally broke? Her eyes began to water. Just the bright sunlight, she told herself. But it wasn't.

Bethanne pulled into the lake house drive and saw Clay standing at the start of the dock, looking toward the water. Her wobbly fingers took the key from the ignition, opened the car door and slammed it behind her.

A gray cloud covered land and water, like a parasol come to soothe her eyes from the sun. A breeze drifted across the lake, but it didn't relieve the heat and humidity.

Clay whirled at the sound. "I can't stay long. Got to get back to the kids." He gestured with his chin toward the bungalow. "They can't believe Granddaddy's gone too."

Okay, Bethanne thought, let's get right to it. Even so, she paused to clench her jaw and find the strength. "What happened the night Winston died?"

"Whaddya mea…" he started to say, then shut his mouth like a bee'd flown near enough to sting his tongue. He walked away from her, hands shoved in pockets, to the end of the dock.

Bethanne followed, her lips set in a firm line. He'd have to speak sooner or later, and she couldn't trust her voice not to tremble.

Clay kept his back to her. "I finally found the will to open Mom's diary. Just cut the leather strap and started reading."

Bethanne was puzzled. Mary Margaret died nearly three months ago. What did this have to do with Winston dying two days ago?

He looked up at the drifting cloud. "The early weeks were just the usual. Volunteering at The Evergreen Retirement Community. Playing bridge with her girlfriends. Working in her garden when spring came. Then everything changed."

Guilt swept through Bethanne. She should have been the one to read that diary. Why'd she give it to Clay? Why hadn't she been a better sister to Mary Margaret? Maybe none of this would have happened if Mary Margaret had had someone to confide in, something more supportive than a diary.

Clay's voice hauled her away from those thoughts. He scowled. "Dad had this obsession, something to do with sex. He made Mom a solemn promise to quit and get help."

He turned to Bethanne, his hands almost prayerful. "He gave her that Mercedes in token of his pledge. A symbol he intended to keep that promise forever. Even the buttery color was specially chosen to show how much she meant to him."

Clay shifted his focus across the lake, and Bethane followed his gaze. The breeze had died down, and the surface was as flat as the dock. He took a breath and said, "This girl found out some secret about Mom."

Bethanne flinched as he continued, "I don't know what, Mom just wrote 'my secret.' The girl started blackmailing her. Then the girl broke into the chauffeur's apartment and discovered something about Dad too. She began asking for more and more money, threatening to go to the police."

Clay pivoted toward the bungalow. "Next thing, Mom found dirty pictures at the lake house when she was getting it ready for summer. She knew they weren't old ones, because she'd been through the house after his pledge and destroyed them."

Bethanne's mind was racing. Winston and dirty pictures. Poker nights. Jeffries. The camping trip. It was all starting to come together, but she needed more. "So what happened?"

Mary Margaret's golden boy hugged himself as tears began to streak his face. "Mom felt totally betrayed. Dad lied to her. He never meant to give it up. He just gave her that car to get her off his back. She hated herself. She hated him. And she hated that car."

He turned back to look along the planks toward the water. "She wanted to drive off the dock there and then. Destroy the car and herself too."

Bethanne looked out at the lake, flat and gray and shiny. Like the granite on Mary Margaret's grave. She shuddered. She'd been right early on, but it was no comfort.

"She needed to get rid of the girl too," Bethanne said. "So she nursed that self-loathing and came back another day."

Clay turned reddened eyes to Bethanne. "The girl, the car, herself. Roar down the hill and off the dock. Everything in one go." He tried to smile but it came out so full of sadness that Bethanne felt like she would weep.

"Mom always was good at planning," he said, "at holding herself in check and making things happen. She wanted it to seem like an accident. So the family'd be spared a trial with all the scandal coming out in the open."

Bethanne got her own emotions in control and returned Clay's look. Her thoughts filled with his athleticism, his strength, how quickly he burned the photo in the apartment, his cigarettes in Winston's study.

"You've carried all this burden for a while," she said.

He nodded.

"But what happened the night Winston died?" Bethanne held her breath.

34

CLAY PUSHED HIS LIPS forward, then pulled them back in a grimace. "Dad phoned, said Jeffries had called him, and now he needed to talk with me."

Bethanne let out some of the air that had been trapped inside.

"We started out in the study," Clay continued, "but Dad couldn't stand being cooped up inside. Not after Jeffries'd called to say you-all were hot on the trail and it was just a matter of time. Dad calmed down some when we walked to the lily pond. Guess it made him feel better being near something Mom made."

Clay's knees buckled and he sat down on the dock. "He told me, Aunt Bee. Told me what a beautiful boy I was, how he longed to touch me, to feel my innocence enter his pores. How he took pictures of me when I was asleep, to capture that purity. It turned my stomach."

It made Bethanne sick too. How she wished she didn't have to go through with this, that she could run away and not ever have to know. She thought about two girls whispering in an Alabama night, about a tow-headed boy rushing to throw his arms around her, about all the failures in her own life. Surely, just this once, she could do something right.

Bethanne knelt beside Clay. "Was that all it was?"

He hung his head. "Dad swore nothing happened, ever. But Jeffries took an incriminating photo and blackmailed him. Dad was helping me into my pajamas. Something about the camera angle made it look like...you know. Dad paid off Jeffries with legal favors for years. To protect me, he said."

"But you didn't believe him."

"No, I believed him. About what happened at the camping trip. If it'd been anything more than that, I'm sure I'd have remembered."

He sat there in silence so long, Bethanne thought he wouldn't finish. Lucinda's version of the story came into sharp focus. Why had young Clay been crying if nothing bad had occurred? Bethanne tried to keep her voice gentle, recalling her own childhood experiences with a sweating uncle. "Sometimes kids block things they don't want to remember."

Clay looked out toward the spot where this mother's car had plunged into the lake. "I don't really know whether two grown men ruined a boy's life that summer or not. But I've always felt like something was missing, something taken from me. Was that a memory of what really went on?"

"I don't know," Bethanne said. "Maybe. But whatever happened, it wasn't your fault. You have to believe that." She forced her attention away from the night of the camping trip and back to the body in the pond. "Did it make you mad, what Winston told you?"

Clay kept staring at the water in front of the dock, as if he could call back his mother's speeding car and return her to his life. "Seemed like Mom was always trying to protect me from something. Like she'd do anything to keep me from being hurt. I never felt that way with Dad."

Bethanne felt sympathy rise up for Clay. He was literally squirming with the pain of remembering. But her conscience forced her to go on. "Did Winston make you mad, Clay?"

When he spoke, she could hear the tears in his voice, and her own eyes stung, but she made herself keep still and listen. The muggy air felt like a weight on her shoulders, pushing her aging knees deeper into the dock.

"Dad said the whole story was going to come out," he said. "It was just a matter of time. Jeffries'd get caught, and he'd tell the cops everything. He'd show them the photo, and before long, the whole town'd think they knew what kind of boy I was. And wonder what kind of man I am now."

Clay pulled his knees up and buried his head in his arms. The pose reminded Bethanne of how he'd tried to make himself small when they'd played hide-and-seek so many years ago.

She struggled to banish the vision of that little tow-headed boy, but it stayed to nip at her heart. "What did you do, Clay? Hit him? Push him?"

He kept his head down, muffling his voice. "I kept thinking about how Dad had really killed Mom. She gave her life to keep his secret, and he wasn't worth it. I thought about my kids and Lucinda's, about how he was always messing with them, taking photos and videos of them. What else might he do? I wasn't sure what he'd done to me, but I knew if it came out, I'd have to leave town. Move my whole family and start over. Maybe do that anyway, just to protect my kids."

He raised a tear-stained scowl and faced Bethanne. "Yeah, I pushed him. He turned his back on me, ashamed to look me in the eye, and I pushed him so hard he fell in the pond. I was wild with rage. How could he risk all of us for his disgusting obsession? I looked down at him, wallowing in Mom's lilies, and I thought, 'Serves you right, you son of a bitch. Gasping for breath in muddy water. Just like Mom did.' I ran off. Didn't even look back. He wasn't my father anymore."

Bethanne forced the words out. "Did you mean to kill him?"

Clay's face went slack. "I'll never know."

⚊

Course I didn't really mean that Bethanne was a son of a bitch. I was just saying that cause I was so mad. And when she come back from seeing Clay, I told her I was sorry, even though she didn't hear me say them curse words.

She patted my shoulder, smiled down at me and said with so much commiseration, I like to die, "That's okay. We all say things we don't mean sometimes."

I was basking in the moment, but Mae couldn't wait. "What about Mr. Clay?" she said.

Bethanne went over and patted her on the shoulder too. "Clay *was* here Tuesday, but much earlier in the evening. We can just leave that worry alone."

Something about the tone of her voice made me wonder if that was all there was to it. Mae looked at her funny too. But Bethanne said she needed to drive me home to take care of Cruz afore Momma left for her shift. So there wasn't no chance for either of us to ask her questions.

Once we got in the car, Bethanne told me about Miz Gravesly leaving this diary that her son read. And he told her how it backed up what Bethanne first suspicioned. Her sister had killed herself and

Ray-Jean too, cause of the blackmail. It was hard for me to let go of the idea that Jeffries done it, cause he been so mean to me, but I had to accept the proof of that diary, even if I couldn't read it myself. Least I'd been right about the blackmail part.

Bethanne had the kindness not to gloat over being right, and when I looked over at her, trying to drive and not cry, I could see how cut-up she was about it. I tried to comfort her, but I could see it wasn't helping much.

⁓

Bethanne dropped Eden at her trailer and drove back to her apartment. She turned off the engine and rested her head on the steering wheel. Lord, she was tired. And bowed down with guilt at how she'd just steered Eden away from the details of her conversation with Clay.

The heat boiled up from the concrete and through the car's open windows. Something thudded on her windshield, and she looked up. A giant grasshopper was taking off, no doubt looking for a cooler roost.

Mae came out on the kitchen porch. "Miz Bethanne? I fixed some fresh iced tea. You sure look like you could use some."

Bethanne tried to smile. "Best words I've heard all day." She got out of the car and started toward the porch.

The housekeeper smiled down at her, and Bethanne found herself bombarded with memories. Mae clumping up the stairs to help her clean the apartment. Mae stopping work to make her pancakes. Mae bucking her up when she wanted to cry. Mae acting like a friend, even when Bethanne was using the housekeeper for her own ends.

She felt humbled by Mae's generosity of spirit. Even more so when she recalled how she used to think of her as Mary Margaret's colored maid.

Bethanne climbed the porch steps and stood on equal footing with Mae. "Isn't it time you stopped that 'Miz' stuff and started calling me 'Bethanne'?"

Mae grinned. "Come on in the kitchen. I got the air conditioning full blast."

They sat at the big wooden table, their feet up on a third chair, their frosty glasses leaving wet rings on the flowered cloth.

"You going to stay in the apartment?" Mae asked.

"Dunno. Suppose I'll have to. For a while at least. Guess I'm going to have to find a job." Bethanne took a long sip of the sweet tea and felt her fatigue start to slip away. "What about you? I expect Lucinda'll write you a good recommendation so you can get another housekeeping post."

Mae pulled off her apron and tossed it on the table. "Not going to keep house now for anybody but Jim."

Bethanne felt her eyebrows rise. "But you told me you have to work. You two need the money. What're you up to?"

Mae put her feet on the floor and leaned across the table. "I got an idea. And maybe it can help you too."

35

So much happened so fast after Bethanne told me how her sister and Ray-Jean died, it was hard to keep up.

I learned I could live with Ray-Jean causing herself to be killed. After everything that happened by the time summer ended, her death seemed long ago. That didn't mean I was ever gonna forget her or stop thinking about her. She's still a part of me, even now.

But I could accept everything about her, good and bad. And always remember what a good friend she been to me when no one else even thought about it. On some days, when the sun is shining just right, I can still see us running through the woods to her hidey place, so she can show me her treasures.

The State Police was suspicious Gravesly's daughter was involved in her father's death cause she wanted him cremated so fast. They called for an autopsy, but it just showed that he hit his head on the edge of the lily pond, passed out and drowned. There was bruises on his body, but they coulda come from the fall. Or maybe he was pushed, but nobody could say for sure. So in the end, when they couldn't tell whether Gravesly's death was accident or murder, the cops had to let go of their suspicions.

Jeffries never did tell what kinda hold he had over Gravesly. Said there was some secrets he'd carry to his grave. Guess he had a little honor left way down deep after all. And there's a lesson in that, specially for me, still trying to figure out what honor requires a body to do.

That Marlene run off just as soon as Jeffries' trial was over. But not afore I give her a piece of my mind when she come crawling to the trailer, wanting to explain. Made me feel a whole lot better, standing up to her like that. Anyhow, we heard she was making porn flicks out in LA, so I guess she's still following her dream. Just like I'm gonna follow mine.

And I got the money to do it, cause I won me a reward. Seems this rich lady had a daughter who went bad. This girl got into drugs and porn and all kinda stuff and finally died afore she was eighteen. Well, the mother felt so terrible, she set up a fund to reward ordinary people for stopping child pornography. Me and Bethanne got five thousand dollars. Each. Buck too. Fifteen thousand in all. Ain't that something? We done what we thought was right, and we got a reward. Don't tell me there ain't no justice in this world.

Bethanne and Eden inched forward, immersed in the scents of cotton candy and popcorn drenched in something that wasn't real butter. That afternoon's storm had brought the promise of fall so near they could almost touch it. Across the park, the carousel's fake calliope oompahed its way through another recorded tune.

"Don't be like me," Bethanne said. "Go to college and make something of yourself. I've been talking to your momma about this. We both agree. You got the smarts, and now you got the chance."

Eden smiled at her. "Been thinking about that myself. I like learning things. Miss Bailey, she's my favorite teacher of all time, and she's been giving me extra books to read." She licked her bright red candy apple. "I know I got the brains, but that reward money ain't enough to pay for me to go to no college."

Above their heads, the crowd was shrieking. The waiting line moved on a few steps, and Bethanne said, "No, but that money can pay for other things, like books and clothes, room and board, transportation. You need to invest your money and make it grow."

Eden's nose wrinkled. "You mean give my money to some stranger? How I know he won't rip me off? I better do it myself."

They neared the front of the line. Previous riders streamed past, and Bethanne felt her chest swell with anticipation.

"You won't have time to learn all you need to know to invest successfully," she said. "You'll be too busy studying hard to get a scholarship."

Eden bit into the candy apple's hard coating, and cinnamon perfumed the air. "Scholarship? Ain't no way some kid from the Happy Hours Trailer Park gonna get a scholarship."

"If you make good grades, you can. We'll talk to your high school counselor when the time comes. In the meantime, let's get your reward money invested in something that'll grow."

"I ain't gonna hand over my money to no stranger I can't trust." She read the "No food or drink" sign and threw the candy apple in the trash bin.

Bethanne let Eden step into the car first. "We can ask Mr. Farnsworth to recommend somebody. He was Mary Margaret's lawyer. I trust him, and you can too."

Eden's eyes widened when the padded bar came down across their laps. "Okay, that's enough for now. I'll think on it, I surely will."

— —

When Ray-Jean died, I thought I'd lost my best friend. And I had, but I found a new one. You know what best friends do when they come into a little luck? They share it.

So me and Bethanne decided to take a little trip over to the this place by the ocean. Just for a couple days to give ourselves a little treat. School was gonna start on Monday, so it was our last chance to celebrate.

I never seen the ocean afore, except on the TV. When we got there, I just stood on the boardwalk, lost in awe of all that water. As far as the eye could see and always in motion, up and down, back and forth. No wonder folks is fascinated by the sea. I have to say, though, for all its glory, the ocean's still not as beautiful as our West Virginia hills.

Later on, I picked up the tab for Bethanne to have a mini-makeover at this spa. You wouldn't have known her when she come out. It wasn't just that she looked a whole lot younger. And pretty even. She was walking differnt and talking differnt. She was a whole new woman. It made me feel grand to give her that gift. The gift of her true self.

Then Bethanne give me a gift. A day at the fun zone. We was going on this old-fashioned roller coaster that went out over the ocean, come back and zipped down this track like greased lightning. I never done nothing like that in my whole life, and I was nervous and happy at the same time. Even if I wasn't brave enough to go on the more modern coaster that did a loop-the-loop so you're upside down part of the way. Decided I could hold off on that til next time.

While we was waiting for 'em to load the rest of the people in the cars, I asked Bethanne what she was going to do with her reward. Mainly I was trying to get her away from talking about me giving mine to some stranger to invest. But I was interested too. Seemed like she had so many ideas about what I should do with my money, she oughta have some for herself.

You coulda knocked me right outta the car when she got a little teary. Made me kinda scared about her answer.

"Turns out the mayor wants to revitalize downtown," Bethanne said. "so the City Council's giving out startup grants. Mae's applying for one to open a gift shop where Perry's Shoe Store used to be, and she needs a partner. What with the reward and the money Mary Margaret left me, I've got enough to pay my share. There's a studio apartment above the shop. After living in that one room over the garage, I'm used to it. Don't even dream about owning a condo anymore."

She grinned. "Well, maybe later. When the shop's going good, and we make some money."

Bethanne looked up the track and sucked at her lower lip. "Figuring on staying in Lewiston. If you wouldn't mind having me around."

I just set there looking at Bethanne, trying to get my thoughts into the right words. Then I took a big breath and let 'em tumble out. "We only met this summer, but I feel like you been my friend forever." Then I had to suck in my own lip. "And I hope you will be."

—⁓

Bethanne's emotions surged when the roller coaster grabbed the chain that pulled the cars up the first incline. The memory of Clay's confession filled her with conflicting reactions. Her heart felt too big for her chest, like it was pushing against her breastbone to get out.

She took a long breath and examined her conscience one more time. Yes, she'd done the right thing. What could be gained by making Clay confess to the police, in sacrificing other lives to the Gravesly secrets?

If the police investigated, Clay would have to confront whether or not Winston had abused him as a child. Bethanne had had to live with such memories, been stunted by them. And Lewiston would be abuzz for weeks about what had happened at the father-son camping trip. Everyone would look at Clay differently, sniggering behind his back and whispering the tale when he passed. When his wife passed. When his children passed.

Clay was haunted by what he'd done to his father. If he was convicted of Winston's death, he'd go to jail. His children's lives would be ruined. Three generations of Graveslys destroyed for Winston's obsession. Was that really justice? She stroked her sister's filigreed bracelet. Whatever Winston had done deserved to stay hidden, along with Mary Margaret's secret love child.

The riders squealed as the roller coaster swooped down through a corkscrew of turns. Then the car climbed up another incline, and the ride smoothed out. So did Bethanne's emotions. She was going to be partners in the gift shop with Mae. Pretty amazing when she thought back to how Robbie Ray had made her quit working at the gift shop all those years ago. That man was hard all over. Not just his fists, although Bethanne had the broken jaw to prove that. But he hadn't broken her spirit. Life hadn't broken her, no matter how much it tried.

She glanced at Eden's face, hazel eyes shining against tanned skin. How healthy she looked, so full of pride and hope. What losers they'd been when they'd met. Knocked down but not ready to give up. Who'd have believed they'd ever win?

⸺

When they started up the roller coaster, I grabbed ahold of that padded bar with both hands. Round and round and up and down we went. Kind of like the ocean, down below. Folks was screaming too loud for me to say a word. And if I'm honest, I was too terrified to even try.

My stomach kept lurching in every direction, but I managed to hold down our hot dog lunch. Bethanne had wanted me to try fried shrimp in a basket, but I wasn't ready for that. With all them new things coming so sudden that weekend, I just felt the need of something familiar—hot dog with mustard and relish. Didn't have no chili over there in Virginia, so I guess I was a little adventuresome, even with that lunch.

Anyhow, the roller coaster went up this last track so high it felt like we might be going to heaven. That give me a little break, and everybody else too, I reckon, cause they all stopped screaming.

I let my eyes wander across the ocean. Out there was the whole world. Places I only seen on the TV. But I could go there. Maybe. If I worked hard like Bethanne said.

I looked over at her, and she was looking right back. Such a beautiful smile on her face. Made me think about her staying in Lewiston, how we both got the money to make our dreams come true.

And I thought I might die with the joy of it.

QUESTIONS FOR
READING GROUP DISCUSSION

1. How did you feel about Eden and Bethanne at the beginning of the story? What words would you use to characterize each of them at that point?

2. How did you feel about Eden and Bethanne at the end of the story? What words best describe them now?

3. Does Eden seem mature for her age? Why do you think she might be that way?

4. Bethanne and Mary Margaret were sisters, raised in the same home. Yet their lives were very different and they ended up estranged. Why do you think this might have happened?

5. What was your reaction to how Eden dealt with Jeffries' guard dog? Was it believable? Why or why not?

6. As the story goes on, Eden's impressions of her friend, Ray-Jean, change. What lessons do you think Eden learned from Ray-Jean's choices?

7. Is Bethanne an alcoholic? Has she conquered her substance-abuse by the end of the story?

8. What did you think of how Mary Margaret solved her dilemma? How would you have handled it?

9. Most families have complex relationships between siblings. Who is stronger in the Gravesly family—Lucinda or Clay? Why do you think that might be?

10. Who's right about Winston's obsession? Is it Lucinda—He's a nineteenth century romantic who idolizes children? Or Bethanne— He's a pervert? Or do you see it a different way? How do you feel about him?

11. What do you think really happened between Winston and his son when Clay was a boy? What did Jeffries' photograph reveal?

12. How much does Lucinda know about the family secrets? What is her relationship with her father?

13. Why did Bethanne give the diary to Clay? Would you have done the same?

14. Did Winston really love Mary Margaret? Or was he just using her?

15. Throughout the story, we see Mae through Bethanne's eyes. How did you react to her changing views of Mae?

16. *Child's Play* is the first in a trilogy of mysteries set in Lewiston, West Virginia. Eden and Bethanne won't be the central characters in the next book, but they will reappear. What do you think will happen to them next?

Nancy Swing's next novel is also set in Lewiston, West Virginia. Here's a preview of the first chapter.

LAZARUS

1

THE SUMMER MY DAD was killed, I turned sixteen and fell in love.

When school let out, I had no idea two of them things was gonna happen. Not losing Dad and finding love. But they did, and they changed me for life. Left a lotta dreams behind. But got hold of some new ones too.

It sure hurt, Dad dying like that. Made me grow up faster'n I wanted to. But somebody had to take over being the man of the family, and me being the oldest, it was up to me. Soon as the funeral was over—only right the West Virginia Coal Company paid for it, him being killed when the tunnel caved in. And they give Mom something "for compensation." A pay-off we all thought, but what was she gonna do? Sue 'em? What with? How'd she pay a lawyer? So she took the money, and I went to work once we got through the funeral.

Used Dad's old truck to get around. Bagging groceries down at the Busy Bee, washing cars at the Pay-Lo Gas Station. But them two jobs together didn't pay enough. Mom had five children to feed, and that pay-off wasn't gonna last for long. I needed me a real job, but I didn't see how I was gonna find one, cause I was just too young. Didn't even have a high school diploma, so who was gonna hire me?

Then I heard about this widow come to live outside Lewiston on the old road to Moorestown, the one nobody takes no more, cause it's too curvy. Rather use the Interstate. Gets 'em there faster and safer. Anyway, I heard from the manager of the Pay-Lo that she was looking for somebody to help fix up this old cabin she'd bought. Dad was handier with tools than I'll ever be, but he taught us boys everything he could, and I figured I could hammer and saw with the best of 'em. So I drove out there one day, between bagging at the Busy Bee and washing cars, hoping she'd see the advantage of hiring someone cheap cause they was young and eager.

I knew where that cabin was. Musta stood there two hunnerd years at least, always in the Thomasson family. Then Floyd Thomasson took it into his head to go work in some Cleveland plant, and the whole place fell to ruin. I turned onto the dirt track that led down into the hollow where they built their cabin, and the first thing I saw was the roof caved in. Not all of it, but bad enough that it was gonna take some work to keep the rain out. The walls looked okay though, thick, made of logs from trees so big you don't see 'em like that no more. Them logs needed chinking, but I knew how to do that.

Parked the truck in front of the sagging porch and couldn't see a window that wasn't busted out. Called out "Howdy" a bunch of times, but didn't seem to be a soul about. Knocked on the door and peeked in one of them busted windows, but wasn't nobody to home.

Inside, I could see where the rain'd come through the caved-in roof and made a mess. Them wide-planked, hand-hewn floorboards was covered in wet leaves, and the smell of rot and mildew was everywhere.

Sure was gonna be a lotta work, getting that old place back in shape. And that was a good thing for me, if not for the new owner.

Looked around outside some, and all I could see was destruction, from the tumble-down stone walls that marked the property line to the overgrown vegetable garden them Thomasson women musta tended for generations. The chimney looked pretty good, though, the mortar just needing a little patching here and there among the field stones. Still, it was a gloomy place, set under giant trees that cast deep shadows even though the sun was full out. The smell of rotten wood was everywhere, what with some of them old trees falling down and being left to lie in the moldy leaves. Hard to imagine why a widow'd want to live alone in a place like that.

Started back to the truck and took a fall cause of a hole some critter'd dug. Fox, maybe. They do that if they smell something underground. Rolled over, looked in that hole and let out a little gasp. There was bones down there, lying every which way. Fox musta done that. Stirred 'em up myself, trying to figure out what was buried there. Didn't want to think it was one of them Thomassons, even though people did bury their dead on the farm back in the old days. Finally decided maybe some Thomasson had buried a dog. Least the bones wasn't human, cause the hip bone was all wrong. Kinda give me the shivers, though, and I set off for the truck at a trot.

Picked up a scrap of paper lying on the dashboard and wrote on it to say I'd be glad to help. Signed my name and phone number, and tucked it in the cabin doorjam. Then drove back to the Pay-Lo just in time to put on my coveralls and get to work.

Well, the widow called me that night and suggested we meet at the Quik Treet the next day. That's this drive-in, been here long before them fast food chains arrived, and I hope it'll be here long after they're gone. Food's a lot better, and you know you're dealing with somebody local. They got a few tables inside, and that's where she said we'd meet.

I set down facing the door, and it wasn't long before this woman come in who didn't look like nobody from around Lewiston, and that's for sure. Looked like she'd lived in the city for a long time and was trying to fit in but didn't have the hang of it yet. Jeans too new and big bucks. Same for her shoes and handbag. Looked like money'd come to her easy, and she knew how to spend it. Even her hairdo was wrong. High-style, like something you see on TV.

Well, she come right over and introduced herself, so she musta figured out who I was too. Anyway, I stood up and shook her hand.

She sure smelled nice. Not that drugstore perfume some of the girls at Lewiston High wear. Hers was differnt. Sweet and spicy, like them flowers we planted by our church door. Pinks, is that what they're called? Anyway, she smelled just like she looked. Expensive and not from here.

"Hi there," she said. "You must be Jimmy Lee. I'm Sarah Simmons." Deep down, under the education that was plainly there, you could hear just the faintest memory of West Virginia in her voice. Where'd she come from? And what was she doing back here?

Miz Simmons looked me up and down, like she was measuring me for a suit I could never buy. I sure felt awkward, but I held my ground and tried to look her in the eye.

"How old are you?" she said, and I had to tell her my age.

Would've liked to ask hers, but I knew enough to keep my mouth shut. Guessed she was forty or so.

It give me a worry that now she knew I was just a high school kid, but I wasn't gonna give up.

"I may be young," I said, "But I'm big and strong. And I know how to fix most things round a house. I ain't afraid of work, and I really need this job." My eyes got all blurry then, and she musta noticed, cause she suggested we get something to eat before we talked any more.

We went up to the counter, and she said she should pay cause I was doing her a favor to meet her there. Made me feel a little ashamed she wouldn't let me pay my own way, but I tried to be as thoughtful of her feelings as she was of mine. We carried our little red plastic baskets of burgers, Cokes and fries back to the same table and set down.

She dipped a couple fries into the little paper tub of ketchup they come with, chewed 'em good and said, "So tell me why you need this job."

And the way she said it, like she really wanted to know, not just for herself but for me, that warm way of asking made me open up. I didn't feel pitiful no more, and I laid it all out for her. Dad dying in the mine. Mom not having enough to take care of everybody. Me being the man in the family now, and working two jobs wasn't enough.

She didn't lay a wet blanket of sympathy on me. Didn't reach out a hand and stroke my arm with more comfort than I could bear. "Okay," she said. "Let's give it a try. You come out to the cabin everyday for a month. I'll pay you the same thing I'd pay a carpenter, and we'll see how it goes. If we find out we suit each other, we'll carry on. If it's not working for either of us, we can walk away, no harm done. How's that sound?"

It sounded so good I couldn't believe it. But I tried to be a man and said a month's trial seemed just the thing for both of us. Said it righteous, just like she did.

Now, looking back, it seems so easy, how I got on a road that led to misery and murder. Deepest misery of my life. Worse'n when Dad died. You learn to accept that miners can die any day they work a shift. You know they live with danger, and you half-expect them dying anyway. It takes time, but you can get over it.

But when loved ones are taken from you without no rhyme or reason, that kills you too. That was a misery so bad, I nearly lost my mind.

Made in the USA
San Bernardino, CA
20 July 2017